LOVE THAT LASTS

Love that Lasts

KELLY GOODING

~ 1 ~

CARRIE

"**C**arrie, that day I knew that you are the **only person for me in this world,**" Justice Carbone, my one and only husband from this day on, vowed in front of our friends and family.

I've been beaming from ear to ear all day, overjoyed to marry my best friend and begin our white picket fence family. I can still vividly picture this man in front of me at that exact moment. Justice wore a tan suit, a linen white shirt that unbuttoned at the collar, and a lavender boutonniere to match the sea of lavender and white magnolia bouquets my bridesmaids held. The dark locks, cropped short, hugged his Tuscan skin, all gelled back into perfect waves except one strand hanging in front. His deep, brown eyes never failed to pull me into his trance. And, as I looked up at him between "I do's", I waited for him to embrace me and officially end this ceremony.

As soon as the officiant announced that the groom may kiss the bride, Justice placed both hands on my face and longingly took all of me in. My breath. My lips. My heart. It feels like my eyes were shut for an eternity, yet our lips were

1

only conjoined for a few seconds. We pulled apart, walked down the aisle, and partied all night long.

The hangover only lasted until the next morning, but the memories we made continue to play over and over in my mind. The promises made at the altar, the overwhelming support from friends and family, and the forever feeling that has seeped into my entire being. Our love is forever. Justice is mine and I am his. Forever.

I am pulled from a lovestruck daze when Justice places his hand on mine as we begin to lift off. We are off to Barbados for the week, and I could not be happier to escape reality with my new husband, alone on a beach sipping piña coladas.

As soon as we are in the air, I rest my head on Justice's shoulder and knock out. It is crazy how easily planes put me to sleep, but something about flying thousands of miles in the air at an extraordinary speed sends me into a coma.

My head suddenly flops down, jolting me awake as a rush of people scramble to get off the plane. Even though the doors have yet to open, there are always those people who cannot wait their turn to get off. I look up at Justice and find him staring back at me.

"Hey, sleepyhead. I didn't want to wake you until we had to get up."

I give a sheepish smile, still awakening from the slumber that felt shorter than the actual flight. "I can't believe we are here already. I didn't think I slept that long."

"I guess sleeping beauty needed her rest," he teases.

Finally, the mob of people begins moving again, signaling that the doors have opened. Justice grabs our bags, swinging them over his shoulder and onto his back. I have always been amazed by his strength. Sure, he is 6'1 and built, but I have known him since freshman year of college, so sometimes I still see him as that athletic yet gawkish boy who stole my heart. Fixing my gaze ahead, I lead the way to the exit. Justice hands me my bag once we have entered the airport and pulls out his phone to call the car service we booked before our trip.

As soon as we step outside, the sea breeze overwhelms my senses, and I can't hide the smile that screams, *Yay! Much needed Vitamin D!* Justice finishes his call and ushers me to a black SUV waiting for us by the curb.

"Hi, sir, how are you doing today?" Justice is such a gentleman and always feels the need to make the driver comfortable anytime we are their passengers. I like that he makes people feel comfortable and secure.

The driver replies and I let Justice take the reins on the conversation so I can enjoy the scenery I imagine will unfold once we leave the airport parking structure. Just as the thought comes, so do the colors of a rich, but quaint beach city. So many colors illuminate each home we pass and bring out the bright blue sky that hovers over them. I cannot wait to see the ocean that I can only assume resembles the beautiful blue sky painted in front of us.

We pass local fruit stands, more homes, and other resorts until eventually, we come to a halt. Again, Justice handles the bags and hands one to me as we make our way up the stairs to the gorgeous all-white resort that I recognize from our online booking. I tug on Justice's arm, unable to contain my excitement.

We walk through the sliding glass doors and enter the air-conditioned lobby. Immediately, we are met with a bell-man who assists us with our bags and completes our check-in. Our room is on the 5th floor, room 305. As soon as we reach our bedroom, Justice sets the bags down and leaps onto the bed. He moves sideways onto the bed and mimics a seductively hot model posing for a swimsuit shoot. Then, he lifts his eyebrows up and down and pats the comforter in front of him, indicating that I should fill the position next to him. I inch forward with a smile on my face. Not only have I been hoping for this moment since we became husband and wife, but he always manages to make me laugh and it's intoxicating.

We've been together for three years, but this really is the start of everything. This. Is. Only. The. Beginning...

Quickly, my brain transitions from dwelling on the sentiment to refocusing on Justice's biceps. The sunshine from the balcony door beams off his muscles and I am ready to kiss that dumb look still on his face. I leap into his arms as he moves on top of me, kissing me from top to bottom.

~ 2 ~

CARRIE

5 years later...

"Only person for me in this world." This would soon be the second time this has become a lie as I glance down at the positive pregnancy test teeter-tottering in my shaking hands. The floor is covered with multiple unpackaged pregnancy tests. All of them plastered with two lines...

How could I be pregnant? I am not sure I even believe it. I mean, there is no way the world thinks that this would be the perfect time for me to carry a child. Everything in my life is a complete mess. *I* am a complete mess. I am not mother material at this moment. The many times I thought about this moment in the past, I never thought I would be afraid to tell the father.

I was supposed to be waiting for the results with Justice next to me in excited anticipation, not alone with anxious anticipation. Tears of joy were supposed to fill my eyes, instead all I can feel is a pit in my stomach. Justice and I always imagined that when we were ready to get pregnant, we would find out together and surprise our friends and family. We were supposed to be prepared for this and I would have had pregnancy tests stored at home. Instead, reality is that I am puking over a CVS toilet in a single, genderless bathroom because this was not planned. I did not have any pregnancy tests at home and, of course, I was too sick to make it home.

I brush the back of my hand over my mouth after spewing my insides out. It is hard to imagine that my stomach will grow any bigger when all I have been doing is puking everything up. I stand up, wobbling from the queasiness I feel either from the 'morning sickness' or the reality of this situation. I wash my hands and then grip the bathroom sink counter, staring at my reflection in the mirror. I look the same as I did a month ago, yet everything about me has changed.

"It's okay. I will be okay. I will pull my life together to give this baby everything," I whisper at my reflection, staring into my soul. I close my eyes to regain peace and balance at this moment.

Knock, knock! My heart races again and I realize that someone's fist is pounding on the door. The CVS bathroom must be popular today. I guess I also took a while puking my brains out.

I sigh and take one last look at myself in the mirror, trying to regain my strength before I walk out the door. I keep my head down as I exit, avoiding any eye contact with whoever was knocking. I am not ready to tackle more than what I just discovered in that bathroom. Honestly, a death glare from a stranger might send me over the edge.

As I escape the labyrinth of the CVS aisles to the exit, I begin to piece together the events that have led me to this. So many choices I made have ruined my relationship with Justice and could have ruined the child that lives inside me. *How could I be so reckless?* I continue to internally reprimand myself while I cross over to the parking lot, making it to my car when I am startled by a noise nearby.

"Excuse me, miss," a man pops up behind me and interjects. "Sorry, miss. But could you spare some change?" The man is brushed with dirt and wearing tattered clothing. I can tell he is homeless and the state he is in tears me from the spiral downfall of my own selfish thoughts. Automatically, I try to recollect whether I have any cash on me.

"Yes, one second," I open my car door and reach over to the glove compartment where I keep a few dollar bills on hand. I carry cash so infrequently that the only reason I have it is because I didn't know what else to do with the change. I paid a restaurant bill for a group of friends and one of them gave me cash for the tip. I left it in my car in case of emergency and forgot it was there until this moment. I hand the change over to the man standing patiently, "Here you go."

"Thank you, ma'am," he replies. The man smiles, exposing a gap in place of one of his front teeth. He pockets the money and turns around to walk away.

All of a sudden, a list of more reasons to reprimand myself surfaces. *Should I have given him that money? Wait, aren't you not supposed to give them cash in case they use it on drugs or non-necessities? I should have asked if he wanted me to buy* *him some food. But what kind of drugs could he possibly buy with $6.00? I hope I did the right thing. Wow, where is my right and wrong compass?*

I can't stop overthinking. *Well, I guess it is out of my control.* Everything could not be more out of control. I can only hope that this was good. Hopefully, this gives me good karma for a change. I need something.

~ 3 ~

JUSTICE

5 months earlier.
"Come on! Carry it all the way! Let's go, let's go!" I can hear my voice and notice I am getting a little anxious at the football game on the screen. It is the Super Bowl and my team, the Eagles, are playing the Chiefs. This is history in the making and I can't contain the jitters I have right now. There is no other team I would root for, especially when the Eagles have an amazing quarterback such as Jalen Hurts. Not to mention, I put down a little money for this game to make it more interesting.

I am part Italian, and I grew up in Philadelphia, so my family and I are huge Eagles fans. Having a home team is less about how good they are or even where you once lived, but more about the memories you have rooting for them. I spent my entire childhood watching them play and attending family Super Bowl gatherings. Now, the time spent watching these games is more for nostalgia than anything.

I glance back at Carrie in the kitchen speaking to one of my friend's girlfriends. I know she is not a huge fan of my friend's girlfriends most of the time, but she seems to

9

be having a good time. I know Carrie thinks that we have outgrown these people, but they were my first true friends when I moved here to Florida for college. Truthfully, I think it says a lot that we have remained friends, even if they are stuck in a "frat" boy stage in Carrie's opinion.

She thinks since we have been married for as long as we have that we should have more couple friends rather than Cruise and Aaron's '2-month stands,' as she calls them. I think it's not fair for her to expect me to stop being friends with them just because they aren't in the same phase as us and it shouldn't change how much time I spend with them. Plus, she's made new friends from her new marketing job and I don't tell her how annoying they are because that would upset her. Rather, I choose to stay home or hang out with Revel on the nights they get together. In the end, it works out for both of us because she gets a night out with the girls and I get a night out with the guys.

"Damn, Justice, your team is getting fucked," Aaron yells loud enough for the entire block to hear. I can admit their language can be jarring for Carrie. She used to get along with everyone in college, but over the years, she lost interest. I just wish she would stay around for me.

"Oh, shit! Looks like you will owe us some shots after this!" Cruise interjects.

I laugh. "Sheesh, I am already three shotguns and three shots in, and I was supposed to drive," I reply.

"Ya, but that is why you have a wife. She is supposed to drive you home on days like this," Cruise teases.

Aaron shoves Cruise's arm and mutters, loudly, "Only reason why I would get me one."

Typically, I just ignore these comments. Carrie thinks that they will influence how I think and that 'talk like that' will seep into our relationship. Truthfully, I think she is overreacting. I don't want to see her reaction behind us because I am sure she will say something on the drive home. I mean, can't a guy just have a little fun?

Just then, one of the Chiefs' offensive players, Kadarius Toney, crosses the line for another touchdown made by the Chiefs. The score is now 28-27 in favor of the Chiefs. This night will not go well if the Eagles let them win.

"Noo!" I yell, pulling at the sides of my head in frustration.

"Yes, yes, yes!" Aaron laughs at my anger and moves to the kitchen counter around Carrie and Cruise's girlfriend. I turn slightly to the right and see Aaron pouring me a tequila shot. *Oh, God. Here we go.* Aaron makes his way back with the shot, moving around Carrie while saying, "Excuse me, ladies, Justice needs a little juice!"

I make eye contact with Carrie, her face filled with concern that another shot is being handed to me. I shake it off and, instead of waiting for the Eagles to lose, I grab the shot out of Aaron's hand and down it. The tequila burns the back of my throat, but I yelp at the sensation, "Woo let's go!"

Carrie has finished the conversation with our friend's girl and has made her way over to the couch next to me. I only noticed because she tapped me on the shoulder and told me she was not feeling great.

"Aw, ok, well you can go home. I will just take an Uber home," I say.

"Uh, ok... I was thinking you would come home with me, though. We can play the game at home, but I would rather be home and, preferably, not alone."

Aaron overhears Carrie and decides to give his input, "No, Justice, you have to stay! I want to see you crushed at the end of this game!"

Carrie is facing me, turned away from Cruise and Aaron on the other side of the couch, so she proceeds to roll her eyes. She ignores him and repeats, "I am not feeling good and do not want to go home alone. You really don't want to go home with me?"

"No, babe," I say with a pouty face to imitate her pleading request. I can tell she is serious and frustrated, but she will be fine. I shouldn't have to escort her home. I mean if we were not married, she would have to get home alone as well, and I don't see why being married means I have to follow her.

Aaron and Cruise are laughing under their breaths at my response. Yes, they are immature. But Carrie should know that I do not pay attention to their immaturity. I am not saying this to make them laugh. I want to stay to watch the game. That's it.

"Ok, never mind," She pulls away and walks out the door. No hesitation, no goodbye.

Aaron and Cruise, unfazed by her reaction, continue to jokingly berate me about the score. It is not long after that the Eagles lose, and Aaron and Cruise pour more shots in honor of the defeat.

It is late by the time the Uber pulls up to drop me off at our one-bedroom, one-bathroom bungalow. I stumble out of the car, drunk and unstable, and wobble into the house. I can't even remember how many drinks I had. Luckily, my incapacitation helps me get out of a fight with Carrie. Except, maybe I need to say what is lying heavy on my chest. The liquid courage is tempting me to confess.

I open the door to the house and the lights are off. It is quiet, and as I make my way over the bedroom, I can see that Carrie tucked herself into bed. I am sure she is not asleep yet. I look for the light switch in my drunken state and turn it on. Carrie moves onto her back and looks at me with confusion.

"Justice?" she asks as if she just woke up. I jump into bed and cozy up on top of her, unfazed by the time. "Ahh, Justice you reek of alcohol."

I laugh that off and lean in for a kiss. She pushes away, reluctantly. I take the message and roll over to my side, but before falling into a deep sleep I sit up and look at Carrie. I need to say a few things first before I forget tomorrow. I look at Carrie.

"What, Justice?" She questions me again.

"I want to say a few things and talk things out," I stammer.

"Tomorrow, Jus," she says.

"No, now," I say. "You can't just expect me to follow you like your little puppy dog, Carrie. I am your husband, yes, but I am not going to hold your hand in this life." The words flow out of my mouth, quick and bluntly. Carrie starts tearing up. "Babe, don't you want me to be honest with you?"

She looks at me with those beautiful green eyes of hers that are made greener with the tears filling them. "Yes, I do."

"I want to be honest with you, and I just wanted one day to myself to watch the game... And again, you wanted to tear me away. You wanted me to do what you wanted, and you didn't think of me... All I am saying... just one day," I let it off my chest, drifting slowly into a coma. I do not even hear Carrie's side before my brain shuts off and my body gives out entirely to sleep.

~ 4 ~

CARRIE

I woke up this morning with a raging headache and swollen eyes. The typical signs that I had been crying all night. All those signs combined with the hangover feeling of 'why did I allow that to happen last night?' wash over me once again. My pillow is covered with dried mascara and still wet from my tears when I got home alone yesterday. I cried waiting for Justice and then cried after he poured out his feelings in a drunken slur and fell asleep.

I wish his words did not affect me so much, but it is just another wake-up call that we are not on the same page. I do not agree with anything he said to me last night, and, unfortunately, there is no changing his mind. I wish he saw me for me and not as a drain on his life.

I do not want to be a bother to Justice. I do not want to be an irritation or a weight in his life. I try my best to get along with everybody to please him. Anthony and Cruise do not respect our marriage and are disrespectful to me for expecting my husband to support me. They interject all the time and Justice refuses to set boundaries with them. It makes me uncomfortable more often than I can count. I am always kind and entertain the women they bring around, even though they treat them with the same disrespect. This is not what I pictured for our life. I did not picture us continuing to live our lives like we did in our early twenties. I thought that saying "I do" meant that we have each other's backs. That we would continue to grow together. In the meantime, I try and fit into this world that Justice is holding onto, but truth is, it is not doing either of us any favors. And it is clear from last night that it is still not good enough for Justice. The more we grow, the more we grow apart. It is like we are getting pulled at the seams. Justice is staying put and I am getting torn in two.

For so long, I have contemplated, 'Am I the problem?' Everything would have been fine if I had not asked to leave. Or we would be in a better place if I did not get frustrated when he wants to hang out with his friends over me. Even if it has been weeks since we had a night out, I should not expect him to make the effort. I should know that he works and wants to wind down with his friends. I should understand that. I should know that he loves me even if it does not seem like it. Maybe what he says is right. I am making a big deal out of nothing. I am asking for too much. I am too emotional or too sensitive. Yet, after last night, I am starting to think I am not the problem anymore.

I roll out of bed and wash down a few Advil before getting ready for the gym. I like to take out my frustration on Mr. Kick-Me Bag at the local kickboxing gym before work. I make it out the door by 7:00 am and arrive just before my class at 7:15 am. Already, I can see my fellow classmates through the glass window, ready for the grueling workout ahead. I wave to them and rush to make it in before our coach begins going over the floor routine for the day.

--

Ding, Ding, Ding! Finally, the timer in bold, bright red flashes in the center of the wall ahead of us. Each one of us is dripping from head to toe after an extra HIIT cycle consisting of two solid minutes of freestyle punching. Didn't matter how we hit the bag as long as we didn't stop.

I collapse to the ground near a few others talking about an event coming up for members of the gym.

"Ya, it's going to be a beach workout, and new members are allowed to invite a plus-one if they would like. I guess it's kind of like a soft-launch and for members to get a VIP experience," says Gemma, a girl in the group around 22 years old who constantly flirts with one of the male workers at the check-in desk. I am always stuck at the front desk, waving my membership keychain for him to scan while he is distracted, flirting with her.

"Are you going to that?" stated a guy next to me with very defined muscles shining from the sweat coating his body. Anthony is a sweet guy who has made me feel welcome since day one. I get the sense that he likes me a little since he is always checking in with me, but I find it kind and courteous of him.

"I'm not sure. When is it again?" I'm actually pretty sure I have the day open, but I don't want to commit to it until I have the chance to ask one of my friends to attend with me. I already know Justice will not be interested. Not his type of 'thing'.

"I believe it's this Sunday. I mean, I'm not sure who decided to add an intense workout to it, but it should still be fun," he smiles lightheartedly. His ease and banter is contagious, and I wouldn't be mad if he did have a thing for me. I mean, I am not going to entertain it, but it certainly doesn't upset me.

"Ok, I'll think about it," I say with a friendly smile, shoving my gloves into my bag. I could use something to distract me from what has been going on lately, and just because it isn't Justice's 'thing' doesn't mean I shouldn't go. I should experience new outings even if my husband is averse to the idea. If I must, I'll create my own reality separate from him. My own friends, my own hobbies, and my own career can all be separate from him if he is uninterested in my company that much.

As I leave the gym, I pull out my phone, searching my contacts to text one of my new coworkers that I'd love to spark a friendship with. Scrolling to the "S", I click on Sarai and begin typing out a quick invite.

"Hey Sarai, my gym has this beach event coming up next Saturday and if you are interested, I would love for you to come :)."

Dot. Dot. Dot. Sarai replies and she's in!

I am surprised at how excited I am. Maybe this will take my mind off the turmoil between Justice and I lately. Maybe this is what I need. I need to start filling my time with girlfriends and fun events. I need more adventure aside from what Justice wants to do. Let's be honest, he won't even notice my absence.

Approaching my car, I decide to let it all go for the day and focus on the work that I can guarantee is waiting for me at the office. As the marketing manager at a retail company getting ready to launch a new spring line, I have a lot of research to gather if I want to impress our management team with my presentation.

Although this job requires me to put in more work than my previous roles, it has been extremely beneficial in other ways. With hard work comes more growth and this company already has space for me to move up within the next year. I have been working closely with the entire organization and the communication is top-notch. I truly could not have a better team - all hard-working individuals who are excited to see where this start-up goes. I am excited to be a part of a place with a mission statement that I can get behind. I am thankful for this opportunity and am so glad I stumbled upon this job a few months back. And, truly, I stumbled...

As I mindlessly drive the same route from the gym to the headquarters, I reminisce on the bittersweet memory still vivid in my brain. I showed up ready for my interview, wearing a white, silk button-down shirt that was tucked into my grey ankle-high slacks paired with black closed-toed heels. My outfit was planned accordingly - a slim yet sophisticated look to show that I have a good eye for style and aesthetic, yet toned down to make sure I don't stand out like a sore thumb. I was greeted by the front desk and encouraged to take a seat while I waited for the interviewer. I specifically remember noticing the luxurious furniture that somehow did not match the interior very well at the time. As I questioned the interior designers' motives in these purchases, the front desk woman pointed out that there was a coffee counter near the window at my disposal. I waited 5 minutes, but since I was early, I figured I might as well get my morning coffee. To my surprise, the coffee bar had so many options that it perked my spirits up and took my mind off the interview. I finally chose between a latte or a cold brew and shoved the lid on top of the to-go cup just as the interviewer entered the room.

"Carrie?" questioned the recruiter, locking eyes with me as I turned around.

"Hi. Jessica, right?" I said confidently, tapping into my extroverted side and holding out my hand for a handshake. "Thank you for taking the time to meet with me."

"No, thank you. Follow me this way, Carrie," she ushered me towards her office.

Jessica began with small talk, asking, "How is your day going?" as we walked through the doorway and entered the hall. Now, this is the moment in time that my brain loves to humble myself with. Our office has been renovated since then, but at the time, the pathway that lined the way to our offices was this god-awful tile. There were hundreds of brown, square-shaped tiles cemented to the floor. And, of course, one of my black, gorgeous pumps found its way between two tiles that were not completely cemented to the floor. My heel wedged into the crack and stopped me in my tracks, flinging my body forward and forcing my hand to drop the freshly brewed latte. The coffee hit the floor and boomeranged right back at me. Drops of brown liquid all over my white silk shirt and grey pants. I was mortified. Thankfully, everyone was very sweet and apologetic. It turned out that the team was already frustrated with the flooring and explained that though they just leased it for the large space, it still needed to be renovated badly. Thankfully, my reputation remained intact after this debacle, but it's not an introduction I can soon forget.

I make it to the office and park in my usual spot near the side of the building. I do not even make it past the entrance before one of my co-workers stops me. Walker nods to indicate 'good morning' from the coffee bar. I reciprocate the head nod and join him to feed my huge coffee addiction.

"Morning, Walker. Any issues this morning with the specifics to our launch?" I ask, hoping there are none.

"Not today. I thought I may have come across something this morning, but the further I investigated, I ended up resolving the issue. In fact, it was the issue with integrating the free sticker gift along with purchases over $25. Thankfully, IT and I already handled it." Walker is a little quirky, but the more I got to know him, I found out he is a surfer from California. He moved out here five months ago to be with his girlfriend who is a nurse and happened to get into a residency here. So, he still passed the company culture evaluation, and now, his nerdiness is a cherry on top.

"Good. Ok, I researched across comparative company lines on how our launch will be beneficial, if you could add some charts with this data to the PowerPoint pressy?"

Walker stands aside, letting me pour a dollop of half-and-half and a spritz of vanilla syrup, as we discuss today's agenda.

"Ok, ya. Go ahead and shoot it over this morning and I will get that to you by noon," Walker assures me, as we walk past the front desk and through to the offices. We walk down the hallway and into an open space where many co-workers eat lunch or open their laptops to do some casual work. This space is meant to draw people together and offer a team atmosphere. I wish I had more time to sit in this area, but as the marketing manager I am usually tied up in meetings all day.

"Thanks, Walker. I will be in meetings later today, so if you have any pressing questions, then I would ask them before lunch," I remind him and assume he will tell the others in our department since he acts as a floor lead.

As much as I would prefer to work out in the sunshine or in my bed, I do enjoy the setup in my office. My aesthetic is simple with a color wheel of white, tan, and transparent décor. Also, of course, I had to add in touches of pink. Baby pink pens. Baby pink calendar. Lastly, a baby pink rug. My last and most cherished pieces are the pictures of my family and a framed photo of Justice and I on my desk. The photo is a selfie that I took of us amid all the chaos on our wedding day. We are both making goofy faces with our tongues out and I love how this one captures our true selves the most.

Although the professional photos are gorgeous and I do love them, I like to be reminded of the Justice and Carrie that were so uncontrollably happy that they couldn't help but scrunch up their noses and stick out their tongues at one another.

I take a seat in my white fur swivel chair and open my laptop. I wait for my multiple monitors to power on and enter my password, 'Justicexoxo'. At this point, it has been so long that I can't even remember when that was not my password. Thank you, college-aged Carrie. The notifications on my email begin popping up – one hundred and fifty new emails. *Great, looks like I will be answering emails all morning.* I click on the Outlook mail icon and open the first one.

JUSTICE

Carrie's pillow is still warm when my alarm goes off. My job is more relaxed than hers, so she's always up before me on weekdays and it's probably why she gets paid the big bucks. However, this is as far as I feed into comparison because it does not matter to me who makes more. She works hard to be in the position she is in, and I could not be prouder.

I push myself up and notice that her pillow is stained with blotches of black mascara from last night. Oh yes, the unforgettable day that will now be known as yesterday. I shake my head at the memories of last night and piece together the rambling that went on after the truckload of tequila I drank. She couldn't have been too happy with that. She may not have liked how it was said, but maybe it needed to be said. I put the conversation aside and remind myself that today is a new day. It is best if we move on and let it work itself out.

Reluctantly, I force every limb off the bed and slowly move towards the bathroom. Once my eyes have adjusted to the early morning sunshine that has made its way into our bedroom through a couple of windows lining the top of our bed, I begin powering through my morning routine. Brush, spit, pee, dress, and power on the coffee. The Italian in me loves an espresso, but the machine that was given to us at our wedding needs time to heat up. Once I finish making my dark espresso, I dump the coffee grinds into the trash and head to our second bedroom which we made into my office. I work remotely and there is no pressure for me to start my day early since the company I work for is located in California. The three-hour difference usually gives me enough time to sleep in, make my coffee, and enjoy breakfast, and then log on. Last night, I set my alarm a little later for today, so I am planning on sipping my espresso and getting to work right away.

I work for a tech company in San Diego. I majored in finance and took the first job right out of college. I have gotten a few promotions over the years and bonuses, but mainly, I am coasting. Finance has never been something that I was that interested in, but I was good at it. In college, I tested as the top student in my class. They expected me to work for Goldman Sachs or something of that high caliber. Unfortunately for them, I don't find pleasure in spending my days in an office going over projections and evaluations just to please stakeholders.

Instead, I make a respectable salary and don't need to spend my days stressing. I start my days later and end them earlier than the average person, giving me more time to hit the gym and hang out with my friends who either work service jobs or have flexible schedules, too.

Do not get me wrong, this is not my be-all and end-all career. I have other interests, such as photography and videography, which is what Carrie would like me to pursue. She says it would be the 'dream' job. However, I don't think she has considered how much effort and hard work it takes to develop a client list amongst all the other photographer competitors. I am not looking to start a side hustle on top of the job I already have.

My computer is taking its sweet time loading the Excel workbook that I need to start my day. So, I focus my mind on the plans for later today. I am going to the gym and then meeting up with Revel. Revel Waters has been my best friend since we became roommates in college and we have done almost everything together. We even met Carrie together one night at a party. She and I became an item, but Revel still hung around us just as much as before.

The three of us have always been great friends, but Carrie and Revel bump heads a lot. She has told me on multiple occasions that she doesn't understand Revel and that he doesn't 'lift' me up as much as she would hope a best friend would. I can see where she is coming from because he does have a more negative attitude at times, but that's just because he had a rough childhood. Honestly, this is how Revel and I became such good friends–because we were both from middle to lower-class families that could not keep up with our classmates at the University of Miami Florida and their brand-new Jeep Wranglers or Audi R8's. Neither of us felt like we fit in with the crowd, but together we don't need to.

Although Carrie did not come from a rich family by any means, they did support her a lot, and I feel like she aspires to be those Miami Floridian students that she befriended in the past and who have burned her. Now, she is working at this 'bougie' retail company and befriending the same type of people. I am so proud of her for getting where she is today, but if I am honest, I feel as though we are drifting apart on where we see ourselves ending up. Is it fair to think she wants more from me than I am willing to give?

--

As expected, work ends early at 4:30 pm today. I spent a solid two hours working out, swung by the house to shower, and arrived at Revel's house 30 minutes ago. Revel bought a nice two-bedroom home with a backyard in a great location a couple of years ago when the market was low, which is harder to come by now. He works for a tech company that Carrie's company happens to outsource to and makes a nice chunk of change. Revel ranked highly, majoring in computer science, but rarely had to put in as much effort to succeed. While all the other students were studying for exams, Revel and I preferred to hang out at our favorite local bar. Revel came from a trailer park before his mother died and was put into the system at 12, so I am happy to see him doing so well for himself. He deserves it.

We are sitting on the back patio, kicking back a few lagers and smoking Cuban cigars, catching up on everything going on in our lives. Once we finished discussing Revel's love life, he must have felt it was the perfect time to broach the discussion of how Carrie and I are doing. Seems like word got around that Carrie left the Super Bowl party early and alone.

"So, how are things with you and Carrie lately?" Revel asks. He has been looped in on the Spark Notes version of Carrie and I's rocky patch lately, even though talking about my marriage is not something I am usually itching to dive into.

"I don't know, man. Sometimes I feel like she just wants too much from me. She wants me to change my career or make new friends. And, if it's not her asking that we make more couple friends, then it's her asking for more alone time or sex..." Justice replies.

"You mean you don't have sex anymore?" Revel questions, hinting at a red flag.

"No, dude. We do. It's just not as much as we used to, but I feel like, at this point, that is normal. Sex just isn't everything to me anymore and I love how we are already," I explain as much as I can.

Revel has not been in a long-term relationship, let alone a marriage. He can't possibly understand the pressure there is to keep a woman happy. The emotional intelligence they require that I do not feel I can even remotely match. Sex is more than just sex for them. She wants more. She wants passion, lust, and longing that I can't even begin to comprehend how to give to her. I want to please her and excite her as passionately as our love has been in the past, but time adds damage like a tree in a storm. A tree can withstand most things, but with time, there is wear and tear to the tree's roots. Over time, the tree will not be as young and lively as it once was. And, eventually, a storm might come around brutal enough to knock the tree down.

"I'm sorry, Jus. I know it's been tough for you guys lately. I just think you two need to talk it out and make up already. And, possibly add in the makeup sex as well," Revel grins at me. Part of the reason I came to Revel is because he seems to make even the toughest times light-hearted, even if most of his advice is layered in sarcasm. I guess you learn to make light of situations when life hasn't come easy.

I grin back and take another long swig of my lager. "Thanks, Revel. I appreciate you opening your home to me in my time of need," I reply with a line from The Godfather. We both laugh and I mention that I should head out, throwing a few empty beer bottles into the recycling bin on my way out.

I did not want to get into the specifics with Revel tonight, but I can't shake the back-and-forth Carrie and I seem to be having. She seems to be pressing me lately on every issue in our relationship, instead of letting things go. Everything she brings up feels so trivial to me, and yet she cries over it. There are so many tears nowadays.

I remember the first tear she shed in front of me. During our first year together, she never cried around me. She would send me texts in crisis or come to me for frequent venting sessions. I have always been a good listener, something Carrie mentioned was one of her favorite things about me. She felt right away that she could open up to me and knew that I would be intently listening. I knew I hadn't experienced her full vulnerability, but as much as she avoided small talk and opened up easily with others, she had yet to open her complete heart to me. I teased her many times that I wanted to make her cry. The first time I mentioned it, she was caught off-guard and, with a puzzled look, responded, "Why do you want me to cry?"

"Because I believe you are beautiful no matter what and I want to be there even when you are at your worst," I appeased her.

Finally, one night, there was a knock at my door. No text and no plans that night. I made it to the door after a second knock and opened it to find a tear-filled Carrie. She immediately wrapped her arms around my neck in a full embrace, silently sobbing. That night Carrie found out that her father would be starting chemo treatment in a week. They had found a malignant tumor wedged in his back. She reiterated the details her mother had given her on the phone earlier as I continued to embrace her in bed. Her eyes were so green that night from the tears that left her eyelids puffy and red. She stayed strong throughout that season, and I couldn't have been more honored to have been there in case she needed me. Yet, I've never seen her so strong. She didn't need me.

Now, I am proudly bound to her for life. And, suddenly, I am her safe line. When did she become so dependent on me? Is that what marriage is? The woman who used to fight and hold back her fears has been vanquished? The independence we had dissipates altogether and I am expected to be her sole companion? Am I wrong for finding it exhausting?

~ 6 ~

CARRIE

I finished work and got home at 7:00pm. I haven't had much time to go to the grocery store this past week, so there is not much in the refrigerator. I open the refrigerator door to check and all that is left amongst the condiments is stew meat, one red bell pepper, and an onion. I remember that we still have a huge Costco bag of Rice, so I go ahead and cook up a stir-fry.

Justice let me know that he was going over to Revel's after the gym, and I figure it will be a while until he comes home. Once I am done cooking dinner, I make myself a plate, pour myself a glass of wine, and box up the rest of it for Justice to enjoy later. Finally decompressing after my long day, I swirl the wine around my glass and collect my feelings about last night. There are too many emotions clashing inside me. I feel restless, frustrated, confused, and disheartened. Yet, as I sit here by myself, the feeling I feel most of all is... alone. Companionship is all but a mirage in our marriage.

Companionship. Like the relationship we used to have. I smile slightly as I think back to all the times Justice could not get enough of my company. I take another sip of wine and sigh, allowing my mind to mull over the memories. The many nights we would attend the gym after classes and then cook dinner together. The hundreds of times he would drive over to campus to pick me up from my dorm and take me to his place to spend the night. Even if I had come home late from a night out with my girlfriends, he would be on stand-by, answering every text and waiting for the one that said, 'Come get me."

My mind flashes to the pink dress I wore to a country concert with my friends that Justice raced over midway through the show, dragging Revel along. Justice had bought two tickets from someone off the street just to meet me inside when I had texted that I missed him and wished he was there. I mean, I was drunk and practically begging him, but he didn't deny the invitation. In fact, he was more than okay with it. Revel exposed the embarrassing truth a few days later when Justice was teasing him about his latest girl troubles with a hot tennis player he was seeing at the time. "Justice, at least I didn't get ripped off from someone on the street to pay $100 to see the last 15 minutes of a concert." Revel laughed harder when he saw Justice's reaction.

Back then, I had looked at him in awe that he had spent that much just to be with me. The concert had been selling their tickets dirt-cheap, like $20 at most. The street seller had probably not made much all night and wanted one good sale, and Justice's craze to meet up with me was his saving grace.

Justice stared straight at Revel, clearly not expecting his best friend to rat him out. His cheeks were flushed, and he couldn't help but laugh at himself as well. He looked over at me and gave me a kiss on my nose. Nothing could stop him when it came to being with me. It was so easy for him to give in to the idea of 'us'. Ironic that it was harder for me to commit to an 'us' and allow myself to be dependent on him.

I used to be in control of everything. I used to be so sure of myself and was a world champion wrangler of all my emotions. Eventually, life learns how to test your limits. And life did just that.

I was away at college when I got a call from my mom telling me that my father had cancer. I was in shock for the first few minutes. She said she loved me and assured me that everything would be okay. Then she hung up and my world went belly up. In that moment, I knew I couldn't handle these moments of life on my own. I drove to Justice's dorm in my state of shock and knocked on his door.

Though the sentiment of giving up control sounds nice and easy, it was not easy for me. It took time, and it took seeing my father sick, struggling through treatments, before I allowed myself to depend on someone else for once. I had one relationship before Justice, but never truly opened myself up to him. Yet, somehow, I knew that Justice was the one who would take care of me. All I needed was to feel his arms around me and his calming voice as he reassured me repeatedly, "He is going to be okay". And, since then, I never closed my heart to him. I have been vulnerable, compassionate, understanding, and hopeful for the two of us. But if he keeps dismissing me, eventually my heart will harden again.

Suddenly, the front door opens, and Justice walks in...

"Hey, babe," Justice greets.

"Hi. I made some food for you. It is still on the stovetop," I reply and point to the kitchen with my wine glass.

"Thanks," Justice responds as he rotates his body in the other direction and heads through the bedroom to take a shower.

While he is in the shower, I contemplate how to approach him with my concerns. How do I broach a discussion about his disregard for me after telling me to go home without him when he already expressed his feelings towards it with disdain? Do I even bring up how that made me feel? I swallow the last gulp of wine and run through the controversy in my head. I am already anticipating the defensive stance Justice will take.

I head to the bedroom to get undressed and shimmy into my nightwear. I can still hear the shower at full blast when I jump onto the bed and scroll through Instagram to catch up on what all my relatives are doing. My sister-in-law is on vacation in Cabo and posted a picture of her hang-gliding. Justice is the oldest of two. His sister is about twenty-four years old and always looks like she is having the time of her life on social media. I am happy to see her single and thriving since she truly is the nicest sister-in-law one could have. Next, I scroll through my sister's post for the day and see that she took her two kids to the movies. Looks like they watched the newest Disney movie that came out, and it makes me smile when I see the kids' reactions, overjoyed and clapping their hands in excitement. As much as I love my sister's kids, Justice and I have talked about having children and we keep putting it off. Truth is that neither of us are ready to be the responsible adults it takes to have children. Not yet at least.

The shower turns off and I freeze. Even though we have been together for so many years and have had many heart-to-hearts, conflict never gets easier. Wondering how another human being will react is always frightening.

Justice opens the bathroom door with just his towel on. No matter how many years we spend together, I will never get over Justice in a towel. I try my best not to glance in his direction. Despite the conversation I would like to have, the water droplets glistening on his toned arms and defined abs are enough to make me say to hell with everything and to just forgive the man. Unfortunately, that will not change the situation and I know I am forced to bring it up. In the meantime, my eyes deviate from my phone to the muscles on his back as he dresses in our walk-in closet.

For some reason, Justice hates it when I watch him undress, while I am the complete opposite and could walk around the whole house naked if he let me. So, as secretly as a wife can check out her husband, I watch as his towel drops. I am not going to lie... Justice has a great butt. And, truthfully, he can twerk better than me. I quickly divert my gaze back to my phone as he pulls his Calvin Kleins up to his waist. Show is over. Now, back to the not-so-fun part.

"So... do you want to talk about yesterday?" I suggest as he turns around and heads for the bed.

"Sure," Justice replies. Ugh, that response has completely turned off anything I was feeling a second ago.

"Okay... well, I just didn't like that you wanted me to come home alone, especially when I told you I wasn't feeling good," I reminded him.

"I get that. I just thought that if you got home and relaxed that you would feel better and that you wouldn't need me," Justice counters. Sounds like half of an excuse to me.

"Even though I asked you to come with me? Wasn't that a sign that I wanted you to be at home with me and that I clearly did need you?"

"Carrie, sometimes I feel like you ask me to help you with everything just because I am your husband and not because you really need me. Who says I am always going to be around to help you? I can't always be called on to be your waitstaff. Sometimes, I need you to be self-sufficient and help yourself," Justice spurts out.

I cannot even believe him right now. As if I am not my own sufficient woman. He thinks that he can do better than someone like me, who works harder and cares about him more than he can imagine. Who is he kidding?

"You think I am not self-sufficient?" I respond, trying my hardest to keep my cool.

"No, it's just that sometimes I wish you didn't lean on me for everything. I feel like you could be better at being more individualistic," Justice combats.

Is that response supposed to be any better? More individualistic? My initial response of shock wears off and I am now seething. He pursued me. He married me. And now, he wants less of me?

"Ok, Justice. I won't ask you for anything ever again. I don't know who you think you are that you can say that I am not my own person and that I couldn't do perfectly fine without you," I am barely holding back the rage. I take his pillow and grab a blanket off our bed and walk out of the bedroom and into the living room. I throw them both onto the couch and yell, "Have fun sleeping on the couch!"

Justice looks at me with a glazed-over expression that crosses his features from time to time, but that I cannot read for the life of me. If anything, that expression makes me want to shake him and scream at him to show something beyond that blank stare. Instead, I stare blankly back at him and wait for his response.

Justice grabs a hoodie and sweats from the closet and walks out the door. I really hope the couch is as uncomfortable as it looks because I won't be getting much sleep tonight either.

JUSTICE

It's finally Friday and Carrie has been working overtime the entire week, partly because she has a lot of work to do for their launch, and the other part, I am sure, is because she would like to avoid me. Either way, we haven't seen much of each other.

I think separation is not such a bad thing. Many times, when we fight, Carrie will pour into her work, giving me enough time to cool off and start missing her. Usually, by the end of the week, Carrie will be exhausted from work, and we will chalk the fight up to a misunderstanding. These arguments are not that big of a deal and get stirred up from the heat of the moment. I would hate to know that something as small as a Super Bowl tiff would be something that we continue to fight over. Our love is much stronger than that, and at the end of the day, we know that we love each other.

I ran to the store and picked up a bouquet of flowers and purchased two tickets for a movie. I cannot help but picture Carrie coming home from her day at the office, taking off her shoes and flopping onto the couch, but her eyes will brim with excitement as soon as I meet her by the couch. She will break the tension with the good news of her presentation and stick her arms out for "huggies.". I will embrace her and whisper in her ear how proud of her I am and then surprise her with a night of good fun.

I display the flowers in a vase on our living room coffee table. She will be able to appreciate them as soon as she flings herself onto the couch. I begin eating the burrito bowl I picked up from Chipotle on my way home since I have neglected the role of grocery shopping and Carrie was too busy this week. Not to mention, if she wanted to cook any meals this week, she would have had to stop avoiding me.

I finish the burrito bowl at my desk. I am assuming Carrie will get home earlier since her focus has been on rocking today's presentation, so it is my mission to get all my work done before she arrives.

--

I finish work by 4pm and rinse off in the shower to be more presentable for my wife. I shave my 5 o'clock shadow and then I step out to rinse off the water residue. I decide to wear one of Carrie's favorite shirts on me, which is a plain black tee with her initials embroidered inside the left side pocket. She bought it for me a few years back and I wear it occasionally to make her happy. When she gifted it, she said that the initials were perfectly placed where the heart is and that she decided to have it embroidered underneath the pocket so that only she and I knew where my heart truly lay. I pair the black tee with dark blue jeans that Carrie says fit me the best. I toss on some white sneakers and hang out on the couch, watching television as I wait.

An hour passes, so I decide to text Carrie to check in. No response and the text I sent is not showing as read. From the start of our relationship, Carrie insisted that we have our read receipts mainly because she gets anxious waiting for my texts and wants to know if I have at least seen it. I agreed and have kept them on since. Seeing that she has not 'read' the text tells me that she is probably networking with other employees after her presentation. I take it with a grain of salt and continue watching reruns of 'Friends.'

After two more episodes of 'Friends,' I consider that she is not coming straight home. I text her again asking, 'Are you coming home?'

As soon as the text bubble goes through, the text changes to, 'Read at 6:36pm'. Yet still no response. Then, I remember that we also share locations in case of emergencies. Carrie is normally so communicative about where she is that I've never needed it. I click the information icon by Carrie's contact and open the maps that show her location.

She is at the EDGE Rooftop Lounge? Of course, she is at a rooftop bar with her co-workers. One of the most bougie bars in the area to celebrate their job well done, I assume. And probably getting the most spectacular service from the bartenders who will do anything to schmooze their way into the hands of Carrie's "friends" so they can walk away with a month's rent in their pocket. She decides to spend the night out and doesn't text me? This is not like her, and I cannot help but think it is because she has started to hang out with this crowd more often. Carrie is the most communicative person and, at times, overly communicative. Why would she just not respond?

At this point, I am over all the immaturity and decide to spend the night in. I change back into some sweats and a hoodie, ordering food in and catching up on a golf match I recorded.

--

I wake up to a stumbling Carrie. I set my eyes on the blaring red clock numbers on the side table and read 1:00 a.m.

"Hehehehe," Carrie giggles all the way to her side of the bed before she plops down on it.

I roll over and sit up against the headboard. My eyes stop squinting and become more aware of my surroundings. Carrie is drunk. I guess the day was a success and in celebration the team decided they would spend their night taking back green tea shooters.

"Babe, are you good?" I place my hand on her shoulder to relax her and hope that she falls asleep fast.

"Hi babbyyy... you should have -err-... hehe... come out tonight," As soon as she finally gets the words out, she looks directly at me. Her green eyes have become controlled by a goddess who seduces anyone she pleases to. Her energy has not calmed down and she seems more hyper now that she has awakened me. I can tell by that look that I am the fallen prey she has set her eyes on for the night. She wants more than to sleep tonight.

But it is not the night for me to give in to her tricks. For one, she never texted me back tonight, so why would I succumb to her scheming seduction after zero contact this week? Why did she say I should have come out tonight? She knows that she didn't invite me. Not that I would have, but she didn't even text me to let me know. This is not something she would put up with and not something that I should put up with either. I think it's in our best interests to sleep and hash everything out tomorrow.

She places her hand on top of mine, which is still resting on her shoulder and inches closer to me. I pull back my hand a bit to gently remind her that we are not on good terms. In a moment, her eyes turn from pure seduction to whimpering. I hold my stance and give her no validation in response. Sex will complicate my feelings, and right now, I am still processing my frustration. Carrie stays persistent and reaches for my zipper.

"Baby, I missed you this week," Carrie admits. Her eyes are still simpering for the attention she wants.

"Not tonight, babe," I say earnestly.

"Why not?" She pleads with the cute puppy dog face she knows usually does the trick. Yet, we have been doing this back and forth for months now and I refuse to be a pawn in this game anymore.

"Because…" I hold back a response. I would rather not get into this tonight.

Instantly, Carrie's face distorts from puppy dog pouting to actual pout. The defeat is written all over her face. I hate to hurt her and refuse her in this moment. I would rather we be wrapped up in each other all night without a worry in the world. It is just not as easy as our relationship once was.

At the beginning, we had no worries in the world and an all-consuming love for each other. We couldn't get enough of each other. Our friends nicknamed us the 'bunnies' of the group. Apparently, bunnies like to fuck a lot. At the time, there was nothing between us that could stop us from grabbing hold of each other and taking advantage of any moment we had together. Now, in this moment, I wish we had never fought. I wish that we could forego the past couple of months with this back-and-forth miscommunication. I wish that couples counseling wasn't something Carrie had felt necessary to bring up a month ago. I wish. I wish. I wish. I just want to make things better and I don't want to complicate things more than they already seem to be.

"You don't even want to be with me anymore?... in any way?" she hiccups the words between silent sobs.

"Babe, no. I just don't want to tonight," I assure her in a hushed tone.

She stares at me, still silently sobbing. Her eyes are darting between me and the wall in front of the bed. She does this when she is trying to read me, but I don't know what else to say. I don't want to make her feel worse. "Just go to sleep, babe."

Carrie rolls over, heaving between breaths and I decide to let her cry it out. I fall asleep still facing her back and hoping that she is better in the morning so we can work this out.

I love Carrie and, even though it seems that I am the one hurting her, I hope she still loves me.

~ 8 ~

CARRIE

It is midday, and I am walking with Justice along one of our favorite paths nearby, recognizable by the coral honeysuckle that lines the trail during spring and summertime. The red, long-trumpeted flowers bring waves of comfort and remind me of home, not surprising since they are a native plant to Florida. I look down at Justice and I's hands locked together and breathe in a sigh of relief. I place my head against his arm as we walk step by step and enjoy this small moment together.

Ring. Ring. Justice's phone goes off and he immediately tenses. Instinctively, I grab the phone from his pocket and read the name 'Janelle'. In my heart of hearts, I know what this means....

"Who is Janelle, Justice?" I throw the phone on the floor, but not before showing him the evidence.

Justice shrugs. He doesn't reply to my seething question even though I know he can see the look of betrayal plastered all over my face. Does he not care? Could he really have no feelings towards what could be the end of us?

I shake my head and feel tears burning in the corner of my eyes. The anger and frustration so high in the heat of the moment that it is now pouring out of me. I fling myself at him and throw one fist after another at his chest. Simply wanting a response out of him. All I want is for him to care.

Justice stares back at me with a hint of frustration as well. Frustration with having to deal with us. He has grown tired and weary. Justice wants out... My heart falls.

I wake up to a pounding headache. I really need to stop waking up like this. I roll over and onto my back to peek at Justice's side of the bed. Looks like he already got up for the morning. *Justice... Wow, that nightmare felt real.* I hate when my subconscious dreams that Justice has cheated on me. It always spins me for a loop and feels so real. Every time, it takes a while for my heart rate to go down.

I don't have these dreams often, but occasionally my brain likes to play tricks on me. Though Justice has never reacted like that before. Or, not reacted, I mean. The nonreaction was the most chilling part of the nightmare. Normally, it ends in confrontation and turmoil from the injustice that would wreak havoc on our relationship if he were to have an affair. Justice, for the most part, would plead for me to forgive him, but this time, there was nothing. No fight. No reaction.

The nightmare does not help ease my feelings from last night. There is no doubt in my mind that Justice loves me and will always love me. But he doesn't show it. At this point, we lack chemistry, companionship, and partnership. That is why I am pushing so hard for one thing to work. I try my best to portray the partnership I am seeking, but he disagrees and sees it as dependency. I ignore the inconsistency of companionship because I do not want to come off any more needy than Justice has already accused me of being. Justice decides when and how we spend our time together.

And our chemistry is not as it once was. That sounds normal for a marriage and would be if we were not lacking in all the other areas. Instead, it makes me feel like I need to bring us together in some way. Lately, he's turned down my attempts, and it is not even the actual act I seek. I want to feel a connection to my husband. I continue to seek him out because if I am not trying, then who is? After all, what is marriage in the end? It would be naïve to think that marriage is not like this. Right? Marriage is choosing to be with each other even when we are not at our best versions. I picked this life.

As I contemplate life and try to ignore the hard truths, I shove the covers off and head to the bathroom to remove yesterday's makeup. The dried-up mascara and spontaneity from last night rinse off with the help of my oil-based make-up remover balm. I rub off the streaks that ran down my cheeks while flashbacks of the rooftop bar replay in my head.

I remember spending the night networking and bonding with the entire department, but as the night went on, I linked up with Sarai. She is our social media content creator and my newest friend. Over the past year, we have become more than just work friends. At 29, Sarai is just a few years older than me, so it's been easy to become so close.

We left our co-workers and ventured to the other side of the bar to grab a drink and catch up. It was not long before my buzz had me confiding in her about married life. I needed some validation and a place to lay out my insecurities, even though Sarai is single and has had little to no long-term dating experience.

I told her everything from how Justice seems to prefer being on his own and designates all of his free time for his friends. In an attempt to allot time together in his schedule, I have suggested date nights and weekend getaways, all things we talked about doing before marriage. However, the dates we've gone on feel forced and feel as though it is a chore for him rather than an activity. I bet you could have guessed, too, that no action was ever taken to get away for the weekend.

Justice works a mediocre job and would rather sleep the weekends away, while I want to experience more than the walls of my bedroom. I told Sarai that I do not expect Justice to get a fancy new job or whisk me away to a foreign country, but I know there is so much more to life that we are missing out on.

A born genius, Justice has had multiple offers, but he lacks ambition. I know he hates working a 9-to-5 job and the idea of working for a boss whose measure of success is how much money you earn them. I know that is why he chose the job he has now, where it basically only requires that he logs on and off by the end of the day. He has so much more to offer than that. He is a gifted photographer, though it was only a hobby, but when we graduated college, he put down the camera and lost sight of his passion. I'm not sure if it was the pressure of finding a job, the hectic time of wedding planning, or some other excuse he's making. He claims his fear is that the market for a photographer is over-saturated and pointless, which I understand, but if he were to find time outside of work to pursue it, it would bring him a greater purpose and joy.

Finally, I confessed my deepest, darkest fear that Justice has lost his lust for me, and in return, I am losing mine. I have no doubt that Justice loves me, but is it a love that grows or a love that is stagnant? Unfortunately, Sarai's response was not hopeful, nor did I expect it to be. She asserted that I 'deserve' better and 'he should know what he's got and appreciate it.' That made me feel good in the moment and validated that I was, in fact, not crazy. However, in the end, it only enhances my doubts of our future together. My hopefulness increasingly grows dim and something else she said still resonates with me: love is not enough.

Although I am left with more questions than answers, I am grateful for Sarai lending an ear. I have had a hard time finding friends and a community since graduating. I have spent years married to a man whom I am so in love with, but life has proven it is not easy. I am happy to have found people in my life to connect with and vent to.

I dry my face, throw my hair up into a top-knot bun, and head towards the kitchen to check on Justice. He is flipping pancakes and the smell of bacon envelopes the kitchen.

"Did you go to the grocery store this morning?" I rub my eyes in surprise.

"Ya, I ran out this morning for some breakfast essentials. I figured you could use something to soak up the booze from last night."

I smile. With the faint smell of buttery, chocolate chip pancakes and the bacon grease, I forget my lingering doubts and take a seat at one of the barstools at the counter. Justice slides a plate with two pancakes and two strips of bacon over to me. I shovel a couple of bites into my mouth and take in the sight of my husband.

In this moment, I choose to appreciate the small act of making breakfast. Justice is wearing his gray Lululemon joggers and no t-shirt, looking like a natural model. Although he goes to the gym on a regular basis, he has always had a six-pack without even trying. His Italian, olive skin only provides more definition to his abs and biceps. I never get tired of ogling his shirtless body, but right now it's reminding me of his latest rejection. How is it that I can be so entirely frustrated, yet still want to take him to bed? But when I fling myself at him, he clearly does not feel the same way.

Again, my doubts intrude on my thoughts and I finish eating without another word. I cannot bear to continue down this road of begging him to be interested in me. This is the first time he has said "no" to me when I was intoxicated. Normally, the booze takes over and has a mind of its own when it comes to Justice. I will do or say anything to be loved by him and I can't fathom how even the alcohol had no power over him.

"Would you like to go to the movies today?" Justice asks as I move off the barstool to clear my plate.

I stop, swiveling to face him. "Ya, I would love that," I reply, stunned by his initiative. *Did he just read my mind from earlier?* Normally, it is me arranging plans and making sure we get quality time together. Suddenly, I'm hopeful again. Oh, how easy it is to please me.

"Great, Revel and I wanted to go see 'Cocaine Bear'. I'll tell him we can meet him there for the 1:30 showing," Justice replies.

Of course. This roller coaster of hope is getting tiring.

"Sure," I reply less enthusiastically, though he is oblivious to my change in tone. "Let me shower and then we can go."

At least hanging out with Revel is better than Aaron and Cruise. Revel has his flaws, too, and he is not exactly Justice's best influence as a self-proclaimed bachelor, but I can tell he wants someone to share life with. In the meantime, his lack of commitment to a romantic relationship does not deter his infinite loyalty to Justice.

At times, their loyalty to each other conflicts with our own commitment, except Justice would never see it that way. The two have always been inseparable. You would think that they are twins by the time they spend together. Justice, the tall, tan, athletic one, and Revel, taller, gawkier, and moodier. I have been a part of their lives almost as long as they have known each other, yet I have not been able to penetrate their bond. I can tease and hang out with them, but Revel will always choose Justice, and, at times, I think it is the same for Justice. *Is it Revel before me?* The truth is, how can his friends be a good influence when they constantly keep coming between him and his wife? Regardless of their bromance, Revel is a thousand times better than his other friends. For one, his language is not as perverse. *Thank God.* And second, Revel is family. Justice and Revel are so close, they are basically brothers. In that sense, I guess you could say he is like my brother-in-law. He will look out for me no matter what, for Justice's sake. Don't get me wrong, if it comes down to whom to protect, he will always choose Justice, but it's exhausting trying to navigate this unbreakable bond, making sure you are the one that stays tied to it. At least, unlike his other friends, I can tag along knowing that Revel won't overlook me.

It takes me thirty minutes to shower and throw on a sweatshirt and sweats. I don't understand people who wear jeans to the movie theatre instead of something comfortable. I select my favorite sweat set from Pretty Little Thing in a subtle tan color paired with white slip-on Vans. Once again, I throw my hair up into a topknot, trying to make it look effortlessly cute. I follow my routine with face lotion, blush, and some light mascara. This is not a date, and I do not care to impress Revel.

Justice is sitting on the couch when I walk out. He glances up and then goes back to staring at his phone. I see the text he sends Revel as I approach, letting him know we're on our way.

"Wait, babe, I was hoping we could stop by 7/11 for some snacks. We still have some time," I suggest. Usually, Justice and I stop by a local corner store and pick out some candy options for the movie. It started back in college when we were 'starving' college students to avoid paying for the theatre's overpriced candy. We accompanied our secret candy stash with a blanket from my dorm room to offset the air conditioning and the movie-going experience has forever changed since. Partly, wanting to recreate good memories, I thought the suggestion would be fun for our first time back at a movie theater in years.

"Oh, babe, Revel is already on his way. We can buy snacks there if you want," Justice replies.

I pout, but Justice is too busy on his phone to notice. He sends one last text and gets up from the couch, walking out of the house.

"Let's go," he announces.

"Wait," I grab a blanket from the extra pile stacked in a basket and follow him out.

~ 9 ~

REVEL

"Hey, Rev," Justice says.

I look up from my phone to see Justice and Carrie standing in front of the table I chose at the café across from the movie theatre.

"Hey, I already bought my ticket," I look down at the table where I had placed my ticket moments ago.

"Ok, we'll go buy ours and then I guess we still have some time before the movie," Justice looks at his watch to confirm. He glances at Carrie with an aloofness and repeats, "ok, we'll be back."

I am still on my phone for no more than five minutes by the time they make it back. They both take a seat, and Justice takes his phone out as well. I don't look up from scrolling on TikTok, but I can tell that Carrie is watching us. Normally, I don't notice her presence any more than Justices', but I can feel a restlessness on her end that Justice seems completely oblivious to. *Is she annoyed?* I really don't want to be thrown into the mix of their situation.

"So, I got a promotion," I announce.

Justice and Carrie look at each other for a second before responding.

"You what?" Justice asks.

I almost laugh at their reactions since it is obvious they are surprised. I rarely share details of my work life since Justice and I don't really get excited about our corporate work. This is not my first promotion, but I guess it is kind of a big deal. I'm a software engineer at Oracle, but they want me to step into a lead role when new clients need troubleshooting. If there are any issues they want to work with us on, then I would be the liaison. It basically means I will be on call 24/7 and the fall guy if anything goes wrong.

"I got a promotion and will probably be working longer hours," I repeat.

"Oh, shit! Good for you, Revel. Wait, this is a good thing, right?" Justice asks.

"Yah, it is," I say matter-of-factly. Justice's congratulations is overpowering in juxtaposition to Carrie. She is just sitting there, quieter than normal.

"That's good, Revel," Carrie adds. Her response is gentle and genuine–almost how I imagine my mother would respond if she were still here. In all her chaos, she had a gentleness much like Carrie. I am taken aback by how much her response warms me, but I don't react.

"Well, let's get some drinks, then," Justice says. "This café has got to have something, right?" Justice gets up and turns to Carrie, "Want a drink?"

"Ya, sure. Just get me any beer," she replies.

I have third-wheeled with Justice and Carrie for so long that I can't even remember a time when they weren't together. Yet, I rarely spend time alone with Carrie, and I feel slightly awkward. Before I can return to scrolling, Carrie interrupts my thoughts.

"You're not too excited about the promotion, are you?" Carrie asks politely.

I debate whether I care to sugarcoat my response or not. I'm going to go with not.

"Not in the slightest," I deadpan.

"Why?"

"Because I couldn't care less about making the lives of big corporations easier and, in return, making my life harder. I mean, the work for the most part is easy, but the more I am asked to do, the more I couldn't care less about doing it," I admit.

"Ever thought about doing something else?" Her statement falls off her lips so easily, as if 'doing something else' would be just as easy.

"Yeah, right," I scoff.

"I'm being serious. You and Justice should start your own business. You guys have the time since the work is so easy for you, and you might find that the extra work towards something you're inspired by would motivate you."

"And what business would that be?"

"Well, you know how good Justice is at photography and with your Photoshop background... Plus, I am sure you could make a great webpage for the business. I could see it happening," she says confidently.

Just then, Justice makes his way back with three beers on tap. "Hey, guys, turns out there is a brewery on the other side with the same outdoor patio. We lucked out!"

"Thanks, babe," Carrie says and grabs one of the beers.

I sit up and grab one of the other beers from his hand and tease, "Nice.... Get this, Justice. Carrie thinks we should open our own business."

"Ya, I know she has told me before," Justice looks at Carrie and rolls his eyes before laughing along.

"Whatever, you guys, it was only a thought," Carrie pouts. "Let's just drink and get to the movie."

"Wait, we didn't cheers to Revel! To big fat bosses with big fat promotions to fill our big fat pockets!" Justice cheers.

Justice and I bellow with laughter and we all clink our glasses.

~ 10 ~

JUSTICE

What a great way to spend our day. The credits are rolling while the three of us exit the theatre. I put my arm around Carrie and think about how today has been a complete 180 from last night.

I hate knowing that I have been the cause of Carrie's tears the past two weekends, but I don't know what she expects from me. I feel like I am being respectful, but there is always something I am doing wrong. Even when she arrives late and drunk after not responding to my texts, I am still the one who has done something wrong. I just do not know how to keep her happy, which is why I invited Revel today.

Revel and I were already talking about going to the movies, but honestly, I wanted the buffer. I wanted the day to go well and I wanted to avoid it ending in tears. She is always pushing our relationship in some direction. Whether it is her telling me that I need to make better friends, or I should start a business, or I am not loving on her enough, the constant nagging makes a man feel inadequate and more averse to change.

We head towards the parking lot and say goodbye to Revel. Before I start the engine, I see Carrie place her head on the passenger window and close her eyes.

"Tired?" I ask.

She opens her eyes and sighs before responding, "Ya, guess it was a long night last night."

"Nap when we get home?" I suggest.

She smiles at me while I navigate us out of the parking lot. "Yeah, sounds good."

I look forward to lying in bed with Carrie and no one needs to tempt me to sleep more on the weekend. As I park, I notice Carrie is sluggish. *Perhaps she's hungover?* Carrie makes her way to the front door, and as she is unlocking it, I rush over. Placing my right arm around her waist, I lift her from the ground, making Carrie laugh.

"Eeeeeekk," Carrie squeals with a gasp of air from the shock. "Justiceee, let go!" Her demand is stern, but she lets out a giggle that lets me know she is not serious.

I walk us over to the bedroom, tickling her left side and making her squirm. Getting Carrie to laugh is a win for today.

Inches away from the bed, I turn sideways and thrust us both onto the mattress. Our backs slam onto the cushions and we are thrown together exactly as I planned. Carrie is laughing uncontrollably, and her hair is covering the smile that I adore so much. My hand involuntarily makes its way to her face and touches her silky, smooth skin. Carrie stops laughing briefly as she makes eye contact with me. My eyes stay locked on hers as I brush the strands of hair back. There is no denying that Carrie is beautiful and I cannot imagine falling for anyone else. I lean in and kiss the top of her forehead. I pull back and see Carrie's eyes still shut. Wrapping my arms around her, I continue to hold her in my arms as she falls asleep. As I bask in this moment, I can't help but reminisce about the day I fell in love with her.

--

I loved Carrie before she loved me. I was a sucker for her bubbly personality and the way that everyone gravitated towards her. She knew how to reel people in with pure kindness and authenticity. Her down-to-earth demeanor had a way of lighting up the best parts in everyone she came into contact with. So when I met her at a college party one night, I was immediately hooked.

At the time, Revel really was the only person I hung around with. There were girls that would approach us, but I was never interested in keeping the conversation going until I met Carrie. That night, I reveled in her attention. She knew how to keep me talking and we ended up talking all night. Between sipping Cîroc and Sprite, Carrie and I asked each other everything from 'What animal do you see yourself as?' to 'Who would you hate to lose the most?' For me, it took that one night and I was all in. It did not take long for me to fall in love with her.

We spent most of our time together over the next two months, doing everything from grocery shopping to studying together, often crashing at each other's dorms in between classes. I thought it might be puppy love until one night when Carrie came over. We had been officially dating for about a month and our physical chemistry was growing. She arrived in the sexiest, short black dress with a V-neck that dipped all the way down to just above her belly button and drew attention to her smaller, yet perky breasts. The fabric was tight enough to show off her small waist and accentuated her lower backside. Straight from a night out with her girlfriends, she let herself in and quickly closed the door as I remained fixated on the way the dress showed off her body.

I felt irrationally jealous that there were other guys out tonight who had potentially checked out my girlfriend. I felt so possessive and eager as soon as I laid eyes on her that I grabbed her immediately. My hands fell beneath her back and my lips collided with hers. The passion I felt for her in that moment was unmatched. I moved my hands over her butt and I lifted so that her legs came up, wrapping tightly around my waist and lifting her dress so I could feel the lace thong hidden underneath. I remember thinking 'Thank god my roommate isn't here.'

Our lips pressed up against each other and our tongues moved more urgently between each kiss. I drank in her strawberry lip gloss while Carrie held onto my waist with her legs and pressed her body tight against mine as I carried her to my bed. My need for her increased as her hands moved across my back and through my hair. I gently lay her down, making sure that no part of us lost contact and my arm trailed along her thigh up to gently grab her face as I continued to embrace her between licks.

Suddenly, I felt something wet on my cheek and I slowly forced myself to pull away from Carrie. As soon as we made eye contact, I saw a tear running down her cheek. I cautiously looked into her eyes and asked her, "What's wrong?"

"Sorry, I've just never felt this way with anyone before," Carrie responded. We lay there on the bed with my body in between her legs. She opened up about how the last guy she was with didn't appreciate her remotely as much as I did. Their relationship was not as serious and she confessed that she knew it was nothing in comparison to us.

"I think I want to wait with you."

At that moment, I knew. I would wait forever for Carrie. As long as I could hold her in my arms, I was happy to wait. "Take your time," I responded and kissed her tenderly.

She told me she loved me two months later. I never told her *when* I fell in love with her. Instead, I waited for her to say it first and affirmed to her that I loved her back when she was ready.

~ 11 ~

CARRIE

I awake from our nap, surprisingly cold, and quickly realize that the chill sweeping over me is from the empty side of the bed. Justice is not lying beside me anymore. *Hmmm, how long have I slept?* He must have woken early and let me sleep in. I wish I had woken up at the same time as him because lying in his arms would have been a much better way to wake up. Slowly but surely, I swing my legs over to the side until my feet are touching the ground. Once positioned vertically, I gain a semblance of my consciousness and hear Justice talking in the living room. I focus with intent on what he is saying.

"Yah, I will be right over!" Justice replies, "No, she was out late, so I am sure she does not want to come out tonight."

It is clear to me that he was awoken by a call and is now making plans to get out of here. Plans that I am not invited to. I walk out to the living room in hopes that his mind can be changed. It is great that his friends call him out of the blue to hang out, but does he have to jump at every opportunity to leave? I swear I am not as needy as I sound. Just spending time together, the two of us, for the night would be great for a change.

Justice ends the phone call and turns around to face me. "Hey, good morning," he says in a sarcastic tone.

"Hey..." I reply, not in the mood to play along.

"That was Aaron. He wants me to come over for the UFC fight tonight," Justice says excitedly. My face distorts into a not-so-cheery facial expression, and what is worse is that he does not even notice it.

"You don't want to stay and maybe watch a movie with me tonight?" I ask as my face reverts into a soft, pleading expression.

Justice stops in his tracks, already on a mission to head out the door, and looks at me with a hint of disappointment. He perks up for a moment and adds, "You are welcome to come! Aaron invited you, but I honestly thought you would be too tired to come."

"Uh yeah, I don't really feel like going out tonight. Do you have to go?" A few months ago, I would have let him go. I would have ignored my desperation and played the 'cool' girl just to avoid getting into a fight. For one, it takes too much energy to fight about the time he spends with me. Second, I want him to want to spend time with me. However, I am afraid he is never going to change, and I have reached far beyond the capacity to pretend like I don't care anymore.

He plants a kiss on the top of my head. "Sorry, babe. The guys need me, and I am not tired enough to stay home."

"But I feel like I need you and we haven't spent time just you and me lately." I hate this feeling of complete desperation.

"What do you mean? We spend time together at home all the time. Just because you were working all week does not take away from the time we spent today together or any other time at home."

"I mean more quality time together, Justice. Revel came with us today when it could have just been us, and now you want to go hang out with your friends again?!"

"I haven't seen Aaron since last weekend. Plus, you were out with your friends yesterday and I didn't complain about that," he replies. "Why don't you hang out with your friends? I wouldn't mind."

My blood is boiling and all I want to do right now is a mixture of screaming at the top of my lungs, curling up and crying, and bolting out the door so that I can avoid the frustration running through my veins when I look at Justice's unempathetic expression. *Am I going crazy? Why is his defense always to deflect me? Am I being unreasonable to expect that my husband would rather be with his wife than his friends sometimes?* I freeze and look at him with sadness and desperation. Every other instance, I have cried my eyes out unable to control my feelings yet hoping he will see the pain he causes by dismissing me. And every time it has failed. I am left feeling empty and weak. Numb to my pain. "Please, just stay home with me?"

"Babe, I will not be out late," he replies and kisses me on the cheek before walking out the door.

It is 11:00 p.m. and I know for a fact that the UFC fight is over, well, because I googled it! It ended hours ago. Truthfully, I did not think to look it up until my rom-com movie ended and Justice was still not home. But, before I texted him right away, I checked his location on my phone... Ugh, he is still at Aaron's place. Two things I know for sure, now: 1) he is at Aaron's house, and 2) he is intoxicated. I decide to call in case he is too intoxicated to text back right away.

Ring, Ring, Ring. Voicemail beep. No answer. Ring, Ring, Ring. Voicemail beep. No answer.

I text him, 'where are you???'

After a few minutes go by, I get, 'sorry I was playing beer pong.'

I call him. Ring, Ring, Ring. Justice answers the call, "Hey, what's up?" His words a little slurred.

"I thought you weren't going to be home late?" I respond with frustration.

"Ya, but then we began playing some games... You should come out babe!" His drunken state is making him more oblivious to how stupid he sounds than normal.

"No, you should come home!"

"I will, I will. What time is not late to you?" he replies. *Is that question some kind of joke?*

"Now," I reply.

"Okie dokie," Justice replies, "Let me tell the guys bye and I will come home."

I cannot believe I am waiting on him again after he made a half-ass attempt to hang out with me. How old do we have to be to put the beer pong balls down and come home before midnight on the weekends? Truthfully and naively, I did not think I would still be pulling him away from this life after five years post-grad. Though I find myself fuming, I know I need to calm down before he walks through the door.

~ 12 ~

REVEL

I don't know why I am still at Aaron's place. The guy's place is a stuffy one-bedroom apartment full of pointless stuff. Hats are hanging on the walls and a beer can pyramid stands next to the television. It's not the first time I have been here, and yet I am still always shocked by how juvenile it is, but Justice insisted I come by for the UFC fight. The fight ended a while ago, but Justice and his buddies (I emphasize 'his buddies') refuse to let me leave. Of course, I would walk out on Cruise and Aaron without a care, but it's Justice that I am worried about. He doesn't normally pressure me to stick around, but tonight, he is going above and beyond to be the life of the party. It's not Cruise or Aaron driving this kickback as usual. It's Justice hounding us to drink and stay late. It is fine for him to want to let loose every now and then, but I have rarely seen this version of him.

"C'mon, Cruise! You lost!" Justice taunts. "Drink up!" He wraps his arm around Cruise's neck close enough to put him in a chokehold. Justice is a good 5 inches taller than Cruise, so it's not hard for him. However, his hold on Cruise is not on purpose. Justice is grabbing him to keep himself from stumbling.

"Nah, dude, that didn't count," Cruise replies. "I am calling house rules, and I get another try."

I roll my eyes at Cruise's lame attempt to get out of taking a shot. Justice merely laughs with his all-American smile, teases, "Ok, ok, I will take one with you if that makes you feel better."

"Whatever, man! I am thirsty anyway," Cruise shakes off the competitive humiliation and pours the two of them a shot.

In the midst of this childish banter, I hear a ringing on the other end of the couch. Is that someone's phone? I get up from the Facebook marketplace couch that reeks of Cheeto puffs, and search for it. Under a raggedy pillow, I find Justice's phone and Carrie's face filling the screen.

"Justice!" I raise my voice to get his attention. "Carrie's calling you. I think she has been calling for a while—" The ringing stops, and the call history pops up. "Oh yah, looks like she called you twice."

"Oooo better answer that, Jus, or she might close up for business if you don't keep her happy," Cruise hollers.

"Tell her it's boys' night!" Aaron pipes in.

Again, I roll my eyes. I do not know how Carrie puts up with these guys. Justice and I have our moments, but they are perverse beyond belief sometimes.

Justice staggers towards me and brushes their comments off with a wave of his hand. "She's just calling to check in. No, big deal."

I see him type a text and send it instantly.

"You're not going to call her back?" I ask. I think I know what is bothering me about Justice and his attitude. He is acting like Cruise and Aaron. It's not like him to dismiss Carrie so easily. Plus, he is acting like this over-privileged, frat-guy prick.

"Nah, it's fine," He dismisses. Yet, as soon as he finishes his sentence, his phone rings again. "Ugh, okay, one second."

He walks away from the couch and the beer pong table awkwardly placed in front of the kitchen, facing the back wall. I try not to pry, but like I said, it's a small apartment.

I can't help but overhear the conversation -- "Ya, but then we began playing some games... You should come out, babe!" Justice is holding the phone to his ear in one hand and his other hand is covering his ear to block the music out. "I will, I will. What time is not late to you?" he replies. *Wow.* I blow out a breath. His tone is oblivious, but that couldn't have been a more condescending response. Justice finishes the conversation with, "Okie dokie. Let me tell the guys bye and I will come home."

He turns around so his back is no longer facing us. Cruise and Anthony are too drunk to notice him let alone listen in, so I take the time to figure out what's going on.

"Jus, is everything good?" I ask. He almost bombards me on his way back to the beer pong table, but I hold him back for a second to catch up before Cruise and Aaron notice his absence.

"Ya, ya, of course. Why?"

His aloofness concerns me considering the talk we had recently. Things are already not going well between them and the way he is acting is not going to help. I want to be there for him, but, honestly, he is acting like a dick. "I don't know, maybe because of everything that is going on between you and Carrie lately?"

Now, I can see it. Justice diverts his gaze away from me on purpose. He dodges out of my way and daps up Cruise and Anthony as he says goodbye. He doesn't even acknowledge our conversation or say goodbye as he walks out the door. The next time I see him, I know he will pretend like this never happened because Justice is doing what he does best, smiling while avoiding everything.

$$\sim 13 \sim$$

JUSTICE

"Thanks, man, for the lift!" I wave as the Uber driver drives away. *What a nice guy!* We basically talked sports the whole time which made me forget why I was calling it a night and coming home. *Oh, righhht... the wife called me home.*

I stumble on a step up to the front door before entering. The house is eerily quiet, so to lighten the mood and bring some laughter, I yell, "Honey, I'm home!"

No answer. I toss my keys on the side by the entrance and take my shoes off. For a second, I lose my balance taking off one of my shoes with the other foot and cannot help but chuckle loudly. Still laughing at myself, I walk towards the bedroom to see Carrie. In the state that I am in, I cannot imagine being upset, so I should be able to calm her down in no time.

I see Carrie lying on the bed, under the covers, and her head laying on the pillow. I walk over to her and gently ask, "Are you sleeping?"

"No?" she responds in a question as if that was the stupidest thing I could have asked.

"Oh," I respond a little taken aback, "Everything okay?"

"No... what do you mean is everything okay?"

I can sense she is getting more agitated, so I try to acknowledge her attitude calmly, hoping to diffuse the tension in the room. "I mean, you seem upset."

"I am upset," she confirms.

Well, she seems much calmer than I expected when she called me earlier. That is a good sign. Maybe this will not end in a fight. Hesitantly, I ask, "Why are you upset?"

"You said you were not going to be out late. I thought you were coming home after the fight?" she replied.

"Yeah, but we weren't ready, the guys and I just wanted to hang out a little longer. There is really nothing more to it than that, babe."

"Yeah, but I was waiting for you to come home, and you didn't even let me know you were going to stay." Tears start forming in Carrie's eyes. "I am more upset that you don't ever want to come home. You would rather be with your friends, whereas all I want is to be with you."

I shake my head at that statement. *There is no way that is true.* "No, I want to be with you, too. I asked if you wanted to join tonight, but you didn't want to."

"And I asked if you wanted to stay and you didn't want to stay," she replies.

I asserted, "Well, because I did not want to be home tonight." Even as I said, I knew it was not the right thing to say.

"Exactly," Carrie responds.

Exactly? What do I say to that? I have no response and, truthfully, I am confused how this conversation ended up here. Of course, I want to be with her. That is why I married her. But my friendships are just as important. Is it so wrong to want to spend my weekends hanging out with my friends for a bit? I am still young and I do not need someone dictating how I should live. Carrie has already turned over so that her back is facing me, and, since I have nothing else to say, I leave her to fall asleep. I figure we could use the space, so I turn Netflix on in the living room, and am fighting to keep my eyes open as I fall asleep on the couch.

~ 14 ~

CARRIE

Ring, Ring.

"Hey, I'm here," I respond as soon as the ringtone mutes, and Sarai picks up the line.

Sarai walks through the double doors of her city-view apartment over to where I am parked in a red zone waiting for her. She scurries over to the passenger side in excitement as I pull out onto the road and head toward the local beach for my gym's event. I am not sure what to expect, but I am glad that Sarai is joining me.

"Hi!" Sarai exclaims as she buckles her seat belt in the old 2009 Jeep Wrangler I have had since college. The weather is so nice today and rolling down the roof to let our hair blow in the wind sounded like bliss. It is worn down, but when you close your eyes and stick your head out the window, it feels just like riding an expensive convertible. It is all about perspective.

"Hey, how's it going?" I screech back, matching her energy. I am just as excited to hang out with my friend, hit the beach, and enjoy a workout!

"Good! You look cute, Carrie," She replies. "I love that set." She points at my matching light blue sports bra and leggings ALO set, paired with white running shoes.

"Ah, thanks. I love what you are wearing, too," I reply genuinely. Sarai is sporting a tan, cheetah-print sports bra and leggings set that accentuates her petite, yet curvy body. She has that Latin flair that oozes spice I could never compete with. Anything she wears always looks so much better on her figure.

Sarai waves her hand and smiles, brushing off my comment as if she does not quite believe me. "Are you ready for this?" "Yes, I am so ready. Are there any cute boys at your gym that I can meet?" Sarai scrunches her nose and looks at me with a glimmer of hope and humor.

"Honestly, I don't know. I guess we will have to see," I respond. I mean I hope I can be her wing woman, but I really do not know what to expect from this event.

On that note, Sarai and I agree that whatever happens, happens, and we crank up the radio, singing along to Taylor Swift and Bad Bunny as we head over.

Letting loose with your girlfriends is a whole other way to live. Since being married, I have craved the energy and passion that I get from connecting with another woman. Living with a man has proven to be harder than I expected. A man will not pour out their day with you. They will not share the same craving for a wine night or an ice cream fix, all while sharing each other's feelings or goals for the future. Rather, a man needs time to decompress. They need their alone time and are not rejuvenated by conversation.

They do not seek new experiences after a long day at work. Is this all men or am I just describing Justice? Singing and driving along with Sarai reminds me that I need more human connection and conversation in my life. I enjoy venturing out of my comfort zone.

Sarai gasps!

"Oh my gosh, I have had this song on replay, Carrie!" Sarai confesses as she belts the lyrics to Flowers by Miley Cyrus.

"I can buy myself flowers," I sing along.

As the song finishes, we pull up to the beach parking lot. Sarai and I look at each other when we notice the number of people who have shown up to this event. At least 100 people mill about. I am amazed and a little overwhelmed.

Sarai jumps out of the car, already checking out the men in cut-off shirts. "This is much better than meeting men at a bar. Now, I have a better profile screening to put together," Sarai lowers her glasses a tad to properly scan the pool of men in front of her.

I laugh at her reaction. "Glad I could provide you with such a feast," I joke about the drool that is basically falling from her mouth.

We make our way over to a nearby booth and the lady manning the booth hands us a water bottle and a nutrition bar, both covered in the gym's logo. These refreshments are not the only thing that the gym is using to promote its brand. As I look around, there are banners galore staked out to make sure all members and newcomers find their way. There is a plethora of yoga mats placed in the middle of the event for the upcoming workout that members were promised a sneak peek into.

Sarai leads the way over to the yoga mats, and I quickly realize it's because she has already spotted a handsome male in the center of the lined yoga mats. She sets her water bottle and nutrition bar down on the mat directly next to the attractive man. I do not get a good look at the guy until Sarai introduces me with her spunky personality.

"...and this is Carrie, my best friend. She is the one who goes to this gym and invited me today," Sarai opens the conversation and line of sight, turning her body towards me a little. It is then that I notice who he is. Right away, I notice the kind eyes and handsome face from many of my classes. It is Anthony.

"Oh, hi Anthony!" I say, caught off guard. Sarai's reaction is pure astonishment. She knows that I rarely interact with males outside of a work environment. Therefore, the fact that I know a male, let alone a very attractive one, has clearly yet pleasantly surprised her. "Anthony goes to my morning classes sometimes," I fill her in and try to wipe the shocked expression off her face.

"Ahh I see," Sarai smirks, "Seems like I need to start coming."

I instantly cringe at her comment. I do not know whether it is the fact that I have to continue to see this guy in class or if I can't identify with being so forward. Oh well, I guess I did sign up to be her wing woman, and if he doesn't like her for her, then we will take a shot with someone else around here. Plus, many guys like forward women who aren't afraid to go for what they want. I still think it's better to play it coy, but who knows, he may end up liking her, and that would be great.

The background music quiets as a speaker turns on her mic and greets everyone. "Hi everyone, so excited for you all to be here. It is a better turnout than we anticipated and we're so glad to see you could all make it!" The speaker has a slim figure in a matching black Vuori set.

I notice athleisure brands since our company is part of the fashion industry. I also notice her long, straight blonde hair pulled into a ponytail and tucked under a black Nike cap. My envy sparks at how well she embodies the appearance of a gym instructor, gliding through our warm-up, directing us to roll, twist, and turn our bodies to get them moving.

As I do what she says, I can't help but compare myself to her put-together persona and feel quite the opposite. My curly, dirty blonde hair and freckle-faced skin give the appearance that I have been running around all day or basking in the sun. I would like to bet that she has a ten-step skincare routine before she goes to bed. I, on the other hand, still use hand cream for my face. I know I should not compare myself with other women, but I cannot help but feel less than when I see someone manicured to perfection. I cannot help but think that a woman chiseled to perfection must have their life figured out and find myself wishing I could say the same. I cannot help but envy women who have perfectly slicked-back hair and tanned skin. Though I can walk around town with no makeup without looking like a hot mess, I cannot hide the blemishes that have scarred the area around my chin, and I know people can detect the chipped nail polish on my fingernails from miles away. Women who don't have to deal with those insecurities and seem to be magically molded to perfection always mesmerize me.

"Now, that was just the warm-up. If everyone could stand up and grab a set of dumbbells at the front here, then we can get started on the actual workout," amplified the woman with great enthusiasm that can only come from someone who does not have any apparent worries on the horizon. I cannot remember the last time I cheered for a hard, gruesome forty-five-minute workout.

I move swiftly from the child pose we ended the warm-up into a standing position to retrieve a pair of dumbbells for myself. As soon as I lift my head, Anthony is already motioning to Sarai and I that he is on his way to grab a pair for the two of us as well. I knew he was a nice guy and Sarai is just about licking her lips at the chivalry.

"I can't believe you didn't tell me you were working out next to a hot, single guy every morning!" Sarai nudges me.

"I had no idea he was single!" I insist, "Clearly, I am not good at this wing woman thing."

"Please! No ring, no occupied yoga mat near him, and he basically hopped up to get our dumbbells before we had the chance? The desperation just about equals my own," Sarai, surprisingly admits.

I raise my eyebrow. "Desperate? You? No way!" I joke with her as Anthony makes his way back and sets our dumbbells at the foot of our mats.

"Thanks!" We say in unison.

Anthony smirks slightly, giving off a mysterious appeal. He may be somewhat desperate to perform chivalrous acts for two women he barely knows yet his desperation has an appeal that I cannot deny is there. The more I think about it, he would be perfect for Sarai! He is so nice, and I would imagine that his calm demeanor would balance her spunk. Wing woman activated!

The next fifty minutes are utter hell. I guess it was dumb of me to think that a workout on the sand would be more fun than the ones I force myself to do every morning. Don't get me wrong, the view is spectacular and the change in venue favorable, but the level of the workout was not changed in the slightest. The slim, fit blonde pushed us through an intensive HIIT (high-intensity interval training) workout. After we finished a set of 3 rounds, it was on to the next set. By the end of the workout, the sand felt like a reflector of the sun, and the ocean looked more heavenly than ever. When the workout ended and she called for a cooldown, I was dripping with sweat, tongue dry and heavy, and ready to run straight into the water for a much-needed refresh. Instead, I flung myself onto the mat, belly-up. Sarai mimicked my pose and the two of us lay there laughing off the embarrassment of our red, sweaty faces.

Everyone began packing up their stuff and wiping down their mats with the provided alcohol wipes. Anthony walked over with three wipes in hand. I take one of the wipes and start wiping down my own mat.

The three of us are packing up our stuff when Anthony interjects, "I heard there is a happy hour at a local dive bar that most people are going to right now if you two are interested?"

Sarai looks at me with wide, pleading eyes, her head shaking up and down, urging me to say yes. I shift my gaze back to Anthony and reply, "Sure, let's do it."

We head back to the parking lot and plan to meet at the dive bar. Sarai and I smile and wave as Anthony pulls out of his spot. I put my car in reverse once he has backed out and follow.

"So, how do you like Anthony?" I tease Sarai.

"Oh, no, no. Looks like he is into someone else," Sarai teases back as she pokes me in the arm. "Me?" I ask in shock. This whole time, I thought she was googly-eyed for him and that he seemed into her as well.

"Yes, you! Did you not notice the glances he kept shooting your way during that whole workout? Honestly, I felt like I was getting in the way of his eye line," she laughs.

"No way! Then why did you want to go to this happy hour thing? I thought you were telling me you really wanted to go."

"I do want to go! I overheard the guy in front of us talking about going. You know, the tall one with dark hair and abs like a god," Sarai says. I think I took Sarai to heaven, and I didn't even realize it.

"Oh, ok," I say, still piecing everything together.

"You are such a married woman! So oblivious, it's so cute!" She jokes.

I guess I am oblivious. Or has it been so long since I have been in the dating game? I remember being quite flirty in college and could easily detect whether someone of the opposite sex was interested. Even in the years that I was dating Justice, I would get some prospects here and there that I would turn down. Yet ever since I got married, the ring repels any man in sight. The idea of any man coming within five feet of me seeking any interest is unexpected. After a couple of years of marriage, you start to believe that no male would ever be interested in you ever again.

I put thoughts of another man's interest to rest when Sarai turns up the music and is singing the Spanish lyrics of Karol G's song 'CONTIGO' to the pedestrians on our way to the bar. Before you know it, we have approached the local dive located on Main Street and I have to concentrate to find a spot. As soon as the light at the intersection turns green, I make a left-hand turn where a car has just begun backing out of its spot. Golden!

Luckily, the spot we scored is right in front of the bar's entrance and we see Anthony walking up from a spot further down the road. He points at our parking space with his jaw dropped. Clearly, he did not have as easy a time.

"There's your secret admirer," Sarai continues to joke, "...not so secret from where I am sitting." She is laughing at herself, and if it weren't for her contagious laugh, I would have been annoyed with the continued commentary. Instead, I bunch up my nose to show my humiliation and give her arm a small shove.

"Jerk!" I toss back.

Sarai and I hop out of the car and make our way towards Anthony.

"How did you get that spot?" Anthony says with his jaw still slightly open.

"Carrie is a lucky girl, that's how," responds Sarai.

I laugh with embarrassment. "Oh, stop. No, we were pulling up and they were leaving."

"Very lucky," Anthony replies with an air of seduction. Normally, I would wince at the comment and feel like it was too forward for a married woman, but he says it so casually and not at all looking for a reaction. I hate it when a man expects the woman to be flattered. Rather, I can tell Anthony has no expectations and is just being himself. I can't be mad at that.

We follow Anthony inside towards the bar. I notice a pool table, low lighting, and stickers plastered all over the walls as décor. Not much about this place is different from any other dive. However, it does catch my eye that several people from the beach ended up coming here.

I am newer to West Palm Beach and not familiar with this area. I lived in Miami for college and knew all the places to go there, but I feel a little out of my element here. Already, I am getting the sense that it is a popular spot with the locals.

I order a beer at the bar and am happy to find out that it is only $5. I can see why this place is so popular. Sarai orders a tequila soda and Anthony orders an IPA of some sort.

I take a sip of my beer, and it provides much-needed refreshment after the workout we had. I am not much of a beer connoisseur, and most of the time Justice orders for me, so I picked the only one I recognize, a Shock Top, because I like the orangey flavor.

Looking up from my drink, I notice that Sarai is no longer by my side. Ahead of me, I see her dark brown, reddish hair bouncing towards what looks like the tall, dark-haired guy she mentioned earlier. I took two sips of my drink, and she has already left me with Anthony! I am so not in the mood to small talk with a guy right now. I continue to nurse my drink and attempt to stubbornly not engage, but it isn't his fault we were forced into this position.

"So, you haven't lived in West Palm Beach for very long?" Anthony breaks the brief silence that I was trying to hold on to.

"Uhm, no... Wait, how did you know that?" I reply.

"This bar is really popular, and I could tell by your face when we came in that you had never been here," he replies.

"Wow, that's some good detective work on your part."

"Well, you kind of show your emotions on your face. I wouldn't say I solved a cold-blooded murder with that observation," he teases. *He has got good banter.*

Taken aback by his ability to smooth-talk so easily, I decide to elaborate. "I moved here once I got married. More affordable here than in Miami," I reply, trying to gauge his reaction to being married. My comment was completely intentional, and I am wondering if that will deflate his confidence.

"Ahh, yes! You're married. How's the guy?" Anthony smiles genuinely. Although I don't know whether it is all that genuine because, at the same time, I still feel flirty vibes from him. Maybe Sarai's comments about him are just getting in my head and he is genuinely being nice.

"He's good. We met in college and got married after," I answer his question, not really knowing what he is looking for.

Anthony stares directly at me with a furrowed brow and a puzzling look. He replies, "I wonder what you were like before you were married."

Suddenly, the air around us has tightened around me and I take in a small breath. Knowing full well this is heading toward murky waters, I quickly look around to see if I can spot Sarai before I ask, "What do you mean?"

"You just seem so uncomfortable around me, and I have a feeling it is because you are married." Anthony's kind smile draws up on one side into a smirk. He is playing games with me and right now he is winning.

"Maybe, maybe not. Maybe I just don't like you," I say teasingly. Not flirty! I am trying to make this a more light-hearted conversation because right now, he is making my face burn and the butterflies in my stomach activate.

"I highly doubt that. Remember, it's not that hard to read your face," he replies with a huge grin, knowing it is game over for me. He found my weakness and knows I can't lie. Therefore, I wouldn't dare deny that I hold any dislike for him.

My face is on fire now and I am feeling too exhilarated by this conversation. I scan the room for Sarai again and know I need to escape.

She is standing by the pool table, twirling her hair, and sipping her cocktail, oblivious to the monsoon that has trapped me. It feels like I am swimming my hardest, gasping for breath when I get up from the table I sat at with Anthony.

"I've gotta go," I reply to Anthony and tread my way over to Sarai.

I tap Sarai's shoulder to get her attention and beg her to leave. "Bring whomever you want, but let's go somewhere else." Sarai nods and invites the tall, dark guy she ditched me for to come with us. Honestly, doesn't matter to me as long as we get out of here.

We make our way to another bar a block or so away and I buy the three of us a drink since I dramatically demanded we escape from the bar that included all his friends. However, he seems unfazed and continues lapping up everything Sarai is saying, while I sit there as a perfectly content third wheel. The only thing that was bothering me was Anthony. *How could he be so forward with me like that?* I wish I hated it, but I didn't. That feeling I got when he was forward with me made me crave that attention again. It is as if the bear that was sleeping inside of me has been awakened, and now, I need to eat.

~ 15 ~

REVEL

Justice and I are sitting on my backyard lawn chairs. Justice has been over more than usual lately and he brought some microbrew from a local brewery.

"So, where is Carrie today?" I ask.

"Out with a friend at some gym event or something."

We are already a couple of beers in and past the stage of small talk, moving on to what's really on our mind. That can range from a whole deep dive into our fantasy football line-ups and who got signed to what team. That conversation is usually led by Justice. Or it can be the time to tell the hard truths. I can remember when I told my hardest truth to Justice here...

I have only had one true love in my lifetime - Raven. Since then, I haven't found anyone like her and still remember the mornings I spent playing with her long black hair, caressing her porcelain skin, spotted with rosy cheeks. She was beautiful.

It took me weeks to wear her down and break through her hard shell. She spoke her mind and didn't believe in being cordial just to appease others. I wondered if she would get along with Carrie and Justice, questioning whether Raven would let them in like she did with me. Yet, what took me weeks to do, Carrie did in one night.

Carrie has this ease and understanding about her that even I cannot deny. I must admit that my walls have almost shattered amidst her presence, but I am better at hiding my feelings. Yet, with Raven, she hit all the right spots. It was checkers for her in a game of chess. Eventually, Raven cracked a smile, which led to a night full of laughter. They would probably still be friends if we hadn't broken up.

As much as I loved Raven's hard exterior and strong opinions, it made it hard when we disagreed, and we disagreed on everything. It was always something important too. I wanted to be exclusive. She didn't. I am a democrat. She was Green Party. I believe in a higher power. She is an atheist. Somehow, we always ended up in opposing parties. Our last disagreement was the final straw. I wanted children. Raven didn't.

I called Justice over for a night of hard truths that night. When Justice walked in, I had already drunk most of the tequila bottle and had to brace myself over the island kitchen counter to pour a shot for Justice. As soon as I filled it to the brim, I gave it a little push and the shot went sliding towards him. Justice got the message and swung back the shot without question. He didn't need to ask. He knew that Raven and I were no longer together. We spent the rest of the night passing the shot glass back and forth as I eventually told him every detail.

"...remember that night last year when we drank tequila all night and tried to forget the shit that went on with Raven and you?" Justice is looking at me, concerned as if the mention of her name will break me.

I let out a laugh at the thought of the two of us being able to remember anything from that night and sarcastically respond, "I'm not sure I do remember."

Justice gives me a light-hearted smirk but returns to a furrowed brow. "That night, you admitted to me something that you had been holding onto... I think it's my turn to do the same." He lets out a deep breath. "I know you've known for some time that Carrie and I aren't on the same page. Things have not been good for a while, and we aren't happy. Well, she isn't. I can't make her happy and I am not sure whether it is possible anymore. No matter how much I love her. It doesn't seem to be enough anymore."

Wait, what does he mean by 'I admitted'?... Suddenly, the memory comes flooding back. Yes, the confession that I made to myself and told him that night rises to the forefront of my memory. "Jus, she doesn't want to have children, and she won't be enough". I didn't want to admit it, but I had to. After growing up the way that I did, it was hard to believe that I could ever aspire to have a family. That growing up poor, fatherless, with a drug-addicted mother, and pushed around from foster home to foster home, would leave me wanting a family of my own. But that is all I have wanted. As of now, Justice and Carrie are the closest thing to it. That is why it is crazy that Justice is saying this. He can't be serious.

"What do you mean it's not possible?" I say, dumb-founded, "You guys are married. It is just tough right now."

"No, Revel. I am happy with Carrie, but I don't think this life makes her happy. I love every part of being her husband. All the mundane shit I can do. Working every day with the same job, day in and day out. Taking the trash out, cooking dinner at times, or cleaning the house before she gets home. The simple life was made for me. It's not made for her," he shakes his head dubiously. "She needs more. She wants adventure and spontaneity. I am afraid she has figured out that a life with me is not enough."

"Jus, that is crazy. Carrie loves you. So, what if marriage is a little boring? Life gets boring occasionally."

"Not just occasionally. I like boring. I don't need a roller-coaster life."

"Haven't you always loved that about Carrie? She gets you out there and experiencing life," Revel insists.

"Ya, I have always been attracted to her fiery energy. But it is like she wants to change me, and I don't want to change." Justice is looking at me with trepidation before continuing, treading carefully. "I don't know, Revel. Ever since we got married, it's like I'm on a hamster wheel trying to keep up with Carrie and her emotions. What I do or who I am or how I love is never enough. I don't know why the person she married is no longer good enough. She clearly wants more out of life, and I am happy with where we are at."

Could it really be that bad?

I am not sure what advice to give, but I'm shocked that he wants to give up. "Jus, you can't hold her back like that. If she wants to grow, you have to grow with her."

He stubbornly puts his head down and shakes it in frustration. A tear spills from the side of his eye. "Why is this so difficult, Revel? Should it be this hard?"

I lean forward onto my knees to get closer to him. I frown, "I'm afraid I think so."

Justice leans back into his chair and lets out a deep breath. "What's it like not having problems? I mean, coming home to this with no worries... No one to disappoint."

My eyes narrow and the corners of my mouth fall further. "Justice, you don't want to be me... You don't get it, do you?... You have everything."

~ 16 ~

CARRIE

Sarai grabbed a ride from the guy we met at the bar, Travis, so I don't have to stop by her place on the way home. I can't shake the thoughts that keep growing louder after my interaction with Anthony. It is like the doubts that I have been pushing to the back of my mind have taken up all the space in my head, and I can no longer ignore them. Anthony made my skin tingle more than I have felt in a while. The hairs on my skin and the butterflies in my stomach have not reacted that way since before being wed. So many doubts flood my mind. Is it doubt or is it fear? Fear, that's what this is. I'm terrified I was wrong about marriage and now I am trapped. The fear that I am supposed to stand by someone who lacks the same passion, interests, or desire to evolve. The fear that if I already feel this way just five years in, then how will I feel ten or twenty years down the line? Will I be committed to a life of comfort and stability, but one that no longer involves passion or adventure? Is life about finding security and comfort with one person, to be contained to just that? Will I soon be a victim of the sad truth that many men reveal about themselves when their wives grow two sizes larger from the baby they have birthed, and cellulite soon ripples down our thighs? Will I, then, be even more undesirable? Will I find myself seeking interest elsewhere because my husband no longer pays me any attention? Will I continue to wonder 'what if'? 'What if' I had not married the first man I loved? 'What if' I had never gotten married? I know this game is dangerous. I try to ignore these thoughts, but they refuse to go away.

I drive on autopilot, passing each intersection, contemplating why I am struggling so much with our marriage. I never struggled with being committed for the four years together before getting married. I never looked at another man and I was so in love with the idea of marrying Justice. It hasn't been until now that I feel an itch that I need to scratch, and the more I ignore it, the worse the itch gets.

I shift around in my seat and lower the radio playing 'Cake by the Ocean' with Joe Jonas in the background. "Cake, body, ocean..." I need silence to continue this little therapy session.

Ever since I can remember, I had the idea that *my* marriage would be idyllic. I never had the perfect picture marriage to look up to. My parents managed to stay together; however, their union was not one that I wanted for myself. I always admired their ability to stay together no matter the difficulties, which were abundant considering they were not the best pairing. Public affection between the two of them was not something I saw often, and their interests could not have differed more. If anything, I constantly questioned what was keeping them together. As I grew up, I thought how great it would be to marry your best friend. To have someone whom you shared the same interests and where love was undeniable. So, when I met Justice and we became inseparable, I thought this was it. Justice and I were an example of what love should look like. There was no doubt in my mind. Now, I think I was naïve to believe we would be any different from my parents. No couple can avoid the difficulties that come with marriage, and I have come to realize that marriage is not idyllic.

I pull into our driveway, feeling defeated. I pull the key out of the ignition, but instead of getting out of the car, I drop my head onto the driver's seat headrest and let out a deep breath. As I inhale another deep breath, I notice that Justice's car is not in the driveway. He is probably at Revel's house.

I am not ready to give up on us. I am craving Justice's attention and I will get what I want.

--

I step out of the shower, clean-shaven and squeaky clean. As I dry myself off with a towel, I open my drawer of intimates and reach all the way back for a brand-new lingerie set. I bought a bunch of lingerie pieces a while back, hoping it would pique Justice's interest. After a few tries, I realized a lingerie set cannot mend intimacy in a rocky marriage. Justice was interested for a moment, but nothing changed, so I stopped wearing them. As I select a black, strappy two-piece from underneath the piles of underwear, I consider 'why would things change now?' Am I kidding myself? I shake my head. I love my husband and I always have. I do not want that to change. I want him and I want him to want me.

I'm still in the bathroom brushing my teeth and running the water when I hear Justice sigh and the thud of his body hitting the bed. *Here we go. Confident!*

He is laying on the bed looking at his phone, unaware of my dramatic entrance. First blow to the ego. I walk over to the foot of the bed and see him catch a glimpse of what I am wearing. He puts his phone down, and I can see the surprise in his eyes, lust mixed with confusion. *Did I catch him off guard?* I make my way onto the bed, on all fours, and crawl on top of him.

"Hey," I break the silence, flashing my best seductive smile. Justice's brow is furrowed, but a smile curls up on one side of his mouth. His hands meet my face, and he brushes the curls back behind my ears. Justice has always loved playing with my curls and I find it comforting. I lean in to indulge him with a kiss that I have been longing for. Forget being on the same page; we could be on different ends of the book, and I would still long for him in this way.

I continue to kiss him longingly as he responds enthusiastically. His hands grip the sides of my face tighter, and he pulls me deeper. I place my hand on one of his hands, pulling apart for a moment to look into his eyes. I want to see if his desperation for more matches my own. His face is stern, almost as if he is hardened by the long day he has had. But, underneath, I see the flicker of desire for more.

I straddle his body and begin kissing down his neck. His hands fall from my face and trace down my back, slowly stopping at my exposed butt. His touch sends a burning, fluttering sensation throughout my body. My heart flutters and my lips make their way back to Justice's lips. I can feel him loosening up as he moves his hands up and down my bare skin. His grip tightens as he grabs hold and flips me onto my back. Justice looks at me with a yearning desire that sends a euphoria shooting through me. I lock eyes with him just before he pulls his gaze away and caresses my entire body. I let go of my fears and doubts and enjoy his touch, his desire for me, and his aroma. Justice smells faintly of beer and a more enticing smell, teakwood cologne. Very manly. He moves through me, and I can feel the intention he is putting behind every movement. His hands run through my hair occasionally and he whispers over and over, "I love you."

"I love you, too," I whisper back.

$$\sim 17 \sim$$

JUSTICE

I arrive home around 3:30 p.m., drained from the emotional spiel I poured out to Revel. I appreciate Revel being there for me so I can spew out all my worries and doubts. Unfortunately, I do not feel any better about it. Revel encouraged me 'to stick it out and things will get better'. But what does he know? I would never choose to leave Carrie, but I cannot be so sure she won't leave me. And, if that were to happen, I am not sure there is much that I can do. I do not have the strength to make her stay.

I walk in the front door and make my way to the bedroom, throwing myself onto the bed. I'm facing the bathroom and I notice the light is on. Assuming Carrie is inside, I turn onto my back and pull my phone out. After the confessional I had with Revel, I don't want to talk anymore.

I am mindlessly scrolling and deep in thought when I catch a glimpse of Carrie at the foot of the bed, standing in a sexy, strappy black lingerie outfit that I have never seen before. Her perky breasts are popping out in the thin layer of lace that is covering them. A smile twinges the left corner of her mouth when she notices my surprise. After the day I had, I was not expecting this, but it is exactly what I needed. I put my phone down and give her my full attention.

I can feel my brow furrow, conflicted and processing what is going on, yet I encourage Carrie to continue. We have been so disconnected lately, but I want to pretend this will rectify the issue. Carrie inches her way on top of me, flashing her sexy, cute smile, and I melt under her seduction. She lays her weight on top of me and sheepishly says 'Hey' to break the tension in the air.

I shoot her a smile and reach for the curls that are falling in front of her face. I love playing with Carrie's curls and how bouncy her hair is. It captures her beautiful and fun personality. But, as much as I love her hair, I brush them away, and it is her face I am truly in love with. Carrie is the most beautiful woman I have ever seen. Her deep green eyes are big and Bambi-like. Her button nose is covered in freckles and looks the cutest when she scrunches it. Her lips are small yet plush. I have fallen under her trance and all I can do is lie here waiting for her to make the first move.

Carrie takes advantage and leans in for a meaningful, longing kiss. I indulge in her kisses and think to myself, 'If there is one thing I need right now, it is to burrow myself in Carrie and hold on to her in this moment. Carrie loves me. I love her. Right now, I want to believe that will never change.'

Both my hands are planted on Carrie's face, taking in her whole mouth and breath, lost in the sweet taste of her. Frantically, we are fighting for more until Carrie's right hand makes its way to her face, and on top of my left hand. She pulls a part for a second and I can see it. Desperation. The same feeling that I have for us. I look back at her with the same desire. I am desperate for her just as much as she is for me. I want to make her feel it. I may not live up to it every day, but here and now, I am all in.

Carrie breaks eye contact and moves into place. Her legs now straddling my sides and her lips are sending vibrations down my neck as her kisses move further down. My hands have moved from her face to trace up and down the back of her until I can't take it any longer. I need to take hold of her. I grip just below her butt and take control, flipping us so I am on top. My chest on hers. My stomach on hers. My breath on hers. I pull at the strings of her hair and whisper three words that will always find me when I think about Carrie. "I love you, I love you, I love you".

She doesn't need to say it back, but she does, "I love you, too".

--

'7:06 a.m.' is the time blaring from my phone screen. Somehow, my body has woken up before my alarm. My brain is racing over all the work I have to get done today. Projection reports, budgeting, review work, Revel and I's talk yesterday, Carrie... my brain will not stop thinking. I turn onto my side and look at Carrie's face, resting peacefully. Her hair is wilder than ever, but her face is relaxed. She's beautiful. Yet, even amid such beauty, I am riddled with guilt and worry.

I cannot deny how amazing last night was, but I cannot forget everything I told Revel. Carrie and I's relationship used to be so definite, and I never worried about where we were. Yet somehow last night I held on so tight to Carrie because I felt like I might lose her. I'm frustrated at the weakness and vulnerability I succumbed to last night. I was not myself. I was grossly desperate.

I try to forget my behavior from last night and sigh one last time, forcing my body to get up. I throw on a pair of shorts that were thrown to the side of the bed and make my way to the kitchen to make myself a cup of coffee.

As the coffee machine gurgles, I run the water for a shower and hear Carrie's alarm blaring. Hopping in the shower, I focus on the sound of water hitting my body and the tile, letting the pressure and heat of the water soothe my mind.

I do not want the issues between us to keep me from being the rock in our relationship. If the man she had last night was the man she wants, then she doesn't want me. I do not want to be that guy. I am happy being who I am and sorry if that does not suit her, but I am done with trying to constantly please someone. I am who I am. Take it or leave it.

~ 18 ~

CARRIE

"**S**hut up!" my brain screams when the obnoxious alarm begins blaring. I groan and shut it off as quickly as my immobile body can muster. I stretch and slowly open my eyes. I glance at the clock to make sure it was set right. I better get up if I want to make it to work right at 8:00 a.m.

As much as I didn't want to wake up, I have a smile on my face and still feel flushed from last night I brush my fingers over my raw lips reminding myself of all the kisses we shared. I am a little saddened to see Justice's side is already empty, but I hear the shower and feel better knowing he is still close by. Taking a minute to get up, I continue to think about the connection we shared last night. I felt so safe and secure. For once, I felt like Justice let down his walls and I was able to see how he truly felt. I love him for the stable companion that he is but, at times, it is hard to read him and know what he is truly thinking. Especially through struggle and discomfort, it is like he completely shuts down... or shuts it all off. But last night felt like a turning point. *Maybe, he can open up to me!*

My hopefulness makes it easier to get ready for the day. I throw on a white pinstripe, navy blue oversized suit, and pair it with white New Balance shoes. I make my way to the bathroom when I hear Justice climb out of the shower.

"Good morning," I say with a sweet, goofy tone.

"Hey," Justice replies, monotoned and uninterested.

Uh, okay, that was weird. I ignore the weird vibes and brush my teeth and hair. I glance at Justice in the bathroom mirror and watch him throw on a Vuori sweatsuit in our room before heading towards his computer desk to start work already. I finish putting deodorant on and spritzing perfume before grabbing my bag and heading out of the bedroom. Instantly, I smell the sweet smell of dark roast coffee. *Mmmm, just what I need.*

"Jus, did you make me coffee?" I shout out. No answer. Oh, he must have his headphones in. I walk over to him and pop my head in front of him.

He takes one of his AirPods out, "What?"

"Is some of that coffee for me?" I ask.

"Uh, no I just made a cup for myself," he says and quickly fixes his gaze back on his computer, placing his AirPod back in his ear. I do not move, hoping to keep his attention and thinking he will take his AirPods out again. He looks up at me when he realizes I have not moved. "Need something?" he says.

"Is there a reason why you did not make me coffee?" I ask. He shakes his head.

"No, you always get it at work," he replies.

"Not ALWAYS. Just when I do not have time in the morning to make it, but looks like I would have had time," I respond in a non-threatening tone.

"Ok, well, how am I supposed to know that?" Justice questions me.

"What do you mean? You know that."

"Carrie, what do you want me to say? I didn't make you coffee. Just grab some at work," he says, his tone growing frustrated.

I am shocked. I was not expecting this hot and cold reaction from him this morning. "Ok, I was just wondering." Justice pulls his gaze away from me and puts his earphones back in.

"Ok, well, love you," I say, backing away from him, knowing he cannot hear me anymore.

Why is he being so weird? Why does he put me on this emotional roller coaster? Tells me he loves me repeatedly and the next day will barely look at me for even a second. *And you wonder why I crave his attention so badly.* One moment he makes me feel on top of the world, and the next, I wonder if he even likes me. Whatever. Suddenly, the hope I felt when I woke up this morning has dissipated. I trudge out of the house and make my escape. As I ignite the engine and back out of our driveway, a million questions flood my mind. Is this what marriage, ultimately, is? I was never one to think that marriage would come easy. However, I never felt this way before, and it is not something you can prepare yourself. The feeling that you can be loved by someone and yet so misunderstood by them is overwhelming.

I make it into the office around 8:15 a.m. and head straight to the coffee cart. I am hoping the caffeine will curb my incessant questioning.

After a wave and morning greeting, I sift through the pile of work on my desk. Although our launch went smoothly last week, there are still a lot of tweaks and future planning to assess. Our company, Finesse Yoga, is a start-up and is growing rapidly. When I was hired, they had only been established for three years. At the time, no one recognized the company name. Now, I see our logo every time I attend workout classes. It started as a niche company geared toward the yoga market, but it has grown exponentially and expanded to loungewear and all types of athletic wear. And, because athleisure has become a staple in everyone's closet over the last couple of years, we have continued to flourish in the market.

I love being a part of something new and exciting. It is like we are tackling the world together, and as a Marketing Manager, it has been exhilarating to study the market and grow as a brand. Right now, I am reviewing the sales we have made from outsourcing our clothing to workout studios, such as Rush Cycle, Pure Barre, and Yoga 1. We work with a lot of local studios as we slowly inch our way out of Florida, but we opened a store in Nashville and Philadelphia this year and are projecting to open seven more next year, including New York.

The growth is amazing, and I love building something from the ground up. As the manager, my bosses have high expectations, but the highest standards are held by my own desire to accomplish my goals. I grew up with two working parents and saw how hard they worked to put food on the table. Don't get me wrong, we were not poor and lived without a worry in the world as children. Not many people get that luxury. However, I was not oblivious to the work that my parents put in to get us there. I have two siblings and providing for all three of us was not easy. My older siblings struggled to provide for themselves in their early twenties. As the youngest, I did not want my parents to struggle because of my inability to provide for myself. Plus, I had the luxury to witness the mistakes my siblings made and knew I wanted more for myself. I attended the University of Miami and wanted to gain experience in the business world. With my creativity and brains, I figured a Marketing degree would best suit me, and I was right. Ever since my first day of classes, I have been working my way up to this position.

It is 1 p.m. by the time I finish comparing revenue, costs, and researching other profitable marketing strategies in the area and my stomach lets out a loud groan.

"Wow, what was that?" Sarai is standing under my office doorway.

"I guess it's time for lunch," I reply.

"Perfect, Chastity and I were just going to ask whether you wanted to join us for lunch," she points to the other end of the office where Chastity's social media team has dropped in to work for the day. "Chastity is just getting her stuff together and then we were thinking of some good Greek food at Acropolis?"

"Yeah, sounds delicious!" I turn my computer onto 'sleep' and grab my purse.

The three of us make our way out of the office towards my car. We do not always get the chance to grab lunch since Chastity and Sarai don't usually come into the office, and when they do, their time is usually filled with in-person meetings and collaborating with other colleagues. Thankfully, it is the week post-launch, and we could really use the much-needed downtime to enjoy lunch.

The three of us are venting about work and deadlines when we pull up to the restaurant. I am glad to have female colleagues that I can talk to and who understand the pressures of a start-up. Making friends at work is funny because, though personalities might be completely opposite, you're bonded through the work you do and the company environment that no one else can understand.

Sarai and Chastity are way more high-maintenance than I am, always spending money on the next clothing line launched for Finesse Yoga or the latest trending beauty treatments, so conversations often revolve around Botox, nails, and skincare. I have yet to dip my toe into the Botox world and still switch between the luxury of acrylic nails and glue-on nails sold at Target. It all seems a little unnecessary to me, but I am the only married one in the group. Sarai is still single, unless her status has changed since meeting the guy at the bar, but I doubt it. She loves being single and does not understand why someone would want to be committed to one person forever. She is always saying how she does not know how I do it because she could never handle one dick for the rest of her life. Chastity, on the other hand, has a fiancé and is getting married in two weeks. The two of them met six months ago and are already tying the knot. Chastity is the romantic, Sarai is the free spirit, and I am the realistic one. *Boring.*

The hostess is at the front when we enter the restaurant. She asks us how many people will be sitting for lunch, and we reply, 'Three'. Picking up three menus, she leads us to a table by the window. We open our menus and peruse its contents. I am drooling over the hummus platter and gyro listed.

"Would you guys like to split the hummus platter for a starter?" I mention.

Both Chastity and Sarai chime in, "Ooh yes!"

The waitress makes her way around asking if we would like to order any drinks. Chastity and I order an iced tea and Sarai orders a cocktail. *Like I said, free spirit.* The hostess asks if we are ready to order and we oblige. All starving to get food in our bellies, we respond with our orders one by one.

Once the hostess leaves with our orders, Sarai wastes no time catching us up on her new 'bae'. I say bae lightly because we all know that by week 'two' she will be onto a new bae. Or should I say 'aae', after anyone else?

"You would not believe the experience he has in the bedroom," Sarai goes on to say.

"Sarai?!" I exclaim. I don't know why I am surprised that she would be so forthright about her intimate life so early into our lunch. Nothing holds her back, and to think she has not even had a sip of her cocktail, yet.

"Wait, I want to hear," Chastity replies. I look at her, a little shocked and she shrugs her shoulders. "What? Jared and I are experimenting as well, so I am a little interested."

"Oh, that's good," Sarai replies to Chastity. "Carrie just doesn't get it because she has had same dick energy for so long. Carrie, you can't tell me you haven't tried changing it up after four years of marriage?"

I blush, not because I am too shy to talk about sex, but because of how difficult intimacy has been for Justice and me. And, to think that the two of them have no worries in that department makes me a little ashamed. But I am not a good liar, and maybe sharing would not be so bad.

"Um, to be honest, it's harder than you would think to get him to have sex in the first place." As soon as I say it, I see their mouths drop. "I mean, we had sex last night after a week or so and it was very good. Like I enjoy it as always, but after a while, the passion is not the same, I would say. I think that's just normal in long-term relationships."

I do not think I have ever seen the two of these women stunned before. Finally, Sarai speaks up. "See, this is why I couldn't do it. Carrie, come on, you are so hot. How is he not drooling over you?"

"I don't know. Because he is tired when he gets home from the gym, and it is partly my fault because I don't have the patience to wait for him to make the move. I don't know, sometimes I find it more of a chore and I wish it were more spontaneous like the two of you describe," I confess.

Chastity chimes in with puppy dog eyes filled with pity, "Carrie, I am sure a relationship as long as yours comes with its struggles, but part of that is appreciating what you have in front of you. It sounds like he is not doing that. You shouldn't have to apologize for not being appreciated."

Sarai adds, "Ya, fuck him."

I laugh because I know she doesn't completely mean that and said it more for female empowerment.

The hostess comes back with our drinks. Sarai takes a sip of her cocktail and continues, "Actually, don't fuck him. You should be open to fucking other people."

I shoot her a look like 'you're kidding, right?'

"Hear me out! If he needs a break and doesn't want to have sex with his wife, then show him what he is missing. Honestly, I have heard of many married couples coming back together after experiencing other people. Carrie, do you think this is really working out how you thought it would?" she pauses, but I am speechless. "Then, why don't you give an open relationship a shot for a week or so? Otherwise, the two of you could very well end up divorcing and this may be the thing that wakes him up. Or, maybe, you find better. Sorry, I just could not hold onto something that was holding me back," Sarai unloads. As much as her confession stings, she also has a point. I don't want to be held back anymore either.

I inhale a deep breath that puffs my cheeks out and vibrates my lips together as I let it out. Sarai jokingly cheers the air since she is the only one with an alcoholic beverage on a Monday afternoon and takes another sip. Her humor lightens the mood. Chastity and I look at each other with a shrug and we all let out a burst of laughter. Sarai could not be more unapologetic. As her friends, we know what to expect and truthfully admire the confidence she acquires to voice her opinions. In fact, I don't just admire but envy her ability to be a free spirit.

The kitchen door swings open across the room and the three of us turn our heads as the aroma of the freshly made food fills the air. We admire the plates balanced on the food runner's hand as he carefully makes his way over to our table. He sets each plate in front of the correct customer and sets the hummus platter in the middle. We dive into our meals, eating, gossiping, and bitching about the past week. Our meals look like vultures attacked and left no remains. We split the bill and prepare to make our way back to the office.

Pulling up to the building, we spot Chastity's fiancé outside. "Is that Jared?" I interject over the music playing on the aux.

"Ya! I was having cramps earlier, so I asked if he could bring some Motrin for me since the Advil in our office doesn't work the same," Chastity replies.

"Oh, we could have stopped by the store on the way if you wanted to?" I suggest, letting her know that in the future she shouldn't be afraid to ask. Calculating the miles it took Jared to drive over, including the pit stop at the store on the way, it seems unnecessary.

"No worries! Sometimes we just like the excuse to see each other," Chastity says with a huge grin and a pep in her step as she hops out of the car and over to Jared.

I look at Sarai and we both raise our eyebrows, fully aware that our friend is head over heels for this man. They are full of love for each other and have no reason to hide it. I take a little longer getting out of the car while simultaneously experiencing an ache in my stomach. I remember that desperate need to see one another. I remember all too well the validation you get when your man is standing outside waiting for you with a bottle of Motrin simply because you asked and he misses you. I remember the undeniable feeling you have when you walk up to him, kiss him, and leave without a doubt in your mind that this man loves you. What would I give to feel those butterflies again?

--

After lunch, I work like crazy to catch up and prepare for another board meeting. This time it is about the budget, so the expectations are high, and the margins are low on money spent versus engagement received. Therefore, I have spent a good amount of time reviewing the material while drinking a LOT of coffee.

By 7pm the office is empty. Sarai and Chastity said their goodbyes an hour ago. It can be a bit spooky when the office is empty, but I am relieved to have time to myself after a long day. Part of me doesn't want to go home at all. I make myself a cup of herbal tea with my office Keurig to offset the jitters from the coffee and relax in my chair.

As I reach for my tea, a knock on my office door startles me and I spill some tea on the floor. I turn towards the door in trepidation, having assumed I was alone, to see Revel in the doorway.

"Sorry, didn't mean to spook you," Revel responds.

"The mere presence of you is spooky enough to make me jump," I reply with a snarky tone. I look at the splotch of tea that dripped on my shirt and the puddle on the floor. I point to the communal sink on the other side of the room behind Revel. "Could ya?"

Revel walks over to the paper towel dispenser and grabs a few squares. He hands me the stack and I begin cleaning up the mess.

"What are you doing here so late? Justice might get the wrong impression of you working late and not coming home to him," Revel smirks. He is, clearly, kidding and I do not think he realizes how far from the truth he could be. I am the last thing on Justice's mind right now.

"I have a board meeting to prep for," I reply, "What are you doing here?"

"Helping the finance team with some tech issues we are seeing since the increase in revenue." Revel works for Oracle, a well-known tech company that implements the infrastructure and systems for our company. I'm not completely sure all that he does. He typically works at one of Oracle's off-site offices, so him being here is not a normal occurrence.

"Bummer, well, hope you have a good night," I say, sipping my tea and turning back to my desk.

Revel smirks and invites himself in, pulling the chair on the other side of my desk and taking a seat in front of me while placing his laptop on my desk. "Actually, our meeting just finished and now, I have a few things to fix before going home. You mind? Your office is way nicer than the shitty room they put us in," he taunts me.

"Revel, no way," I reply, "I was looking forward to some peace and quiet." He looks at me with humor in his eyes and his fingers pull an invisible zipper over his mouth. "I mean, without you!"

"Come on! I promise I won't bug you, and I will even order us some food if that will make you feel better. Come on, Chinese food always makes everything better," he pleads, imitating a little boy.

"Ugh, fine," I concede. Though Revel can be irritating, I do have to admit that his antics make me laugh. *Only somewhat!*

We put in our order for delivery and I make him a cup of peppermint tea. Of course, I made fun of him for wanting tea by calling him 'so dainty'.

"A guy can't do anything without a woman picking him apart, can they?" he jokes, grabbing the tea from my hands and making a show of sipping with his pinky in the air.

I crack up and, suddenly, the idea of working anymore has lost its appeal. I look at my screen and take a few more sips before finding the courage to ask something that has been on my mind since the last time we saw each other.

"So, how is the promotion going?" I ask.

Revel barely looks up from his computer as he replies, "Err, you know, it's going."

I notice the energy shift and bluntly ask, "Why do you and Justice always avoid talking about work?"

Revel replies with a sarcastic tone, "I don't know. Maybe because it's work, and I am already here eight hours a day. So, why would I want to talk about work after working?" He looks up after that and sees that I am a little thrown from his response and further explains, "I mean, I don't know... I guess I can't speak for Justice, but this job is just a means to an end for me."

I respond, "If it's a means to an end, can I ask... what does the end look like to you?"

Revel closes his laptop slightly. Clearly, he is impressed by my line of questioning. "Not sure. Haven't figured that out, yet." His response was so nonchalant. As if the future of his career is just an afterthought. Sometimes, I just envy men's brains. It is like they don't find the time to worry. "What about you? Tell me, what is work like when it is not a means to an end?"

"It's great. Don't get me wrong, work is not going to magically become the most fun thing to wake up for day after day... but, I don't know, this job gives me purpose," I crinkle my nose at the sound of that. "Does that sound dumb?"

"A little," Revel jokes and brings his finger and thumb almost together to sign a tad bit.

I think more about my response and elaborate, "The responsibility can be tough, but I love it. I love creating something and presenting a finished product to our crew. I love knowing that when our teams succeeds then the whole company succeeds. But mainly, I love what this job gives me outside of work." I withdraw my gaze from my desk after the trance I was just under and look at Revel. Revel looks intrigued, like this conversation is the first in-depth conversation he has had in a while.

"What do you mean by that?" Revel asks.

"I don't know, I have been thinking a lot lately... about life and what is truly important. I think what excites me most about this job is knowing that the more I succeed, the more I can contribute to a family," I admit. "I guess I am not that boss-bitch girl who sees work as my everything or even a means to an end. Yes, I enjoy it, and I work hard knowing that it will bring me something greater... I guess that is why I asked you what you see at the end of it." Revel is sitting there, stumped. Stupefied is the expression I read on his face. Embarrassed by my vulnerability, I add, "Sorry, that was a lot."

Revel wakes up from his own train of thought and looks my way with more intent, making my cheeks blush. He replies, "No, I get it." Ding. Revel looks at his phone. "Oh, looks like the door dasher is here. Be right back."

A few minutes later, Revel comes bearing bags full of Chinese food to-go boxes and we spend the next half-hour filling our stomachs with orange chicken, rice, and wontons while laughing the calories off. As the time ticks by, I realize this is the most I have laughed in a long while.

~ 19 ~

REVEL

"**T**here is no way that happened to you as a kid," Carrie is concerned yet giggling at my confession.

"I promise you. In fifth grade, I was stalked so tragically by this girl that I would ask the teacher if I could stay inside during recess and even tried not showering for weeks. Nothing worked. She was obsessed." I shrug, jokingly, like it is not hard to believe.

"Honestly, kind of explains a lot actually," she is still smiling ear to ear, with an eyebrow raised in consideration.

"Explains what?" My eyebrows raise with curiosity.

"Why you are so afraid of women or commitment is because you were *tragically* stalked by a ten-year-old girl and you are still scarred by it," she jokes, giggling.

I smile. Then, seriously, I say, "Maybe, I just haven't met the one."

Carrie's smile fades slightly at my serious tone, but she says nothing.

There is a shift of energy in the room and Carrie moves around in her seat. To divert my gaze from her, I reach for the last wonton on her desk. I barely notice she has done

116

the same until our hands meet in the middle and, inevitably, touch. Her touch is warm and soft. My gaze meets hers and she pulls back immediately.

Somehow, I am not startled. There is this feeling I can't explain, but, ultimately, I feel a sense of comfort even when I see in her eyes some apprehension. I decide to be honest.

"You were right."

"What?" she asks.

"This job is a means to an end. But... ever since you mentioned that Justice and I start our own business... well, I can see it." She stays silent. I am not sure what comes over me or why it is so easy to talk to her in this moment, but I keep going. "Plus, I would like my own family, too."

She's back to smiling.

JUSTICE

Work is coming to an end fast today. Normally, my workday starts early since my company is based in California, but last Friday I got ahead of my assigned work and decided to enjoy my morning with a few clicks on the snooze button followed by a workout.

Carrie always nags me when this happens because I could probably work towards a higher position with all the extra time, but I love the flexibility. Why would I give up extra time on my hands? Up for what? Truth is, I could push to be a manager or V.P., but it is not my aspiration to manage others and be held down by the work that they cannot complete. I surpass my co-workers with every project I am given. Thankfully, I am not in an office for them to notice. I am happy that my days tend to be short, but that does not take away from how obnoxiously mundane the work is.

I switch between pulling reports for my financial plan to messaging another financial analyst, Megan, on Teams. Our corporation is global, and the financial team is made up of ten of us, not including Accounting. Megan and I have gotten along since day one when she asked me to pull data since she corrupts everything she touches. Megan is always having issues running reports for herself in our ERP system so I became her 'report bitch'. Megan has a pretty foul mouth, which came through in her messages really quickly. 'Hi, this is Megan, and I am new to the office. Unfortunately, our system is shit and I can't run any reports. And, since it is my first day, I don't want to look like a fool in the office. Would you be able to run some reports for me? Yes, I am asking the co-worker who lives all the way in Florida because I am THAT embarrassed!'

She is lucky I appreciated the transparency and was intrigued to have an interaction with someone from our corporation beyond Teams work meetings. But, when I tell you everything she touches is corrupt, I am not kidding! She has blown through five computers in two years, while I have had two computers over the five years. It is a good thing Megan is ahead of the team like me. I swear we could run the entire team if they needed us to. Megan is up for the Financial Manager Role. She has put in a lot more effort than I have and she deserves it.

We spiral into a conversation about our co-workers and how miserable her life will be when she has to confront Trisha to pick up the slack, Jeff to stop coming to her for advice, and Tyler to rub two brain cells together. It may be mean but being in Florida, I only hear Megan's side of events.

"Jeff just LITERALLY asked whether I want a comparison of all months or just the current. Yes, Jeff, please do the bare minimum," Megan direct messages me with a sarcastic tone.

"Maybe Jeff just needs his girlfriend to help hold his hand while he works on his wittle project," I swiftly reply while my report runs on another browser. I like to tease Megan that Jeff is in love with her since he is always walking up to her desk for help. It is hilarious. The guy has a handlebar mustache and wears cowboy boots to the office. I have seen the handlebar mustache on our video calls, but unfortunately, I have yet to witness the cowboy boots. Megan fills me in on all the details. She voiced her reaction to the boots while mentioning her hatred for all things country. Since then, Jeff has become the butt of the joke, and I can continue to tease Megan.

Megan sends a GIF of Michael Scott mouthing the words, "Stop It!" before sending her next message. "Justice, stop teasing me about Jeffreyyyy! I could never get with a man who probably keeps his cowboy hat on in bed!"

"HAHA I wouldn't be surprised if he let out a 'Yee-Haw' at the end of it," I reply.

"Thank God you have the same humor as me. I do not think I could continue to work here if you ever decide to leave."

"Sure, you could! Jeff would keep you company. And, no, I will not stop teasing you. It is hilarious."

"So, have you heard that we are coming out to Florida for a corporate event?"

"Ya! I am excited to meet the crew. I want to know whether you have been lying about them or not."

"Lying? Me? Never!" Megan replies. And again, I can hear the sarcasm so clearly that it is practically coming out of the screen. Megan replies again while I am copying and pasting my report into an Excel. "I think I am most excited to see you."

I see her response and, internally, feel a little guilty. Am I reading into this or is she flirting? Or is this purely platonic? I do not want to come off as if I am full of myself and assume she is hitting on me, so I reply with, "Ya, same here."

Was that the appropriate response? Am I emotionally cheating on my wife, or does it have to be intentional because this was definitely not intentional? No, there is no way. She knows I am married, and we are just co-workers. If anything, we are just friends.

The three dots form on the page in front of me and Megan replies with a smiley face. Ok, purely innocent. Nothing to worry about.

I spend a full day finishing up a few projects at work and am heading back from my workout for the day. It is still early in the day, so I decide to check if the fridge has something to make for dinner tonight. A dinner spent with Carrie could be just the thing we need right now. Hmmm, leftover spaghetti sauce on the refrigerator door and pasta in the pantry. I laugh to myself, 'Well, she doesn't love me for my cooking.' She'll be happy to see anything made when she comes home. I turn on the stovetop and place a pot of water on it, noting the clock reads exactly 5:45 p.m. Carrie, normally, comes home around 6:00 p.m., I believe. Then again, I don't always keep track since I spend a lot of time at Revel's after my workouts.

Three hours later, I had my dinner, and the pasta noodles are sitting on the counter, cold and far from fresh. I am sitting on the couch on my phone when Carrie trudges in and throws her keys on the kitchen counter.

"Hey, how's work?" I ask her. She looks irritated. Maybe, from a long day of work?

"Good," she responds politely but with no emotion. Not like her.

"I made pasta," I interject. "It is on the stove if you want."

"I already ate," Carrie huffs.

"Oh, with the girls?" I ask, intrigued since this is not a usual occurrence for her.

"Uh, yah, with the girls..." Carrie mutters and walks toward the bedroom, and I can hear her turn on the shower. I follow her into the room while she puts her work bag away and undresses. I feel an issue looming in the air between us. Carrie looks at me unbothered and says, "Chastity's wedding this weekend, by the way."

Her tone was quite scornful, so in my attempts to relieve the situation, I respond with a calm voice, "okay."

and walks towards the bathroom. She turns the shower on and closes the bathroom door.

~ 21 ~

CARRIE

"So, I hope you have a suit or something to wear," she responds. She drops my clothes in the laundry in our closet and is rummaging through my closet. I am assuming she is looking for the suit that I have not yet bought. To be fair, she mentioned it months ago, and I can easily wear a button-up with dress pants to a wedding. I do not need an entire suit, so she is stressing about something that is not as big of an issue as she is making it.

"I will," I reply calmly to her condescending response.

"You will? So, you don't have it? Why couldn't you do one thing for me?" she replies, like this is a testament to my love for her. Like if I bought a suit for this wedding, it would be the equivalent of renewing my vows to her.

"Carrie, I will get something before this weekend. It will be fine," I insist.

"Yeah, Jus. Everything will be just fine... fine," Carrie shrugs her shoulders. She looks at me, defeated.

--

It's 2pm on a weekend and the white sheets that blanket my bed are still covering my naked figure. We have resisted every attempt to get out of bed. Justice's chest is slightly leaning on top of mine and his arm is resting against the side of me. His hand is framing my face and his fingers are playing with the curls that coil lay in every which way around my face.

I am looking up at Justice and admiring the smile plastered on his face. He is enthralled by crazy curls always made me feel a little insecure next to the blowout beauties that the men of this world usually worship. Yet, Justice smiles in amusement, twirling and fiddling with them. Looking at him so happy to be with me puts a smile on my face and I cannot imagine feeling better than I do when I am with someone who cherishes me, bare-faced and naked from head to toe.

I pull a strand of hair off the pillow and place it between my nose and mouth, pretending that the strand of hair is a curly, funky mustache. Justice takes one look at the fake mustache paired with a classic duck face and belly laughs. He kisses me with the mustache still in place. And again, the little kiss he gives me turns into a longer and deeper one. After a night spent together memorizing each other's bodies, we finally fell asleep only to wake up and continue the game we had fallen asleep to. Every kiss we exchange turns into something more. His kiss is intoxicating. It is like our lips fit perfectly together. The warmth of his mouth and gentle licks fill my heart with a sense of security. I feel so safe with him that I dive headfirst into passion. He quickens his kiss and sends vibrations throughout my body. My skin is burning and my nipples harden with pleasure. Nothing feels as euphoric as this does. I can tell Justice feels the same way. Anytime I pull away for a breath, he pulls me back in.

This is love. I guarantee I have never felt so many emotions that I can only describe as being head over heels in love. I told Justice last night that I loved him for the first time. Before tonight, we were waiting to have sex until I said the three words. Justice didn't know that I was waiting for it. I have had sex before, but the men before him never treated me the way that Justice did. He was so attentive, and you could tell that he was not the game-playing type. I have always felt myself around Justice. I knew that dating Justice could turn into something real, and I did not want to mess that up by getting into bed with him too fast. I knew I could fall for him quickly, and I wanted our first time to mean more than sex. But I never could have imagined that it would be this great.

We have been kissing all day, our lips swollen and tender. Therefore, as much as we want to continue wrapped up in each other, Justice pulls slightly away with every kiss he places on my lips. His lips move to my ear, and he whispers, "I love you, I love you, I love you..." He continues to say it between kisses as he makes his way from my ear to my neck to my collarbone to my stomach, and again, I am gripping the sheets beneath me.

--

Present Day

I haven't talked to Justice since I blew up on him this past Monday. The combination of the weird coffee interaction we had that morning and then him not having his suit yet that night has accumulated into a thick, harsh tension meandering through our house. I have left the communication up to Justice this week, and so, of course, we have not talked much, if at all.

Chastity's wedding is today, so the constant talk of wedding nuptials has added pressure to my week that is weighing me down. I am the one married with the experience of spending eternity with a life partner. Yet, every time she mentions love, I feel overwhelmed by my frustrations. Chastity has more than enough reason to share the details of her wedding. I am excited for her and that is why I volunteered to help with any last-minute details. I am not a bridesmaid, nor did I attend her bachelorette; however, her family and friends are mainly from the Upper West Side, so it is difficult for them to help from afar. When she told me she was born and raised in NYC, it made so much sense and explained the privilege she had grown up with. That is also why her wedding will be top-notch, and her honeymoon will take place in Mykonos. Two weeks of passionate sex on a hut on top of the clear, blue ocean. What a life.

So, with all that this week, I avoided talks, expectations, and fights with Justice. Better to not deal and get nowhere than to deal and still get nowhere. Yet, in my attempts to avoid, I am lying in bed this morning, reminded of the time Justice and I spent the entire day in bed after I told him I loved him. That was the height of our great passion. A time I never could have imagined the passion would run out.

I turn my gaze from the ceiling and turn to my side. The right side of my face is resting on the pillow and my left hand is touching the unoccupied left side of the bed. I know Justice is at the gym getting a workout session in before we need to get ready, but somehow, I am mourning the relationship we had. The times we spent the morning together.

I know it is unhealthy to dwell on the days we had raging lust for each other, but it reminds me of what this is all for. A tear escapes the corner of my eye and drips onto the pillow. I wipe it away, dreading the wedding agenda for today.

--

I am zipping up my own dress when Justice makes it home. He spent a long time at the gym and now we are behind schedule. I am not in the wedding party, but I let him know that Sarai and I wanted to arrive early. Instead of getting upset with what is out of my control, I texted Sarai to pick me up on her way to the venue. I did not bother to let him know that he was running late and I was having Sarai take me instead.

I finish zipping my dress and walk out of our dressing room. I am hopping on one foot as I round the edge of the door frame to face the full-length mirror beside it. I securely fit the foot raised in the air with a tan-colored sandal heel. I press my hand against the wall to keep myself from toppling over and switch hands to secure my other foot in the air with the other heel. I turn around and stand about 2 inches taller in the mirror.

I brush the front and sides of my dress after the brief chaos of securing my footwear and stare at myself, pleased with my efforts. My hair is pinned back with a few curls framing my face. I am wearing a silk green dress that hugs my curves and stops just below my knees. The neckline forms a deeper "V" than I normally wear, but it sits and frames my breasts exquisitely. Sarai helped me pick the dress out when we went shopping for the wedding and her exact words were "Hot Mami" in her sexy, Spanish accent. I stare at my reflection and smile at how carefree I feel in this outfit. I feel sexy and beautiful. Two things I do not normally feel when I look at myself. I move my gaze from the dress to my face. My hair is pinned back with a few curls framing my face and my ears are adorned with yellow gold dangling diamond earrings. Justice saved up and gifted them to me for our first Valentine's Day married. I have only worn them a handful of times, so they have not lost their sparkle. I take a second look at my makeup to make sure there are no smudges and reapply my lipstick as Justice makes his way into the bedroom. I glance at him through the mirror and I continue to smack my lips together to make sure it's even. His reaction is visceral.

"You're already ready?" Justice asks.

"Ya," I reply casually, "I decided to have Sarai take me since we wanted to be there early and you were still at the gym."

"Oh, yah, I remember. I just thought you would text me," Justice replied.

"No, it's okay. I'll just meet you there. You still have an hour and a half. It doesn't start until 2pm," I remind him. Just then, my phone rings and Sarai lets me know she is outside. "See you."

I blow Justice a kiss with a hint of pettiness. *I am not going to lie to you. Truth is, you can't keep a girl like me waiting around.*

~ 22 ~

JUSTICE

"Come on!" The tie around my neck is too tight and not settling nicely on the white dress shirt I am wearing. I use the rearview mirror to adjust it. I give up after a couple of tries, honestly, ties are not for me. I pull one end of the tie and loosen it, letting out a breath, "God, that's so much better."

I glance at my rearview mirror again and see someone tailing me. I am on my way to the wedding, and I'm not in the mood to deal with reckless drivers. I am fifteen minutes from the venue, and it starts in twenty-five. That hour and a half that Carrie warned me about seemed shorter than normal. Now, I am trying to beat the traffic and have someone tailing my car's rear end.

"Hey!!" I yell in response to the car behind me as he approaches an inch too close. I wave my hand at him to go around.

My phone rings and I see it's a message from Carrie. I need to open my phone with my password before I can read it, but I have no time, and I can already guess what it says— she is frustrated and texting, 'Where are you?' rightfully so.

Sorry, Carrie. After her obvious tactic of leaving with Sarai this afternoon, I know this is only going to make things worse. Not to mention, it is one of her close friends from work and she wanted me to be there. I would rather be anywhere else than at a rich couple's wedding with every bell and whistle in the package reeking of snobbery and privilege. I already have a headache thinking about the millions of people that the bride and groom invited, yet they only know half of. But I should be there for Carrie.

Oh no, the millions of people. Parking is going to be a nightmare. Not to mention, they had to pick the most pretentious wedding venue in the area. The Hyde House is completely modernized and boasts nothing unique besides pretty scenery for good photos to post on social media. Knowing Carrie's friend, the venue is not the only cost they doubled down on to create their magical evening. I can guarantee there will be appetizers handed out by waiters in white coats. If I ever make it!

I'm following a few cars ahead of me towards the venue. I am not excited about the spectacle that I can only imagine awaits. Carrie and I's wedding was so perfect. It was come as you are, not a huge show for everyone to pay tribute to. Rather, we invited only a few friends and family for an intimate and more affordable celebration. We were young and got married right out of college, so we didn't have the means or the richest parents to afford an expensive ordeal. And yet our wedding was perfect.

We chose Sunken Gardens, home to an enclave of plants and critters, as our venue, and the idea of birds dressing her that morning would not have surprised me. The landscape painted a beautiful fairytale scene in which the princess marries her prince, and all her animal friends are there to appreciate it. Sunken Gardens was the perfect choice for us and the one place that Carrie had spent many times visiting with her father growing up. It had so many memories for her and watching her father walk her down the aisle was a full-circle moment. Her father watched her grow up there and was able to experience this next chapter in her life, something she was afraid at one point would have been stolen from her.

I still remember the nerves I had that morning. I can still picture the paper with my wedding vows all crumpled and damp from my sweaty, fidgety hands. I practiced them all morning, hoping that my feelings and devotion to Carrie would show through in the words I spoke. Yet, as I saw Carrie walk down the aisle, I felt calm for the first time that day. She took my breath away and eased my worries with one look. The vision of Carrie walking toward me is an image I will never forget. Her dress was long and fitted to show her curves, covered in lace. I was enraptured by her. She could have worn a paper bag, and I still would have married her on the spot. It was not the dress or the hairstyle she wore, but her beauty shone from within.

She was beaming as she walked down the aisle, and I could feel her happiness radiating. Carrie was the true star at our wedding. I couldn't and still cannot believe she chose to walk down that aisle toward me. She chose me.

I still have those vows memorized. I held onto the paper with my vows with white knuckles, yet the truth is, I didn't need it. I knew them by heart:

"My vows are simple. I vow to love and accept you for who you are from this day forward. I vow to be there in sickness and in health. I vow to continue vowing all my days to be the better version I can be for you. The father and the husband that you dreamed of. Since the day I met you, Carrie, I could never have imagined someone more perfect to spend the rest of a lifetime with. You were my dream come true and all I want to be is yours. The day I said I loved you was months after realizing it myself. It took two months to fall for you. Before you knew it, I knew. I always knew. Carrie, that day I realized that you are the **only person for me in this world.**"

Finally! I am driving past the venue, following the pin Carrie dropped earlier as a suggestion for where to park since the lot was so busy. Thankfully, someone is pulling out of their spot right in front of the venue. It's a two-hour parking spot, just enough time for me to make it to the ceremony, and then if Carrie wants to stay longer, I can move it. I pull into the spot, fiddle with my tie one more time, leave it be, and then fast walk to the entrance.

Phew, just in time with five minutes to spare. I look at my phone for the first time since Carrie texted me in the car. Turns out she had called 3 times since. I unlock my screen and call her back.

"Hey, I'm here," I respond when I hear the line is picked up.

"Glad you made it. Where are you?" Carrie replies. Her voice is not as angry as I thought it would be, but she might be holding back.

"I am by the huge bar, I guess," I reply, unsure. I entered the front doors and walked past the mingling guests into a large ballroom. Other than the sea of people and tables set up for the guestbook and small bites, I find myself standing next to a large bar that takes up one full side of the wall. I could use a drink after the cortisol spike from my drive. I squeeze between a couple talking on barstools and a group of friends circled around another set of stools.

"Ok, I am coming from the bridesmaid's room. Stay there," Carries responds.

"Okay."

Carrie hangs up and I motion for the bartender. The bartender nods his head towards me, indicating he will take my order next. He pours a wine glass for an older lady at the other end of the bar and then maneuvers his way over to me. By the looks of it, no one is handing the bartenders their cards to cash out tabs– one thing to love about an overzealous wedding is the free booze.

"Can I have an old-fashioned on the rocks, please?" I murmur to the bartender quickly

I watch as he muddles the bitters and pours the whiskey into a glass while simultaneously nodding to the next guest in line. They really work fast. He sets the glass in front of me, and just as I pick up the glass, I spot Carrie a few feet away.

I take a sip from my glass and smile at her. A gentle smile crosses her face. I can tell she was worried I was running late, but she remains composed. I close the gap between us and place my hand on her lower back. I press my lips against her cheek and hear her sigh. *Let it out, Carrie. I am here now.* As my lips pull away from her cheek, I look at her with sorrowful eyes. I can feel the tension she has been holding onto, and I want to relieve her frustration. Just as her body relaxes and her furrowed brows loosen, people begin to take their seats. Carrie and I follow the guests and find two seats towards the back. I let Carrie pick the seats and reserve the aisle seat for Sarai. Sarai gallivants toward us with a freshly made drink in her hand and a smile from ear to ear. Carrie pats her leg and giggles back at her while placing her pointer finger in front of her lips to quiet her friend.

A trio of violinists begins playing and I note the wealth dripping all over, from the groomsmen dressed in white tuxes, which look like they have a taper candle stuck up their asses to the imported chandeliers hanging above our heads.

Everyone turns their heads as Carrie's friend begins walking down the aisle, taking the slowest steps known to mankind. My Apple Watch wouldn't even be able to pick up the pace she is walking at. I am sure she is walking at snail speed to relish in the limelight for as long as she can. It does not help that Sarai is oohing and awing at the sight of Chastity from her seat.

"Oooo so gorgeous," Sarai whisper shouts while Chastity walks by us and moves her head towards us to repeat herself to Carrie, "Wow, she looks amazing." A drunk giggle escapes her, and I am humiliated for her.

Carrie stiffens and, again, puts her hand on Sarai's thigh. She whispers something in her ear that none of us can hear. In response, Sarai puts her pointer finger to her mouth and nods her head up and down.

Thankfully, Sarai is quiet for the rest of the ceremony, but it was still unbearable. The vows were long and full of cheesy phrases, such as 'you make me better' and 'I could not picture this world without you'. I know that I also veered on the cheesy side with my own vows, but they were short and simple. Just like how simple it was to fall in love with her. It wasn't an act, and it wasn't a performance. This wedding feels over the top, from the violinists to the flower petals and candles lining the aisle. Chastity is even wearing a crown of some sort. The ceremony comes to an end, and I shift my gaze from the bride and groom to the bar in the back, already anticipating my next drink. My eyes flicker to Carrie and I focus my gaze on her to realize that her beautiful, green eyes have welled up with tears. Instinctively, I place my hand on her left knee to comfort her. She stiffens and continues staring ahead at the newlyweds.

I am still studying her face and trying to comfort her with an empathetic look in case she decides to make eye contact. Everyone stands for the bride and groom. The audience is cheering and hollering at the couple's elated faces. I clap for the couple and find a smile cross my face. I guess, no matter the production, we can all appreciate the sentiment of forever. Again, I turn back towards Carrie just as she is turning away. Is she crying? Carrie is not the type to cry at happy moments. She cries when she is deep in thought.

Carrie pushes past Sarai and slips out the back without anyone else noticing. Everyone is focused on the couple posing in the famous "kissing sailor" for the cameras. I shuffle closer to Sarai and towards the aisle, "Hey, mind if I get through?"

Sarai nods. She has a concerned look as if something is wrong. She was just giggling like a hyena. Something seems off.

Thankfully, I slip past the back few rows unnoticed before the bride and groom make it down the aisle. I spot Carrie standing on the balcony across from the bar at the back of the room. I glance at the aisle, ready to make a run for it, and see that the newlyweds are slowly making their way down the aisle, soaking up every moment of the spotlight. I move towards Carrie and push open the balcony door.

The balcony door closes behind me and the noise of the crowd hollering behind us is drowned out in an instant. Carrie is staring out at the view before turning towards me.

"Carrie, what's wrong?" I take two steps forward, giving her enough space, but trying to close the gap wedged between us.

There is a pause and then I can only make out a few words from Carrie as she trails off under her breath. I hear "can't", "want", and "I'm tired" all in the same muttered sentence.

"What?" I repeat.

Again, a moment passes before she breathes out, "You."

~ 23 ~

CARRIE

I often live in my head because it is more romantic than real life. I am a romantic at heart and life is not as idealistic as a dreamer would like it to be. I fight to be content, but I want more than that. I want pleasure. As I sit, watching our friend walk down the aisle to her forever person, I cry. I do not just tear up like the other family members in the audience, appreciating the beauty of this moment. I sob.

I make sure to slip out past Sarai and avoid the pitying look she shoots me as my emotions take hold. I spent the time before the wedding with Sarai and the bridesmaids in the bridal suite. I expressed my frustration about Justice in the car on the way to the venue and made snide comments in the room over a couple of sips of champagne. Embarrassment is already catching up to me as I realize the comments are coming from a deeper place and Sarai is picking up on it.

I am holding it together as much as I can as I make my way far away from the ceremony and slip out onto the balcony. Thankfully, my sobs are silent, and some of my embarrassment subsides once I remind myself that the audience will never notice that one friend/co-worker sitting in the back row leave.

Now, far away from the excitement, I look out at the city and take in the view. I look down and see some teens running around with ice cream cones dripping down their hands. Two girls are laughing so hard over something that they are struggling to walk, gasping between bellowing laughs and one girl is grabbing onto the other for stability. Innocence. Happiness. Pleasure. The sight of the two girls reminds me of who I was before a man became my life. When the presence of my best friend was all that mattered. When the possibility of a boy falling for me was still just a daydream. The butterflies you would get from something so small, such as a glance from your crush. Justice and I met when I was still new to dating. Everything felt so new. The first night when we talked all night, or the first time he held my hand, when we knew something was starting between us. I remember when it was still new and we would joke about having staring competitions because we constantly found each other gazing at one another. We were both so entranced that we couldn't stop studying the other person. Breaking eye contact seemed like the hardest thing to do at the time.

The balcony door opens, and I know it's Justice. I turn away from the two girls who have walked off into the distance and turn my attention towards him. He is standing in a gorgeous gray suit and a button-down white dress shirt. He ditched the tie and still looks divine. You could argue that he looks better with the definition of his pecks peeking through his button-down, contrasting perfectly with his tan skin and wavy brown hair brushed back in a perfect swirl.

Justice walks slowly towards me but remains an arm's length away. "Carrie, what's wrong?" he breaks the silence.

I murmur. Anything I say in this moment could quite possibly tear us up. I am a terrible liar, and I could never look into his eyes and lie. My heart is too open to him for such foolery. But I have been thinking about us for a while, and for god's sake, I am crying at a wedding because it has become so overwhelming. I am constantly fixating on us, and I need a break from it.

"What?" Justice replies, clearly not picking up on the gibberish I spew.

I take a deep breath and decide to come clean. "You."

My heart breaks as I see Justice's face fall into a frown and his eyes turn from deep brown to hazel. It feels like this whole week, he has been putting on a face and trying to be the rock holding up our relationship. He took my place in anchoring our ship. I thought if I anchored the ship that we would make it through the storms, but to fix the ship, we need to get it ashore. I do not know how else to get there than to jump out and swim. We haven't been able to sail in a while. What makes him think we still can? Something tells me from the expression staring back at me that he doesn't know anymore either.

"Justice, you!" I repeat a little louder than the whisper I stammered out a second ago. I want to grab his attention and get him to answer me.

"Carrie, what do you want from me?!" Justice replies a little louder than normal. He's getting angry and turning red, a vein on his forehead popping. He turns his back, brushing his hand over his mouth and through his hair to calm down. I am silent, not wanting to provoke him anymore. Justice turns back to face me, back to a lost puppy dog pout. "Carrie, why are you crying? What do you want from me? I will do anything for you."

"I need space, Justice," I reply, "How can you give me everything if I do not know what that is anymore? And how can I do the same?"

Justice stands there, jaw locked. A tear rolls down his cheek. I approach him and hold his face with one hand. I brush away the tears and look up at him.

"Justice, we deserve better. I know you tried, but we need a change."

Justice leans his head on mine, holding it there for a second before pulling away altogether and walking away.

--

I watched him walk past the ceremony, open the entrance door, and exit the venue.

The tears I struggled to hold back come bubbling up. I rush towards the bathroom in the back. Thankfully unoccupied, I pace until my heart rate slows and I can face the mirrors. The makeup I had carefully applied has formed into a watercolor mess on my face. Mascara has clumped into bags under my eyes and my nose is red with snot. I close my eyes, not wanting to take in the sight anymore and breathe in deeply.

Clank! The bathroom door opens and hits the wall behind it. Sarai barges in. "Honey, what's wrong?"

I shake my head with shame, knowing that today should be about Chastity, not me. "I'm sorry. I've been a mess all day and now look at me. I just couldn't help it when I saw how happy they were coming down that aisle. That used to be me."

I was expecting Sarai to talk some sense into me. She is great at giving tough love. Instead, she walks towards me and pulls me into a hug. "Don't be sorry."

Surprisingly, her reaction calms me. I wrap my arms around her and take in the much-needed comfort. Sarai holds me tighter and speaks up again, "I am proud of you. You are being honest with yourself. It's not easy, but I know you will get through this and come out stronger than ever."

Wow. Sarai always puts on this demeanor that she is confident and unaffected by others' struggles, but in this moment, her walls are down and she is convincing me that I am strong. The vulnerability from Sarai gives me the confidence I need to compose myself. She is right. Admitting this to myself and to Justice was a long time coming and I will be damned if it ruins my opportunity to celebrate Chastity's beautiful day. I pull away from Sarai and shoot her a smile, "Let's get a drink."

Sarai nods and lets out a bellowing laugh like the teens outside. "That's my girl!"

--

A multitude of drinks later, a tweak in my neck, and the sound of coffee grounds grinding all combine to make a morning headache made worse. I slowly become aware of my surroundings, still in my dress from the wedding, lying on Sarai's couch. It all comes flooding back. After Justice left and Sarai and I had our little pow-wow, I made it a point to still have fun. Sarai and I agreed as we clinked glasses right after our talk that I would come home with her for the night and forget about my drama. I guess that didn't stop her from bringing a guy home last night because he is currently the one grinding coffee grounds and making my head throb.

I rub my eyes to get a clearer visual and notice that the man is shirtless and pantless. *I mean, thank God he is wearing underwear, but what the hell!*

"Morning, would you like some coffee?" he asks.

"Er no thanks!" I blurt out. I straighten and hop off the couch. I grab my shoes and start walking towards the door. I look over at the man with glaring, chiseling abs and cover my eyes out of instinct. This is so inappropriate. With my hand still covering my eyes, I amble towards the door, "Actually, I should be going. If you could tell Sarai..." Oomphf. I bump straight into Sarai.

"Tell Sarai what?" Sarai laughs at my embarrassment. "Josh was just making some coffee. You want some?"

"No, no... nice of you to offer, but I really got to go," I admit and rush towards the door. "Thanks for letting me stay here last night. I owe you!" I open the door and close it hurriedly.

My back presses up against the door and I notice how fast my heart is beating. A laugh falls from my mouth, and I smile. *How did I end up here?* This is probably the most spontaneous thing I have done in a while, and man, did that feel exhilarating. My body relaxes and I feel more in control than I have in a long time.

I was right. I really needed to get to the bottom of everything with Justice. As much as I love him, I want more of this feeling of control that has evaded me. He cannot take care of my needs, and it is time to take things into my own hands and be unconventional.

I am wearing my confidence on my sleeve and shouting out the lyrics to 'Flowers' by Miley Cyrus while I drive home. It is not about Justice. This is about me. And, in some way, it will be better for him, too. I know it will be hard to convince him, but I need to try something new.

A few intersections and boss bitch songs later, I make it home. The confidence that was so prevalent a moment ago dissipates as I stare at the home the two of us have been sharing since we wed. There is no shame in failing. And, who says we have failed? Sometimes it is just about finding your footing.

I make my way through the front door and find Justice on the couch watching golf. I walk towards the kitchen and set my purse on the kitchen barstool.

"Justice, can we talk?" I speak up over the TV.

Justice sits up and looks over at me. He grabs the remote to mute the game. "Sure," he replies with no emotion. Typical Justice. Stoic as always.

There is no point in sugarcoating what I am about to say, so I blurt out, "I think we should try something new and see other people." I am standing by the kitchen barstool, the inevitable gap still wedged between us. My heart is racing as I wait for his response and try to read his demeanor. However, unlike yesterday, he was anticipating a conflict today and is not emoting anything.

"I think I can manage that," he replies. My heart sinks. Was I expecting a different answer? Was I hoping he would beg for me or get hot-headed or cry? Why am I shocked by his response? I try my best to stay as stoic as he is and explain.

"Okay, I just think that it may be good for both of us and it might give us that outlet you are always looking for," I muster out in a tone that is hopeful yet I am holding back the fear that he truly has no feelings for me.

"Yeah, ok," Justice replies, brushing off my explanation. Our communication is as weak as ever.

I realize, now, that this was never the reaction I wanted.

I wanted to anger him or send him into bargaining mode. Agreeance was not the plan. It's as though Justice had turned from my partner to a guy friend in the span of one second. I felt as though he might high-five me, pass me a beer, and begin the process of scouting chicks right then in that moment. His reaction destroys any belief that we ever had anything special and proves it was just a fleeting love.

"Okay, well then, maybe we should set up some boundaries," I reply. The thought of talking about other lovers and the limits on how far we can take it makes me sick to my stomach. But I am not going to let him read that all over my face. Instead, I am determined to push through.

Justice perks up from the couch and replies right away, "Okay, sure, but later. I am meeting Revel. There is a game on later and I told him I would go over now."

As much as I don't want to talk anymore, I also do not want him to leave. But what else am I supposed to say? This is the start of me not being so dependent on him. "Okay, I'll see you later."

The last view I see is watching him grab his wallet and keys from the dining room table and walk out the door. No uproar or disagreement. Rather, he left with a smile on his face. How does nothing affect him?

The house is silent and I am engulfed in loneliness that feels less like an acquaintance and more like my shadow. I search for my phone and pull up Sarai's contact number, pressing the call button. The phone rings and I am about to give up when Sarai picks up.

"Hey, Carrie. How'd it go with Justice?" she questions.

I am a little surprised, but realize that we were all expecting some sort of confrontation today. "Fine. We both decided we start seeing other people. I think we need the separation."

"And he was okay with that?" Sarai presses.

"More than okay," I say while taking a deep breath and letting it go away from the microphone.

"Ok, then. Let's get you set up on Hinge. You need to get out there and have some fun. It's about time," Sarai pleads.

"Ya, tomorrow," I reply, "Well, anyways, I just wanted to update you and again thank you for letting me stay over last night."

"It's more than okay. Talk to you tomorrow."

I hang up the phone and, in the most depressed state, drag myself to my bedroom. My limp body barely makes it onto the bed. I guess this is the end of an era. I'll boss up and be that superwoman, feminist, individualist woman later. Right now, curling up in a ball with tears and snot running down my face and tangled golden locks is all that I can muster.

~ 24 ~

JUSTICE

I am sitting here watching golf, yet my mind is elsewhere. I couldn't care less about who is leading or who is under par. All I can think about is where Carrie is. She texted me yesterday that she was with Sarai and wouldn't be coming home. I barely slept last night thinking about where she ended up and why she wouldn't want to talk this out. She hasn't spent the night away since being married. Now, it is 9:30 in the morning and she is still not home.

Normally, I try not to worry about things that are out of my control. Carrie's emotions tend to fall under that category. Yet here I am twiddling my thumbs and ignoring the television, just waiting for Carrie to arrive. I cannot help but worry about what happened last night because when I left, I walked out on more than the wedding. So, I am worried that something happened last night that, honestly, I would not be able to play victim to. If Carrie wound up in another man's arms, then I could not help but blame myself. We didn't agree to that, but I haven't been fulfilling my obligation to be there for her either. If someone else did, it would kill me. But if that's what she needed, and I was not there then how can I blame her?

The front door opens and Carrie walks in. My thumbs stop fidgeting and my worry subsides only for a mere matter of seconds until I see the state she is in. Her beautiful golden locks have fallen out of the bun she had it in yesterday and are ruffled more than usual. She is wearing the same thing she wore yesterday, and her makeup was not wiped off either. Basically, she has done the walk of shame into our house. I keep my worry and anger under wraps because I will not let myself get out of line like I did yesterday on the balcony.

I only looked at Carrie for a second when she walked in and turned my head back to the golf match in front of me to avoid showing my frustration. I am anticipating she will want to talk, but for now I need to get my temper under control. In order to calm down, I am focusing on every movement Carrie is making behind me. She has made her way over to the kitchen and set her purse down on one of the barstools. She seems to have paused until... "Justice, can we talk?"

I turn the television on mute and turn around to face the inevitable. "Sure."

In less than three seconds, Carrie blurts out, "I think we should try something new and see other people."

I knew it. She slept with someone else and wants to spring this on me like it is a new idea of hers. As if she didn't just have sex with someone last night. I mean, here she goes again. Bouncing off walls and making decisions because she can't be fulfilled with what I have given her. I am not enough once again. I can feel my face turn to rock and my breath halts. If this is what she wants, then I will give it to her. I want to make her happy and, clearly, I am not making her happy.

I respond, "I think I could manage that." I can read on her face that that was not the response she was looking for. Good. I mean, how can she be upset? Is this not what she wants?

"Okay, I just think that it may be good for both of us, and it might give us that outlet you are always looking for," Carrie encourages with a twinge of a smile that I can tell is fake.

"Yeah, ok," I hate to admit it, but maybe it will be easier. Maybe it won't hurt so much when she doesn't rely so heavily on me. Maybe she will be happier and in the long run, we both will. I hate to admit it, but in this moment, I have ignored the vows I made and let her go.

"Okay, well then, maybe we should set up some boundaries," she replies.

As much as my 'yeah' agreed with her suggestion, I am not ready to talk more on the subject. I quickly make up an excuse and reply, "Okay, sure, but later. I am meeting Revel. There is a game on and I told him I would go over now."

I jump up from the couch and beeline for the door. I can't sit here and pretend that I am not already picturing Carrie with someone else. The thought of her in someone else's arms is sending me into a complete rage. My mind is racing with so much anger that I can't even make out Carrie's response as I walk towards the door. I need to talk to Revel and let him know I am spiraling. I thought I could man up and handle our marriage on my own, but I can't. And now it has all gone to shit.

--

I can't remember the route I took to get to Revel's or if I drove through red lights. It was a blur, but the mind games replaying in my head were as clear as day. Is Carrie moving on? Has she moved on? I bet her friends are relieved and setting her up on dates already. They never liked me. I was never on their good side, nor did I try to be. Is this Carrie's decision or did they influence it? Was I naïve to think we were forever?

I knock on Revel's front door and open it before he can register who it is. I usually let myself in and today especially, I am not waiting. The rage inside me has overcome my patience. Yet, as the door cracks open, I can already see someone else in the house that I do not recognize. A woman. Revel, the womanizer, has lured another woman over and it looks like she has her clothes on from the night before. I can tell because it is far too revealing for the daytime. A flashback from Carrie walking through our door this morning in yesterday's clothes with her hair in dismay clouds my mind. The image of this woman suddenly irks me to my core and I don't hesitate to take it out on Revel.

I look past the woman and towards the back room, "Revel, where the fuck are you?"

Instantly, Revel pops his head out from where the open layout kitchen ends and extends into his pantry and laundry room. He makes eye contact with me and doesn't hide his surprise. Rounding the corner, I see he is holding a bag of bagels. Oh god, I just walked in on breakfast.

"I need to speak to you," I continue, "...without her." I look at the woman with slight distaste. She is really a pretty woman despite the morning-after, smudged makeup look, but I couldn't care less. There is one thing on my mind and one thing only. Carrie.

Revel nods his head and motions her over. I roll my eyes as he rubs her arms up and down and whispers something I can imagine was an exaggeration of how last night was so amazing. I know his tricks. I spent his college years with him and, if anything, he has only gotten better at the whole 'bachelor' thing. I have never cared to be the bachelor he is. Even before Carrie, I always imagined finding that one person. I didn't expect it to be as easy as it was with Carrie, but I always figured there was something more out there. Revel, on the other hand, has jumped from girl to girl. He was close to having that special something with Raven, but their baggage was ultimately too much.

The woman smiles up at Revel and stands on her tiptoes to give him a kiss goodbye. He smiles back at her and as she is turning away, he looks at me with a frown on his face. I look at the woman who is walking towards me, still anxiously standing by the door. She flashes me a slight smile before walking out. I couldn't even muster a polite smile before she left.

"What's wrong?" Revel finally says once the door is closed.

"It's over, Revel," I spew out and begin rambling, "...the wedding was yesterday, and I left early because we argued. Then, she came home with the same clothes from the night before. She texted me last night that she was staying at Sarai's, but what am I supposed to think? And then, she wants to see other people. I mean, what's going on?"

Revel shakes his head from side to side and questions, "Wait, what? She wants to see other people? You are sure about that?"

"Revel, she was so upset yesterday, and then today as soon as she saw me, she said that she wanted to see other people," I reply.

"What did you say?" Revel questions the situation again. He is so calm and collected. Is he not listening to what I am telling him? It is only making me angrier that he is so calm. Did he expect this to happen? Am I the only one who feels blindsided?

"I said 'ok'," I reply, confused. "What else was I supposed to say? She isn't happy with me anymore. It is what I have been saying all along. I can't make her happy as much as I try."

Revel blows out a deep breath at the news. "Justice, she loves you. You need to go back and let her know that you love her too. I don't know any couple that is a better fit than you two. I mean, if you can't make it, then I don't know who can."

I know he is trying to make me feel better, but he is acting like it hasn't taken everything out of me to just try to make this work the last few years. And this attitude that everything will work itself out on its own doesn't feel possible now. It feels naïve. I am done being naïve to the situation. "No. Let her walk out on us." I say, knowing fully that it isn't only her walking out. I am.

~ 25 ~

CARRIE

It's been a week since I told Justice I want to see other people. It was a night of many tears and puffy eyes. Yet, since then, I feel more in control than ever. My thoughts don't revolve around him anymore. I do not have any intention of seeing anyone, but I needed to break the tether between us that was dragging me down.

I haven't seen Justice much. It seems he is off with Revel, and I have spent much of my time with Sarai outside of work. We haven't even had the boundaries conversation because of how little we have seen each other, and anytime I am home, it seems like he is avoiding me at all costs. Many times, he rushes out the door before we are together in the house for more than five minutes. However, I am not shocked. He had been one foot out the door for a while. He might as well commit to it.

I just left work to meet Sarai at a local yoga studio for a workout and a coffee. I need the break and the caffeine kick afterwards. I have been burying myself in work this past week, scheduling meetings and deadlines, trying to ignore life. However, to my luck, our team meeting ended

155

earlier than expected and I arrive at the studio in time to witness Sarai chatting up another fella. I park to the right of them and get another glance at Sarai giggling away with her raspy, cute laugh at the guy next to her who has a yoga mat swung over his shoulder and a topknot bun. Typical yogi. Honestly, how does Sarai always end up finding that one guy who attends yoga class or is walking by a gynecologist on his way to another doctor's office? Even with the slimmest chance of meeting a guy she somehow always does, and I am not surprised when they are enthralled by her looks and charm.

As I make my way over, Sarai spots me and I hear her say, "Ok, well, it was nice to meet you, and I can't wait to do downward dog with you in a bit." They laugh off what seems to me as a very forward comment, but to him was probably charming. He steps away and heads into the yoga studio. Sarai opens her arms with a big smile and gives me the biggest hug as if we haven't spent almost every day this week together.

"Hey, cutie!" She squeals. "Ready to get your sweat on?"

"Yes, I am!"

The yoga session was 45 minutes and hot! I have done hot yoga before, but this room was sweltering. I am so glad to be back outside, where the temperature is, as usual, a balmy 65. It should be a sin to put the temperature up that high in Florida. Doesn't everyone know how hot and humid it already gets here!? Why make it hotter?

"What did you think of it?" Sarai asks me. Again, she is barely sweating in comparison to the Niagara Falls falling from my forehead to my breasts.

"Great, loved it," I say with a sarcastic tone that Sarai does not pick up on.

"Oh, good, I am glad you came. I love this studio," She squeals, "Ok, there is this coffee shop nearby that I was thinking we could go to?"

"Yeah, take me wherever as long as they have caffeine," I reply.

We make it to a shop called 'Coffee Cruisin'. It is half coffee shop and half surf shop- 'Coffee' for all the coffee addicts and 'Cruisin' for the surfers. I can already tell Sarai is a regular. She is waving at the baristas, and as she is giving her order, the cashier nods like he already has it memorized.

The cashier finishes inputting her order, "Nice to see you come by again, Sarai."

He leans over the register to get a little closer before she replies, "Nice to be back." Her mouth curls on one side to flash him a little smirk.

Oh, I get it. They have slept together. Makes all the sense now why she likes it here so much.

The cashier then looks at me for my order. "Can I have the iced oat milk vanilla latte, please?"

He nods as he types in the order on the register pad. I pay him and realize that Sarai did not have to pay for her latte. If I had that kind of treatment every time I ordered coffee, I would save so much money!

We find a table by the front window and wait for our coffees.

"What do you think of him?" Sarai points at the cashier who just took our order.

"Oh yah, he is cute," I say, assuming she is asking for confirmation on her hookup.

"I could get you his number!" Sarai perks up.

"No way! You have already slept with him," I reply with a laugh.

"True, but why does that matter?" She replies.

"Because I can find my own guy when I want. No need to worry about it."

"Ok, well, have you started your Hinge account?"

"No," I am so not in the mood for this conversation. I thought putting myself on the market again would make it easier to move on. But truthfully, I am more of a monogamist than I thought. I do not want to be as forward as Sarai or seek out man after man like she does. I would rather not have to meet someone on a dating app, and I want to share my intimate life with someone I truly care for. It is funny, when you are married, you think life as a single woman with so many options will be so fun and glamorous. Now, as a woman on the market, I just want to feel secure and safe with one person again. I guess the grass is always greener on the other side.

"I can make it for you! I promise I will make you look hot," She suggests.

"No, I will meet someone when I am ready and in person," I persist.

She frowns a little but looks at the to-go table to see if our orders are ready. She heads over to pick up two iced coffees waiting there. As she heads back over with our orders, she says, "What was the point of asking to see other people then? If you wanted to stay celibate, then you didn't have to say anything at all to him."

"Because it wasn't about the sex at all," As I am talking out loud, I am listening to what I am saying as well. I don't think I have fully processed everything until I gave it up. Now that Sarai has asked, what was it all about?

"I loved Justice, but I forgot what it was like to love again. You know when something good happens in your life and you can't wait to tell that one person? Or, when you could only picture them in your life and no one else? The desire you feel when you went a week without each other and somehow you knew that if you ignored the tension between the two of you that it would only take a second before he was forced to make the first move. I remember the days we spent all day in bed, embracing and studying each other's faces and bodies. And then as the years passed, I somehow forgot what all that was like. Anytime I had good news, I forgot to tell him by the time I got home. It was like I had been disappointed by his lack of attention for so long, it didn't matter to me anymore. When I went to sleep, I stopped dreaming of him and started dreaming of other lovers. The spark left and as much as I tried to keep it alive, it wouldn't stay lit. Instead, I was constantly questioning if he loved me at all. I lost myself in the process. I lost how to feel and what to think. So, it was not about sex, and it was more about how to get back to love."

During my speech, my eyes drifted to my hands fiddling with the label on my drink. I shift my eyes back up to see Sarai in awe. "Wow, that was the most poetic speech I have ever heard."

We leave the conversation at that. I know Sarai cannot fully relate to everything that just came spewing out, but I am glad I said it anyway. I needed to voice that and understand what I am truly feeling throughout all this.

--

I make my way back to the office, still sweaty and dressed in leggings and a sports bra. I had changed into my workout clothes before leaving so I would not be rushed in the studio. Since we sell athletic clothing and it is part of the wardrobe here at work, I am not entirely insecure when making my way inside to our office bathroom to change. Thankfully, the clothes we sell make up about 50% or more of everyone's closet, so it is not unusual to spot someone in athletic wear at work. Yet, shirts are typically required in an office setting, so I nod to the front desk receptionist and put my head down as I rush to the nearest bathroom.

It is too late when I notice the feet on the ground in front of me are incredibly close... "Oof." I look up from the crash, mumbling, "I'm sorry..."

Then, just as sudden as the crash between our bodies is the surprising presence of Revel. Ever since Justice and I agreed to the new terms or change to whatever we were, Revel has avoided me at all costs. He never came by my office after that night eating Chinese food, even though I have been working late, and I know his team has too. He avoids eye contact from across the room, and when I spot him randomly, he always turns away. It is like he anticipates my every move and makes sure not to be present. Until now.

Revel is staring back at me with a stunned expression, clearly not anticipating this very moment. One of his hands is grasping his phone and I notice an iMessage response in process. So, he was on his phone. Amateur move. He should have known that would distract him from avoiding my existence.

"I guess this was bound to happen," I speak up and, suddenly, I am aware of the perspiration glistening all over my body. I am sweaty, probably have a lingering odor, and I just rubbed it all over him while we collided. I can feel my cheeks flush as I think about it.

"What do you mean?" Revel knows exactly what I mean, but again, he is avoiding the situation.

"You know, running into me when I know you have been avoiding me." I purposefully avoid mentioning why.

Revel looks behind him in embarrassment and, I think, partly to make sure no one is near us to hear this conversation. "Okay, yah, I am avoiding you... I just don't know how to react with everything going on... you know...."

Ya, of course, I know. "Just because things are not going great between us doesn't mean you have to come to work and act weird."

Revel runs his hand through his hair as a nervous tic. Very much like what Justice does when he is nervous or frustrated. "Yah, you're right." He gives me a smile that just very slightly twinges on the right side of his mouth. Unlike Justice, Revel is mysterious in a way that is moody, not in the 'I don't know what he is thinking' way. In fact, I can read his emotions far easier than it is to read Justice's. Just now, I can tell there was a change from discomfort to relief just by reading his expressions. And can I spot a twinge of excitement? My heart kicks up at the thought of that. I can't help but indulge in the idea that I might be able to read Revel's mind. The ease is a relief to the unemotional chaos with Justice. The tension between us at first crash relaxes and we both fall into comfortability. Something I am not used to but could get very used to.

I mean, the inability to read a person's mind is exhausting and frustrating. I am too tired to play games. I need some ease in my life and the inability to read Justice's mind was fun until it wasn't. At first, it was fun guessing what he was thinking about, and the emotional and physical tension between us was so palpable that it wasn't hard to imagine his thoughts. At that point, there was no need for me to guess because his actions told me everything. Just when I could feel the tension between us become unbearable, he would pull me into an embrace and kiss me with confidence. Or, in that year I got our family's bad news, he made it a point to be available whenever I needed him. You wouldn't believe it now, but in the past, he wrote love letters and surprised me with gifts. I didn't need to ask repeatedly how he felt about me. His actions told me everything. Even in the beginning years of our marriage, when it wasn't as new and hot as the beginning years of dating, he would text me during work hours or out of the blue, something that let me know he was thinking of me. A video he came across on Instagram or TikTok that included puppies or baby ducks, something that he knew would make me smile. It was such a simple act, but it helped me gauge that he at least thought of me. But, as the years went by, the texts stopped coming, our chemistry dwindled, and his interest fell on other things. It is for that reason that I knew he had lost interest in me.

Yet, standing here with Revel, I could guess what he was thinking without asking. And that twinge in his smile and sparkle in his eye is one that I haven't noticed before. I am intrigued.

"What was that?" I reply with a slight smile. His response was quiet, and I wanted to make him say those three words louder again. Of course, in a teasing way.

His smile widens and he replies, "YOU ARE RIGHT, CAR-RIE."

I blush and look behind me now. His response was louder than I was expecting and ballsy if I must admit. I should have known. As much as Revel was acting nervous and tentative at first, I know he doesn't actually care what people in this office think about him. Perhaps, he only cared at first for my benefit. I look back at him and giggle. Full on, little girl giggle.

Then he looks me up and down and replies, "Where did you go?"

"Oh, Sarai from marketing and I went to a yoga class. I know, I look disgusting," I point down the hall towards the bathroom. "I was just about to change."

"You look far from disgusting, Carrie," he says it so fast, almost automatically, that I can see him recoil instantly. "Um, I better go... I promise I won't continue to ignore you." He gives me a genuine, innocent look. I definitely have never seen that expression on him before. To be honest, it scares me a little. That is a look that I would only ever expect him to give a girl he was interested in.

~ 26 ~

REVEL

Honestly, what is wrong with me? I just gave my best friend's girl a compliment. Something I didn't even recognize when it came out of my mouth. Thoughts of the perspiration gleaming off her chest are flickering in my mind, and I can't help but crave the smell of her perfume that hit me in the face when we crashed into each other. And what is up with me feeling fidgety around her suddenly? I must be going through something and projecting it onto her. I mean, my emotions have always taken control over logic when it comes to these things, but this cannot be happening. I look at myself in my car mirror and slam it shut.

My phone dings... Justice's name pops up. "When do you get home today?" I shut my phone off and instantly decide not to reply. I'll just see him when I get home and I am not in the right headspace at the moment.

I am going through something. That must be it. I just don't get how she and Justice could be fighting. Her? Carrie. It is like she is a completely different person over the past month or so. I can see more to her that Justice is overlooking. And the more he has overlooked it this month, the more it escapes her. It is a longing that I believe I am looking for. A depth that I can pick up on that others can't relate to. Carrie seeks the same thing that I lost when Raven left.

It has been a few years since Raven left. The only girl I ever loved. I haven't met anyone as special since then, and it has kept me longing for a partner who is loving, understanding, and supportive. I had that with Raven, but lost it when I found out she didn't want children. It was another desire that I couldn't give up. I did not have the best childhood. It was full of poverty, emotional abuse, and an addicted mother. It made me into the emotional mess I am today. However, I made it a point to break the cycle so that someday I could give my child a better life. It seemed impossible before meeting Raven, and even after that, I haven't found someone to share life with. But the candle of hope never blew out.

For many years, I felt like I was playing catch-up with Justice because he had the career, the house, and the girl. I had the career and house, but finding the girl proved to be harder than expected. I would not be surprised if it is because of my previously unresolved trauma and coping mechanisms. The life they built always seemed rosy and perfect. The one I looked up to, but never truly understood. Yet, now, I am thinking that it was all premature.

They have a hard time communicating and Justice wants to give up. Justice grew up differently from me. He never experienced childhood trauma. He had a mom who drove him to school, made him lunches, and was there to pick him up after school. He never witnessed his mom passed out on the tattered couch in the trailer home we could barely afford. He never had to force-feed her when she was too high to eat for days at a time. I envied Justice. Not in a vindictive way. In a way that I looked up to and aspired to create a life like that for myself. But it never worked for me. He didn't appreciate it. Their relationship had barely experienced any turmoil until now. It was easy enough for Justice to play the role of doting, loving husband until it was not. And it is not even his fault! How could he not feel discomfort in the turmoil and change? It's something he never had to deal with.

I know this sounds crazy, and maybe I am, but I am conflicted between being there for Justice and seeing Carrie for who she is. Carrie and Justice were a pair for so long, it's hard to think of them as individuals. I've been happy for him and their love for as long as I can remember. But I never imagined how I would feel when he neglected her. I mean, there is an instinct that should be there still. An instinct to protect her and understand what she needs. One I could feel. I could see what she needed. I knew she needed to hear she was stunningly gorgeous, no matter what she wore or how sweaty she was. She wanted someone who recognized she stayed late at work and was achieving so much. She craved the company of her person on late nights or long weekends. She wanted someone to make her laugh and also be serious when needed. But mainly, she needed someone to recognize her pain and understand her. Something I understood.

I must get to the bottom of this. I must convey this to Justice for his own sake because I can't let him lose her. Eventually, they will forget this nonsense about an 'open' relationship because I know there is no way in hell this is what Carrie wants. Carrie? Carrie, who just recently told me she wanted more out of life, was not possibly talking about this. She is probably just trying to get a reaction out of him. Hoping he will fight for her. I know he is not doing that now, but there must be a way for him to see what I see. Only time will tell when they get back together. Then, maybe, I will stop thinking about her.

~ 27 ~

JUSTICE

I wear denial just right. Fear is no longer strapped so tightly around my waist and ignorance fits like a glove. I have managed to avoid my worries and the breakup as much as possible. I may sleep next to Carrie, but I have treated Revel's place as my own Airbnb. It has been over three weeks and my interactions with Carrie are minute. I don't make the effort to tell her good morning. I don't make her coffee in the morning. I don't kiss her goodnight. Our relationship is almost non-existent. I have had more conversations with an old roommate.

Yet, she looks better than ever. She spends most of her days out with her co-workers and comes home tired from the fun she has had that day. She has no interest in my arrival or my departure. We have no worries when it comes to each other. No worries at all.

I open the door to Revel's for the third Wednesday morning this month. I moved my computer PC and laptop to Revel's the Monday morning after Carrie told me her plans for our relationship. As much as she needed a break, I needed an escape. This is not what I would have dreamt of.

Yet, I cannot control the future. This should be just as much her dream as I want it to be mine. And it no longer was.

My PC is set up in Revel's spare room upstairs. I head to the kitchen to toast a bagel from the pantry before getting started on the workday. It has become my routine. Bagel, work, and then go for a run.

Revel is a top-tier tech analyst, so he is already at work when I come over in the mornings. Last night, he came home just before I was on my way out for a run. He stopped me in my tracks and asked what my plan was.

"What do you mean?" I replied. He has all the right to ask this question. It has been almost a full month and I have shared nothing with him about Carrie and I's dismal relationship.

Revel looks past me for a second and then stares into my eyes once again as he asks, "I mean, are you going to go home anytime soon?"

Avoidant as ever, I couldn't answer him. "Ask her," I shrug.

Revel stares at my expression for longer than I feel comfortable with. He is trying to read me and my feelings. I bow my head and turn towards the door. I am not in the mood for a staring competition or, better yet, I am not in the mood for a therapy session. Truth is, I may be giving Revel the impression that Carrie is the one making the decisions, but it is all I can do to cope. It is easier to blame her for everything than to put in the effort. It was easier to express my emotions and understand how I feel when I was expressing feelings of love and devotion to Carrie. Yet, now that there are more nuances to our relationship, I can't give her what she needs. I cannot match her whirlwind of emotions and it overwhelms me. All I can do now is get my bearings and run, run, run. I have run about 4 miles each day this week, and my head is not any clearer.

Today is another bagel. Another bagel, another workday, and another run to look forward to. I take my toasted, cream cheese bagel and head upstairs. My computer takes about five minutes to power on. I work for about three hours before my co-workers are online. It is almost noon when I hear a 'swoosh' blare through the speaker.

Megan has messaged me, "Countdown begins." Another swoosh. "Tomorrow morning, we are flying into Florida!!"

"Exciting! When are you supposed to get in?" I reply.

"5:00! And then we are all going to dinner at 6:00 in the Malibu area. I am so excited I have never been!" Megan almost screams through the screen with excitement. "You are coming, right?"

"Yeah, a free hotel room and food on our company's dime? Of course, I am there," I joke.

The dots show on my screen a little longer than usual before Megan asks, "Is your wife coming?"

It takes me a few seconds to respond with a legitimate answer. "No, she has work." I think about what I just typed and remind myself that it is a completely viable response considering they are flying out Thursday and leaving Saturday. No working spouses can possibly make it to that.

"Oh true. Forgot people will be working lol," Meghan responds.

A few moments pass in which I have left Meghan on read, distracted by the open tabs on my desktop. While flipping through tabs, I notice the dots appear again and Meghan has responded with, "I am trying really hard not to think about whether Jeffrey will be bringing swim trunks to Miami lol".

Poor Jeffrey. He is commonly the butt of our jokes, but maybe he would be happy to know that his unique characteristics have bonded two of his co-workers who live on opposite ends of the country. Without him, we would not have gotten so close. "Ask him!" I tease.

"You dare me?" Megan responds. I have yet to meet Megan in person, but I can already tell she is someone who likes to test her limits.

"I dare you," I type.

A few more reports run, and pivot tables refreshed before I receive a response. "In 24 hours, you and I will be witnesses to what Jeff is hiding underneath that suit of his."

"No way, he said he was bringing it?" I ask.

"Yes. I couldn't make that up even if I tried, haha," Megan clarifies.

"Haha, that was gutsy," I reply.

"Dare me to do anything and I will."

I leave Megan on read once again and get back to work.

Thankfully, my workday wraps up around 4pm, and I am guzzling water in the kitchen after my run when Revel walks through the front door.

"Hey, Rev, early day for you?" I ask him as I set the cup down and am making my way to the stairs for the shower. I am still not in the mood for chit chat, so I hastily move past him, hoping this conversation will be brief.

"Yeah, you know the team went out for happy hour and that is not really my thing," Revel responds. I am about to begin climbing the stairs when Revel swiftly faces me and blurts out, "Jus, have you thought about what I said earlier today? I really think you should talk to Carrie. I am sure this is all a misunderstanding and you both just need to get on the same page."

I don't reply. Revel scratches the back of his head as he rambles on, "I mean, you haven't really said much about anything. Are you okay with this whole 'open' relationship thing? Because, to be honest, it does not seem much like either of you. I mean, it might do more harm than good."

I feel frozen in place. What am I supposed to say? I failed. I am a failure. I vowed to my wife that I would love her and be there for her forever. I vowed that I was the only person for her. Of course, I don't want an open relationship. We were supposed to be our one and only forever. So, I stay quiet.

Revel looks at me with hesitation and astonishment. "Jus? Do you have anything to say?"

I shake my head.

"Jus, come on! What are you doing? You love Carrie and, as your friend, I can't just watch you throw your life away and bum it here," Revel responds.

I scoff and shake my head some more.

"What? Do you find this funny that I am genuinely concerned for you?" Revel raises his voice. "I mean, fuck, you're acting like a huge dick! Is that why she left you? Cause, God, I would too if this is how you have been."

I know he is trying to get a reaction out of me. Revel and I could say anything to each other, and we know that at the end of the day, our words would never affect our friendship. So, he does this whenever I am not in the mood to talk, and I do it, well, when he is being a dickhead as well.

"Don't test me right now, Revel," I reply, getting more irritated with him. I should just storm up these stairs, but fuck, I am not throwing a temper tantrum like a fucking four-year-old.

"I will test you! You have been moping around for almost a month and I am fucking sick of your attitude. You fucked up! You are painting this like it is Carrie's fault, but you know that you gave up a while ago," Revel pushes back.

My blood is boiling! I can feel it pumping from the valves of my racing heart. Heat waves move through my veins. Fuck! He thinks he knows everything. Was he there every time Carrie looked at me with hurt behind her eyes and pleaded that I love her when I couldn't possibly love her more? Does he know what it is like to let someone go whom you love because you have exhausted all other attempts to reconcile? No. He doesn't even know what it is like to live day in and day out with the same person for more than a week. This has been seven years of my life.

"Fuck you, Revel," I am so angry I can barely get out any words.

"No, fuck you, Justice. You made vows! Why don't you try a little harder!?" He steps towards me, pointing his finger as he speaks. Suddenly, my lid pops.

"You think I haven't fucking tried? You know what, Revel! You are lucky you are so fucked up in the head that you don't have to have the only person in your life that you give a fuck about sit you down and tell you that you aren't good enough. Maybe you are lucky that you can't hold up a relationship for longer than a good fuck and breakfast in the morning to experience any type of heartbreak!" I am pacing back and forth in front of the stairs before I end with, "God! You are the last fucking person I would talk to about any of this!" I turn around to face the wall, and before I know it, my hand has made its way through. The black that blurred my vision just moments before lifts. All I can see now are the dust clouds that surround me and the wall caved in before me. I fall to the floor, holding my injured hand. I lay my head against the wall and feel the wet warmth of water seeping out from my eyes. My eyes close, and when I open them, I see Revel staring at me in awe.

"I'm sorry, Jus" Revel apologizes. "You know I had to do that."

"Ya, I know," I assure him and let out a small laugh as I say, "Because I was being a dick, right?"

Revel lets out a breath, finally, now that the mood has lightened. "Fattest dick I have ever seen."

We both laugh. I stop laughing once I look down and notice my injured hand. Again, I take in the heaviness of the situation and realize the damage I caused.

"Don't worry," Revel replies. "The place was too nice before you smashed a hole into it."

I flash a half smile and lean my head back on the wall once again. Revel joins me on the ground before the stairs and leans his head against the wall as well. We sit in silence. The truth is, I said all I needed to say to Revel. He does not need to know everything. He just needed me to feel everything. To let it out.

--

It is Thursday evening, and I have spent the last four hours driving to Miami before checking into my hotel room for the night. My company gave us an itinerary for tonight and it looks like dinner is at 6pm, like Megan had mentioned. This work event couldn't come at a more perfect time after the blow-up I had with Revel yesterday. I'm glad he got through to me, but as we sat there for thirty minutes under the hole in the wall, we both came to terms with reality. We can't control everything. Sometimes you must let go to get something back. And, right now, I can't think about what I could be losing by letting go. I can't even imagine what she is thinking of me right now. This morning, before she left for work, she noticed my hand while I was brushing my teeth. I stopped brushing when I noticed her stunned expression. She looked directly at me rather than through the mirror and asked, "What happened?" Her face was genuinely concerned and the last thing I want is for her to worry about me. So, I told her I fell on it while running. Unfortunately, it was not the best lie, so I am sure she still has concerns.

Our office asked that we attend in formal attire, so I bought myself a new navy blue suit paired with a black button-down. Leaving two buttons undone because if I am forced to wear a suit, I am not tying a noose around my neck with a tie as well, I begrudgingly use some gel to hold my curls in place, but the messy locks are undeniably a part of my look no matter what I try. Lastly, I pair the outfit with black dress shoes and head to the banquet hall.

I have already spotted our company name (along with a few other company names) posted in front of two double doors down the hall from the lobby. I am a little nervous to meet my co-workers from across the country. I mean, they are basically strangers. I walk in after a group that I do not recognize from any Zoom calls, assuming they must be from another company. As I watch the group in front of me conversing and laughing, I regret coming. I plan to grab a drink and call it a night if I don't recognize anyone by the time I finish it.

My legs feel like weights dragged against the floor and my stomach flip-flops anxiously as I head to the bar. The bartender is busy on the other side, so I take a moment to peruse the crowd in hopes of recognizing someone. Nope, no one. But, then again, it is fairly crowded. There are probably around seventy people in this small banquet hall, and I am looking for at most 5-10 people whom I have only met virtually. I give up and put my efforts towards getting the bartender's attention.

He finishes topping off the last drink for the group on the backside of the bar and looks up to find his next customer. I make eye contact with the guy and nod when he raises his index finger to motion 'one moment'. I am awkwardly sitting on the last barstool of the bar next to multiple groups of people. Somehow, I am the only person alone in a sea of groups of people. I order an old-fashioned, and thankfully, with the herd of people around me waiting for drinks, he does not beautify it. He simply throws together some sugar, water, an ice cube, and whisky on top. Just as I like it.

"Justice?" My ears perk up and, suddenly, my face flushes and my stomach is full of nerves. I turn around to finally meet Megan. In this light and in real life, my mind cannot help but recognize how pretty she looks. I mean, she has always been fairly pretty, but in this banquet hall, dressed up, she looks more than just pretty. Her dress happens to be a deep purple color, almost like the deepest waters of the ocean or the sky on a moonless midnight. They highlight her cat eye make-up that surrounds her blazing irises. I never noticed her eye color before, but right now, they are pulling me in and it is hard not to try to identify this color I have never seen before. The dress must be bringing out a new shade altogether because it is a fusion - too dark to be blue and too vibrant to be brown. Everything about her is complementary. Her makeup complements her eyes, her dress complements her irises, and her irises complement her hair. Her eyes pop against the deep brown hair that turns reddish in the fluorescent lighting above us. I shake my head in disbelief and remember this is Megan. Say hello.

"Hi..." I let out a small gasp of relief and embarrassment, "Megan?"

Megan seems way more comfortable in a social setting and wastes no time with the greeting, automatically pulling me in for a professional hug. Megan has arrived with some of our other co-workers: Sheila from AP, Sean from AR, and Trish from HR. I go around giving each one a professional side hug that was not as pleasant as the one with Megan, but rather very awkward. It looks like the four of them have all banded together. There is no cohesion in this group besides working for the same company. Sheila is about 60 years old and wearing a brown, rustic-looking dress with a white scarf wrapped around her neck just where her short, gray hair ends. Sean is stern-looking, around his early 50s, and his presence screams, 'I hate social crowds.' Lastly, Trish is in her late 30s and looks like she prefers dive bars and smoking a pack of cigarettes a day. Interesting crowd.

After a little bit of small talk, Megan's pleading eyes meet mine. Sheila, Sean, and Trish are all oblivious to the telepathic message she is sending me, but I can see it loud and clear. "Get me out of here!" I smile at her invitation to leave and take charge immediately. I down the last bit of my drink and ask Megan in front of the others if she would like to grab another drink with me at the bar. She smiles nonchalantly as if that was completely out of the blue and not part of our great scheme to ditch everyone else.

We make our way over to the other end and squeeze in between two groups of people to two available barstools. The bartender is busy assisting one of the large parties, so instead of trying to get his attention, I turn to Megan and teasingly ask, "So, where's Jeffrey?"

Megan lets out a small laugh and teases back, "Waiting for me back in my room?" She throws in a wink at the end, which is playful and sexy.

I laugh nervously and look down at my hands so she can't see how much her remark had me swooning for a second. "Oh really? If that's the case, then why aren't you there right now?"

Again, she replies with a hint of seduction, "I like to play hard to get".

I am looking into her eyes this time and I can see a glimmer of hope. I feel the chemistry flickering between us. The virtual messages that teetered on flirting for the last couple of months brought me to this moment. A beautiful woman right before me, in whom I have no reason not to engage. As I process this, the tension between us grows thicker. I pull my eyes away and turn my attention to the bartender, flagging him down a few moments later to order another old-fashioned. Megan asks for a Chardonnay, and it is only mere moments before we are handed our beverages. I try to focus on our drinks to cut the tension a little. Feeling awkward, I take a sip and steer the conversation to another topic.

"So, how has Miami been since you arrived?" I ask and then add a touch of flair to my question, "Have the people of Florida done their job to make you feel at home?"

She giggles and replies, "Yes, everyone has been nice, and it is much more tropical here. I love it!"

"Yeah, I have never been to California, but I hear it's overrated," I reply sarcastically.

"Don't get me wrong, I like it here, but I would never move here! I mean the alligators alone." She replies with vindication.

I laugh. "There are no alligators here."

"Personally, I find they are too close unless they are on the other side of the country," She exaggerates.

As we are laughing and continuing to spar over which state is better, the groups that are on both sides of our chairs are pushing closer together. More people are entering the banquet hall, and, in the process, we are getting squished closer and closer together. Someone's elbow makes its way into my back and knocks my body forward. The whisky I am holding is jerked in the process and a splash hits Megan's hair, chest, and the top of her dress.

I quickly scramble to my feet, looking for napkins while apologizing, "Oh no, I am so sorry!" I am still scrambling to find a napkin or flag down the bartender, but it's like we are invisible amidst the mass of bodies that have engulfed us. I frown and gesture to the exit doors. Megan and I make our way through the crowd until we are free from the chaos. I repeat, "I am so sorry!"

Thankfully, she doesn't look upset at all and laughs, "No biggie, this just reminds me why I can't have nice things."

I sigh in relief. I was so overwhelmed by the number of people in there, but her laugh was all I needed to take the edge off.

"I do still want to wipe off the stickiness, though, if you don't mind?"

"Sure, I understand," I reply. I stand still, assuming she will want to freshen up in her hotel room and then meet up later.

She hesitates and says, "Want to come with?" I hesitate but she continues, "Come on, it will be quick, and I do not want to lose you to this crowd."

I nod and follow her to the elevator up to the second floor. She waves the hotel key in front of the handle and opens the door.

"Go ahead and make yourself comfortable. Please, don't mind the mess."

As I make my way into her room, I notice it is clean except for an open suitcase. On top, a red bikini and a black lace bra stand out. I redirect my gaze towards the balcony, so I can respect her space. I hear Megan turn the sink on and decide to take a seat on the bed as I wait for her to freshen up. After a minute or two, she walks out of the bathroom. I look up from scrolling on my phone and, suddenly, I am aware of the setting. Megan's smile twinges at the corner and she breaks the silence with, "I am all refreshed."

I reply, "Oh good. You ready to go?" I stand up and begin moving towards the door. For a second, Megan looks a little disappointed, and I am only inches from the door when Megan blurts out in a nice little tone, "Justice, wait?" She places her hand on my wrist and when I turn around, I see her eyes meet mine, all doe-eyed. "I really did mean I was most excited to see you and that I don't care to go back out there."

I look at her and, for the first time in a while, I feel desired. And, in all honesty, the desire is reciprocated. I have been ignoring the feeling before tonight. Why try to fight it anymore? What am I afraid of?

Her hand is still holding my wrist. I keep my eyes locked on hers and allow my fingers to move towards her hand and lace them together. I inch closer to her. The intensity grows thicker. My heart is beating more rapidly, and I swear she can feel it. I bring my head down and press my lips against hers. It's sweet with a hint of cherry. My heart is pumping, and my mind is begging for more. I lean into it and lap more heavily. Her kisses follow the same rhythm, picking up in pace with each lip lock. I am in shock when she bites my lip slightly and drags my bottom lip through her teeth. Suddenly, every force in me is thinking 'MORE'. My hand moves to her cheek until eventually both of my hands have made it into her hair, moving frantically for 'MORE'. I can feel the intensity from her frantically silent pleas for more as she rests her hands on my back and then begins pulling at my shirt and shifting our bodies towards the bed.

Bed. Sex.

Unexpectedly, everything in me grows cold. Thoughts of Carrie begin rolling through my head. I have had sex with a few women in my life, one of them being my wife for the past seven years. I cannot do this. I am not thinking straight. I pull away from Megan and turn around so she can't see my disbelief.

"I'm sorry I should never have done this," I admit.

"Justice, it's okay," she tries to console me by moving closer. Instead, I turn around, distracted and in thought. "Is it your wife?"

I face her and realize she never asked. She doesn't know how rocky it has been. She doesn't even know we are separated, and that Carrie told me we should see other people. And yet she still wanted to come between us.

I reply, "Yes, it is my wife, and I love her very much."

~ 28 ~

REVEL

I have no more bagels. Why would I have no more bagels? Probably because my best friend moved into my guest room this past week and has been eating all my groceries. Did the guy ever grocery shop? I substitute my craving for a morning bagel with a sad and depressing bowl of oatmeal. Just as I am preparing the heap of gloppy oats, the front door opens and Justice walks in from his morning run.

"Hey," Justice mumbles.

The guy was mopey before he moved in, but ever since he brought all his stuff over and asked if he could stay for a bit, he has been unusually and unbearably mopey! So much so, it is starting to piss me off. To be honest, I really wanted that bagel... "Hey, fuckface! We're out!" I hold up the empty bag he left in the cupboard.

"Uhh, right," Justice shuffles back down the first step of the stairs that he was already making his way up to get a better look at what I am holding. "Sorry."

He sounds so defeated. But why? I can read Justice better than anybody. That is why this friendship works. The mystery to him is less brooding than one may think. Many times, it is nervousness, frustration, or anything with the lack of time to process. Justice and I could relate on a level that our classmates in college couldn't because we had the book smarts. Justice eased through classes just as I did. He was my best friend because he was loyal and would always be there to pick me up. He sat with me when Raven left, and he was the guy who celebrated with me on my best days. But one thing I knew about him was that he was avoidant. Avoidant of confrontation, processing emotions, and communicating. But I can't understand what sent him over the edge. Something happened this past week that he is not telling me.

Ok, sure, he punched a hole in my wall last week, but I saw that as a breakthrough. The moping around, running to numb himself, and isolating himself in my guest room is a bit pathetic, but it's his way of avoiding the situation. I knew I had to intervene and that meant forcing him to feel something, even if that something was anger. Justice is a better man than me. We all know that. Which is why he bottles up anger, bitterness, and sadness. He pushes down anything that he feels will make him less than. I am not his therapist, nor would I want to be, but it does not take a degree in psychology to figure out that the guy avoids unwanted emotions. But let me tell you, you can either stay in the eye of the shitstorm. Somewhat safe and content. Or you can escape it by letting it pass you by. If I have to force him to leave the eye of the storm, then that is exactly what I will do.

I feel like the overbearing parent when I yelp at him before he makes it all the way upstairs, "Hey!"

I hear his footsteps stop and he replies with a huff, "...what?"

"Let's do our traditional 'beer night and sit outside' tonight?" I tone down my voice and add, "...I might even bring the tequila?"

"Ya sure," he replies, and I hear his footsteps continue up the stairs.

--

Two beers in and we still haven't gotten past the 'how was your day' and 'how has work been, lately?' small talk. And now that his relationship is off bounds, there is less to talk about, plus his mood is not helping. Normally, this wouldn't bother me. Long, lengthy chats were far from our style. However, I know if he lets Carrie go he will hate himself and me a little for not being a good friend and setting him straight. It was time for the tequila. It was the only thing that got me through my breakup with Raven, and now, it is Justice's turn.

I pour some Jose Cuervo Silver into shot glasses and hand him one. We don't exchange any words. Bottoms up. I pour another round and we go bottoms up again. Justice slams his shot glass on the side table between us and I begin pouring him another. He looks at me with a brow lifted. I pour myself a third and we drink up.

"Ok, talk," I tell Justice.

Justice has his arms crossed, looking straight ahead. "What about?"

"I know something happened," I replied. Justice keeps looking straight ahead and it is almost like the tequila has done nothing to loosen him up, yet. Fuck, I am going to have to pry this one out. "Jus, c'mon. I am not stupid. I mean, look at you. You have lost about 10 lbs. just from running so much. You're moping around my house and hiding out in that room. You owe me this… it's the least you could do for punching my wall. Now, talk." I say the last part as sternly as possible.

He grabs the shot glass he put down moments ago and gestures towards me for another heavy pour. I pour tequila into each of our glasses. We drink up and I see Justice rub his mouth with his hand, partly wiping the liquid off and partly out of frustration at knowing he can't keep up his cold shoulder act. Not with me anyway.

"I kissed my co-worker the other night," Justice grunted. He could barely mutter the words.

My mind is blank. "Okay, so you kissed another girl," I repeated. "Those are part of the rules, though, aren't they?" I was trying to make him feel better while at the same time wrapping my head around this. This wasn't like Justice. It sounded more like me. Carrie was Justice's one and only love. Only, maybe, we were both naïve to believe that.

Justice shifts his weight back in the chair with his elbows on his knees. He is holding his beer with two hands like a crutch. "Ya, I guess. But I never thought… I never thought I would actually use it… I don't know how I ended up here, Revel. I guess I knew she liked me, and I was playing with fire, but it felt like it all came out of nowhere still. I have just been feeling so shitty lately. Once, I kissed her, Revel…" He glanced over at me now. His eyes a little glazed. "I knew it was wrong and that all I have wanted... ever wanted... is Carrie."

"So why are you moping around here? Why don't you tell her that?" I reply. This all seems so simple to me. She doesn't want this. He doesn't want this. Why am I watching their relationship implode and somehow getting wrapped up in it? On one hand, Justice is sitting here telling me he still loves Carrie. On the other hand, he has been telling me this is all Carrie's idea while exploiting the opportunity. Maybe she was doing the same thing. Kissing guys and flaunting herself. The relationship I looked up to is in such disarray and it bothers me. But why?

Justice sits back in his seat and takes a swig of his beer. "She wanted this, remember? I am not good enough for her." His jaw flexes and I can tell he is holding back the whole truth.

"Ya, whatever that means," I reply and take a swig of my beer. I know I should be the supportive friend, but I find it to be utter bullshit. Love should be more. Love should mean more to people.

Justice shakes his head at me. "You know, this is why I don't tell you anything... No, like truly. You don't get it. And why would you? I appreciate the housing and the fucking bagels and that is all I will be needing!" He turns away and I watch him walk away, swiping the tequila bottle as he goes.

CARRIE

It's been a month since Justice and I changed the terms of our relationship. It's been a week since Justice moved out. He moved out and didn't even manage to tell me. It's not like I could tell any clothes were missing. He just never ended up coming home.

Tonight, I am looking forward to a networking event with an open bar and the opportunity to forget with the help of a good cocktail. I have spent the past month hanging out with Sarai and men after men who are only looking to hook up with me or my hot friend. I am not interested. And I cannot help but be disgusted imagining whether that was where Justice's head was when he was gone. I keep telling myself he stayed at Revel's. Except he wouldn't just stay there and not come back. Something in my gut is telling me there's something else.

I selected a silver, somewhat sparkly yet elegant cocktail dress that is perfectly professional in the front but leaves my back fully exposed. It is a little longer than the normal cocktail dress but hugs my curves and slims my figure. My hair is bouncing more than ever in spiraling curls, and I have paired my dress with a simple pair of nude pumps. I am, slowly, walking in my pumps towards the entrance of the venue, located in the heart of downtown. It is large enough to hold our company, plus a few departments from third-party vendors we are currently working with. Our management wants us to mingle and become familiar with the companies we are working with. I am excited to introduce myself to some individuals that I work with virtually to bring our projects alive but have not yet met in person.

"Carrie Carbone," I tell the bouncer at the door.

He checks his list and lets me pass. I am greeted with a champagne flute at the door. Wow, such great service. I pass through the double doors, and inside, there is a wide hallway that extends further than I can see. On the left side, the space opens into a huge ballroom and on the right side is a staircase that spirals up to a balcony overlooking the entrance. As I walk down the hallway and towards the ballroom on my left, I am amazed by the elegance our company has created in this industrial venue. You can tell this place is used for weddings, but tonight it has been transformed into a wonderland. The chandeliers are wrapped in twinkling lights and faux crystals. At the front end of the ballroom lies a sitting area of green velvet and dark wood, set up aesthetically. Large glass vases with candles are standing next to the pillowy, velvet couches to create a romantic ambiance. And, of course, the open bar at the other end of the room is just as elegant. It looks like they rented a dark wood bar to match the dark wood coffee table set up at the front end, and barstools with tables are spaced throughout the room. The centerpieces for these tables are cylindrical vases with pine tree branches and twinkling lights to brighten up and romanticize the room.

I am still in awe when my Marketing Director finishes a conversation with someone and heads my way.

"Hi, Carrie. You look so nice," She gives me a hug.

"Hi, Miranda," I say with a big smile. I am glad she spotted me as quickly as she did, so I was not standing alone for long. It is always tough at these social events to keep oneself busy and mingling. I like people and I am an extrovert for the most part, but I am not as confident in my small talk abilities. "You look great, too!" She is wearing a crimson, silk, high-neck dress. It is gorgeous against her tan, olive skin, and her mocha-colored hair.

Miranda smiles and falls into Marketing Director mode right away, "Okay, so I want to introduce you to a few people. Here, come with me. This group over here helped us with our 'Stretch and Strive' campaign before you were even on board and have helped develop the site since. And then, I want to introduce you to the Reps for the studios we are working with." I instantly try to get into Manager mode to keep up with Miranda and follow her to begin networking.

After four rounds of small talk and three deep conversations with people I will be working directly with in the next couple of months, I am beat. I need a drink. Miranda left me alone halfway through, which was fine since I had warmed up and was in complete Manager mode by then. However, it is time for a break.

I make it to the long bar that hosts four servicing bartenders. I raise my hand when one of them looks my way and shoot a polite smile. The barkeep smiles back and makes his way over after pouring another customer their red wine. "Hi, can I have a dirty martini, please?" I ask before even looking at the menu of special cocktails. *Mmmm espresso martini? I will have to get that next.*

The barkeep responds with a smile, and I think he even flashes me a wink. A little stunned from thinking I may be seeing things, I miss what he says. I laugh it off and reply, "Sorry, what?"

"I haven't seen you much at the bar. Not a big drinker?" He repeats with a grin.

That response confirms that I was not seeing anything. I reply slyly, "Quite the contrary."

"Good, then I will see you again," he flirts, sliding my martini towards me and then hastily heading to the next customer. I smile and sip my martini before noticing Revel standing like a wallflower next to the bar. I might not have noticed him, but he is staring intently at me.

~ 30 ~

REVEL

Only in my world would I imagine a life with my best friend's wife.

I can't explain it and I am completely ashamed of it. It was just last night that I was determined to knock some sense into Justice. But something about his recklessness was starting to chip away at me, especially when I am looking right at Carrie, trying to find a flaw. She is different tonight. The glints and glimmers I noticed this past month are now shining like a disco ball. I couldn't help but notice the chaos she was wreaking havoc on in this ballroom. Making her way back and forth to the bar and flashing teasing glances at any man in the room. She was being careless, and it is taunting me. And, at the same time, it's creating a fire inside me. A fuel of fury is rising inside me and, now, burning at the thought that she is, like Justice, exploiting her right to an open relationship. They were both being reckless, and it angered me more than usual.

She probably didn't know I was coming tonight. I was forced to attend this social event as I work for a company that has partnered up with hers. I am sure her company thought it would be nice to extend the invite. Most unfortunate for me. Of course, when would I have told her that I was coming? There really hasn't been time to since the day we ran into each other briefly. Truth is, I hadn't wanted to avoid her. Every night, after our long meetings, I would see her in her office alone, working late. Every time, I wanted to join her just like the last time we spoke in her office. That night was a breath of fresh air. There is something so sincere and wholesome about her that Justice has been keeping to himself all this time. And, when I see her spending time alone in her office, clearly not wanting to go home, I have thought what a shame he doesn't see more in her like I witnessed that night. I want to say that I understand Justice more than anyone. Sometimes, more than Carrie at times. But I do not understand what happened between them.

As I stand by the bar with a drink in my hand, I can't keep my eyes off her. She has been mingling for a good hour, during which I have staunchly stood here. Everyone she meets, she puts a smile on their face, and every guy in this room, as much as they try, can't keep their eyes off her. Another thought runs through my mind. Carrie broke it off. She didn't give Justice a chance to come back to her. I continue watching and see a few married men turn their heads to check Carrie out when their wives aren't looking, and it aggravates me. At first, I thought it was because I was protective of my friends' soon-to-be ex-wife, but I haven't managed to take my eyes off her either. I am no better than them. I am worse. I am his best friend, and I cannot deny my attraction. It infuriates me even more.

I promise I have never thought of Carrie in this way since she and Justice got together. I mean, I was with him the night they met and could see the attraction. She was enigmatic. And, for the few years of college they were together, they were a force to be reckoned with. Over time, she became more like a sister, and the turmoil between her and Justice only created more tension between her and me. I could tell she wished Justice found some new friends or wouldn't hang out with me as much as he does. I mean, she has been a part of almost every conversation I have had with Justice. All the locker room talk, the debauchery, and offensive talk we have exchanged. She has either ridiculed me for being so crude or has allowed the men to be men. Being able to be myself around her has brought us closer together, but there is no way that I could have seen anything romantic towards her until today.

I saw a different side of her... and, maybe, I wanted to spend some more nights talking. But tonight is making my head spin. This is the first time I have really seen her since the terms of their relationship were redefined. Truly, there is something different about her than what I have seen since the first day. It is almost as if the terms of an open relationship have opened her up altogether. In this moment, it is as if the fences of commitment have come down, and from it arises a woman with little fear. She has taken the crowd by storm. I can tell that she has captivated those around her. Her looks are not the only thing that people are noticing. Rather, she is as radiant as ever because of her personability, quirkiness, and confidence. Then again, I am only observing the clamor she has caused since being let off the leash. I am only observing.

As an observer, I notice Carrie making her way over to the bar in which I have done the kind service of patrolling all night. I'm two whiskey sours deep with the third in hand. Buzzed but nowhere near drunk enough to escape this social climate. Carrie lifts her hand up and makes a swift motion to signal the bartender for a drink with a wide, sparkling white grin. Justice is in big trouble.

The bartender makes his way towards her, and I can already tell what his intentions are. He confirms my judgment when he does not hesitate to wink at her and attempt his conquest. I guess he says something sly because she falls right into his trap and melts at his line. I watch her flirt back and I am fuming just thinking about Justice sitting at home while she is here entertaining every man in the room. The bartender finishes making her drink and moves on to the next person in line, but not without flashing her an obnoxious grin. Carrie is smiling and blushing until she spots me staring at her and I am not hiding my frustration.

"You sure have caught everyone's attention today. Please, don't let me interfere with your chances of meeting the next man on your list," I interject, doubling down on my reputation of hatred for events like these. Carrie is shocked but manages to steady a mean glare at me.

"Please, I'm just having fun, you should try it sometime," Carrie responds as she takes another sip of her dirty martini. "Plus, I don't know what Justice has told you, but I am not looking for anything."

"Justice hasn't told me anything and, for the record, it doesn't matter to me who you smash just as long as you get what you need from it." My third glass is completely empty, and I can see now that the effects have started to take control. Part of me wanted to defend my friend and part of me feels bitter towards her. Either way, my words crossed a line that I shouldn't have. But, then again, that is not out of character for me.

"Fuck you, Revel. You really need to man the fuck up and stop being a drunk on the sidelines as always. Say what you want, but at least I am doing something about my shithole life. It is more than you have ever done." Her big green eyes, black with makeup and fierce with anger, stare deeply at me for a second, and then she pulls her gaze away as she storms off.

Wow, I did not expect that from her. And just as the storm left, so did the whiplash the wind gave me in that moment. I probably should have proceeded with caution, but the whirlwind came out of nowhere and left me completely enamored by her fearlessness.

~ 31 ~

CARRIE

God, Revel can be so fucking obnoxious and pathetic. Justice's friends always gave me headaches, but especially Revel. And, of course, that one just had to be his best friend. I mean I know why the two of them will always be friends and why they lean on each other so much.

Justice is loyal and would never leave Revel, no matter how obnoxious he gets. As much as he would hate to admit it, Revel fears abandonment, and with all his commitment issues, Justice is the only one who has stayed through it all. Revel's backstory is traumatic and is the only reason people give him a pass on being a selfish prick. He grew up with no parents, at least none that ever had the capacity to love and care for him. For some time in his life, he grew up with his mother, but it was not long before she overdosed. I remember Justice telling me the story of how Revel found her. Only ten years old, he was shipped off to live with his grandmother until he turned eighteen.

Thankfully, he is as smart as he is because he got a full ride to Miami University and gained more scholarships throughout his college years for succeeding in his classes.

Now, he works for a successful tech company and lives the ultimate bachelor's life, bouncing from girl to girl. And that is where Justice is hooked. The bachelor's life appeals to Justice and is something he gave up early in life when we met. Now, when he hangs out with Revel, he feels a sense of independence, even if it is a false sense of reality. I always hoped that Justice could recognize the scars that are so deeply embedded in Revel. Because the truth is that Revel doesn't want to be alone. I saw it when he and Raven broke up and, again, when we talked the other night in my office. As much as he puts on a hard shell and pretends everything is fine, I know he is looking for family and more to his life. I guess it was naïve to expect Justice to see the internal scars when he cannot even detect his own emotional intelligence.

I used to give Revel a pass out of respect for Justice. That night we spent in my office eating Chinese food and laughing, I thought that maybe he was not just Justice's friend. I thought that all the time I spent around him over the years meant he cared about me too. But he knew everything that happened between Justice and me, and he chose to ignore me. He chose to walk down the halls of my workplace and avoid even saying hi to me. So childish. So, he can say all that he wants, and it will not affect me. I decided before coming tonight that I am not allowing petty men like Revel to bring me down. I will speak to whomever I want, and it is no one's concern but mine. Because if I have learned anything from these men, it is that you have to protect yourself and can never be too selfish.

I lean back and open my gullet as the rest of my dirty martini slides down. My eyes tingle from the vermouth and I am ready to let the night take me wherever it goes. As I conclude the pep talk in my head, I notice Chastity and Jared at the other end of the hall. I stride over confidently, not letting anyone stop me in my path.

"Carrie!" screams one of the girls. "I haven't seen you in forever! How has it been?"

"Hi Chastity! And, you'll have to buy me a drink before I can answer that one." I say with a lot more charisma than I truly feel answering that question.

"Well, say no more! Jared, can you grab Carrie and me a drink at the bar? Two espresso martinis, please!"

Chastity has more glee than the whole cast of the CBS show. Seems a little over the top for what this whole night is, but in all honesty, I needed this. I need someone to charge my battery and energize me since I have been running on low for so long.

Jared makes his way over with two martinis for 'his girls', he calls us, as he hands over the two glasses.

"Looks like you and Jared are doing well. How is newlywed life?" I ask, not really wanting her answer. Probably amazing. Probably still in the stage of continuously groping each other and saying their "no, I love you, too's." I hate that I am so pessimistic about love. I used to be her for so long, and now I'm that 40-year-old married old hag who imagines killing her husband in the middle of the night because she has four children and hates her life. That is exaggerated, but sometimes I wonder.

"Oh my gosh, amazing! While we were in Mykonos for our honeymoon, we saw so many...." Sorry, I basically ignored everything I heard and, again, leaned my head back to take a few gulps of the espresso martini. Mmmm rich, bitter, and the perfect amount of sweet. I need to order another one of these. "...and we basically sat around drinking copious amounts of alcohol while getting our tan, didn't we, Jared?"

"Oh, absolutely. My color has changed from ghost white to eggshell white. Can you tell?" Jared jokes.

I like Jared, but sometimes I wonder how he puts up with Chastity. She is like the energizer bunny and is always on to something new. She joins a lot of those pyramid schemes on social media and swears by them, but by the next year, she has ended her "sponsorship". And guess who pays for all of this? Ding, ding. Jared. If it weren't for him, she wouldn't have as many followers as she does because she wouldn't have the money to go on vacations and create the content she's had since meeting him. I guess that's kind of why Justice never gelled with them. He didn't come from money and can't fathom a relationship being so dependent on one person's finances. I guess I respect the way Jared provides for her. He loves her enough that he would spare no expense for her and her dreams. There I go again. Cherishing other people's relationships and regretting my own. I down the rest of the martini.

I give a little giggle in return to Jared's joke and interrupt, "Would you two excuse me for one second? I am just going to get another one of these at the bar." I motion to the empty glass that my hand is loosely gripping. "Would either of you want another?"

"Uh, no, we are good…" the two of them respond as I begin backing away towards the bar.

I hope Revel isn't still there. I glance over at the corner he was lurking in and find that he got pulled into a huddle by some men off to the right. Oh, thank God. Why did Revel have to be a smart techy who gets invited to these things anyway? I would like, for once, to escape Justice's world and enjoy a work outing.

I make my way over to the bar and wait for the couple in front of me to order, but they are taking forever!

"What would you say is your favorite drink to make?" asks the woman in front of me. Her tone is flirty and overly seductive for someone ordering a drink at a portable bar booth. Plus, the bartender who handed me my drink earlier looks conflicted by the question and the other people swarming to order a drink. In a quick second, it looks like he defaults to a flirty comeback, "The espresso martini is a fan favorite tonight, which I think you might have in common. Would you like that?" I hear her giggle and see her nod her head up and down.

Wow, so much for being the only woman here that he flirts with. I am increasingly annoyed, now, with the wait time and the special service I got earlier that is not so special anymore. The bartender takes a second making the drink and then hands it to her, already turning to the next customer. He looks embarrassed when I step forward.

Maybe he was interested in me and can now tell that I am not entertained anymore.

"One espresso martini," I interject, sliding my empty class across the bar towards him and turning my back to indicate I am not in the mood for another interaction. I can sense his hesitation before he gets the message and goes through the motions of curating another cocktail. Normally, I am not this bold, but the effects of two martinis in twenty minutes could be taking a toll on me.

The bartender slides the espresso martini across the counter and sympathetically says, "Here you go, miss." I turn around, grab my drink, and head back towards Chastity, who is now chatting with Sarai.

"Hey besties!" I hug the two, interrupting Chastity and Sarai's conversation about Jared and Chastity's honeymoon that I would not like to hear again.

"Hi, Carrie!" Saria replies and hugs me back. In my sad attempt to hug them both, I end up hugging Sarai and flinging my other hand over one of Chastity's shoulders. I can feel Chastity tap my hand and Sarai holding me up as I lose balance for a second. "Are you good?" Sarai asks me under her breath.

"Pshht, yes, of course," I whisper back. "So, how was the resort you stayed at in Mykonos, Chastity?" I change the subject, redirecting it back. I would rather listen to Chastity brag about her relationship than have anyone notice my alcohol intake tonight. I'm just taking a little advantage of the free booze and there is nothing wrong with that.

Chastity continues describing the amazing view and food on their vacation. As she drones on about Mykonos, I take a few more sips of my cocktail, which is now nearly empty. I decide to play a drinking game in my head by myself. I will drink every time Chastity says 'we'.

"We decided to get up early one day and watch the sunrise..." Drink "... since we thought the sunset was so beautiful the night before..." Drink "Then, we came back to an amazing breakfast display..." Drink "We could not believe how fresh the food was there..." Drink.

Whelp! Looks like my drink is all finished. I hold on to my empty glass as I listen to Chastity's monologue. Once she is done speaking on Jared's behalf about their honeymoon, she makes eye contact with him and waves him over. The two of them break off to network with others, still in the phase of being tied at the waist. As they saunter off, I link up with Sarai and convince her to grab one more drink with me.

The two of us make our way to the opposite end of the bar from the formerly flirtatious bartender. However, instantly, I regret the new location. As soon as the new bartender makes eye contact with me, I can tell he is questioning the state of the 130 lb. woman swaying. Why does a girl have to go through harassment and judgment by a man just to get another drink? I roll my eyes and order another drink with confidence. Either it was the confidence or his wish to avoid an outcry.

"So, Carrie, has that guy from the workout day gotten back to you at all?" Sarai presses.

"Back to me? There is nothing to get back to. I said 'no,'" I defensively remind her.

"Ya, but that was before you and Justice agreed to letting go of monogamy, remember?" She nudges my arm, winking at me.

"I just brought up the idea. It doesn't mean it will be what is right for us. We are still figuring it out, okay." I grab the two espresso martinis from the bar top. "Now, can we stop talking about it already?"

"Sure," Sarai says, clearly disappointed.

I spent the rest of the night talking to a dozen more people and downed two more martinis. Five martinis in and a scan of the room to make sure I covered my bases, I realize it is time to take myself home.

The martinis are having more of an effect on me as I walk slash stumble towards the front entrance. I reach for my purse, which is still remarkably hanging from my shoulder, to pull out my phone and call an Uber. I shove my hand into my purse, searching for the phone that seems to be hiding from my drunken self. A few more circular motions stirred around in my bag, and I finally grasp it only to drop it onto the asphalt by the entrance. I bend down, trying not to fall, while remembering to hold down my dress so I don't flash everyone in the process.

"You good?" Revel emerges from the black wall he was standing against and which happened to impressively camouflage his black suit with the dark of night.

"Yes, very much so. Please go away." I purposefully lie so he knows he is not welcome in my vicinity. Of course, this is when I notice that my phone has cracked. I hit the side of the phone against my other hand a couple times hoping to jumpstart the home screen.

"C'mon Carrie, let me help you call an Uber," Revel said, "You may be mad at me, but you clearly need help."

Frustration floods my veins. Of course, I need help! My frustration is erupting from a deeper place, but I can't help it. Justice and I needed support and help, and what has he done? He has been of no help in bringing us together! If anything, he has made it worse. Not to mention, the last thing I need is for Revel to report back to Justice on how much of a mess I am. Suddenly, in the spur of the moment and with the liquor of courage inside me, I let go of what I have been holding on to, "Oh, now you want to help?! Where have you been ALL THIS TI..." Hiccup.

Oh no, not the drunk hiccups! Once I get these, there is no coming back. As soon as the hiccup leaves my mouth and my mind processes what just happened, my hand flings up to cover my mouth. My eyes widen as Revel's mouth curls into a smile. His eyes, which are normally dark and mysterious, glimmer with humor. Revel has always been handsome, but all of a sudden, his dark exterior has warmed up to me. His eyes are now staring at me with burning intention. I have to pull my eyes away because I am now blushing. Hiccup... Hiccup.

"Come with me." Revel grabs my hand and takes me past the front desk and up the stairs that are right next to the hall doors.

"Revel, are we…" Hiccup "allowed to go up here?" I eventually ask through the hiccups that keep emerging.

"Sure, why not?" Revel furthers his mysterious appeal.

He pulls me up the stairs. I'm heavily leaning on him for support. Suddenly, he stops and swings me in front of him, gesturing at a water cooler in front of him. Say no more, I fill one of the paper cups with water. I try the best trick in the book and force myself to drink the water while holding my breath until my hiccups feel like they have subsided. I tilt my head forward again once the chest spasms recede.

"Thanks," I break the silence and take in the area around us. Looks like the second floor is made up of cubicles for what looks like temporary office spaces. "Revel, how did you know there was a water cooler here?"

"Well, I took your advice and decided instead of being a 'drunk on the sidelines' I'd just come and be a drunk up here," Revel says lightheartedly.

I can't help but laugh at that. Even though I have been a complete jerk to him, justified or not, he can still make me laugh. It's a skill I know Justice admires about him too.

Something about looking at Revel and thinking about Justice right now feels wrong. Revel is looking at me with the same expression as earlier and I can't quite read it. What is up with these men and not being able to read their emotions?!

I look away and stare down at my toes, "Maybe, we should order that Uber. I mean, if you don't mind that I go with you at this point?"

"Already done," Revel grabs my hand again and leads me back down the stairs. I don't know if it's because I am drunk, but I don't want him to let go.

I use the railing to make my way down. Revel reaches the bottom first but waits to make sure I don't need assistance. I walk ahead of him and notice a car with its hazards on in front of the building. I bet that is our Uber. I walk towards the car and look at Revel for confirmation. He nods his head and we both climb into the backseat.

The drive is a full fifteen minutes. But fifteen minutes too long to hold in the tension I am feeling. Revel's eyes are darting between the driver and my exposed thighs just before my dress covers them. I am not going to lie to myself and deny that I don't mind entertaining him in this moment. I may be drunk, but the drinks are only reinforcing my interest towards Revel. He makes me so mad sometimes, but something about it is just what I need.

Revel slowly moves his gaze from my thighs to my eyes. It takes a whole minute before we collide. Revel's kiss is warm and sweet, and his tongue knows exactly what it is doing. I guess his experience with all those women has paid off. As much as my mind tries to will itself to think clearly, the last thing I want to think about is who would be affected by this. Not to mention, every responsible bone in my body has disappeared after gulping down five martinis. I kiss Revel back, letting his tongue take control and his hand make his way down to my waist. I let go of all control and let the waves of passion rush between our bodies. His kiss is so strong and assertive that it takes me a minute before

I realize his hand has made its way under my dress, slowly making its way under my boob and just as it does, his licks against my tongue slow until he gives me one final kiss and comes to a halt. My eyes open and he is staring at me wide-eyed. Revel looks down at his hand that is comfortably sitting under my breast and quickly removes it. He jerks away from me and turns stone cold for the last five minutes of the ride. I fix my dress and sit in silence, taking in the consequences of what just happened.

--

I wake up in an oversized tee and my comforter draped over my face. The clock reads 9:00 a.m. Still, my room is dark because the blinds are protecting me from the morning sun. I rub my eyes and am not surprised to feel makeup leftover from last night. Ugh, last night. The memories of last night rush through my head and my hangover sends anxious shivers to my spine. Did I really kiss my husband's best friend last night? I blink and my hands that I just used to rub my eyes are staring me in the face now. The most daunting being my ring finger. I kissed my husband's best friend with my wedding ring still on. I know that is part of the open-relationship gig, and I know we didn't cover the rules of it all, but I do not think kissing his best friend was part of it. Suddenly, the fear of losing Justice creeps in. Maybe we don't need to tell him.

My stomach flips and my fear is moved to the back of my mind because all I can think right now is 'must throw up!' I leap from my bed and run to our bathroom. My stomach begins hurling up all remnants from last night. The vermouth,

the vodka, the coffee. After a couple of minutes, my stomach is completely empty, and as much as it wants to keep
going, there is nothing left. I crawl back into bed and spend
the rest of the night fighting the nausea.

--

Thankfully, it is Saturday because I still feel awful this
morning. Maybe the copious amounts of alcohol weakened
my immune system, and now, I have the flu? Except, isn't
it called a 24-hour bug because the nausea stops after 24
hours? But I still cannot eat anything, and the nausea is persistent as ever. I have not left my bedroom since yesterday,
the thought of it is unimaginable. So, why do I feel like I
need to throw up again.... Oh no. I leap from my bed again
and run to the bathroom.

I am heaving, but nothing is coming out. 'I should probably eat something so I can give my stomach something to
throw up.' I hear a knock on the bedroom door. My ears perk
up. I thought I was alone...

"Carrie, are you okay?" Justice asks.

"Justice?" I respond. So, it's not a serial killer. Phew!

"Yah, sorry, I came by to pick up my spare charger... I,
uhh, kind of lost my other..." Justice trails off and repeats,
"Are you okay?"

An involuntary heave comes up again. "Uhh yah, I'm
fine." All I want more than anything in this moment is to
open the bathroom door and allow Justice to comfort me.
To have someone fetch me water or some chicken soup.
But he isn't that person anymore and I'd better get used to
that now. I don't hear him reply or hear anything over my

pounding headache, resting on the toilet seat. I closed my eyes for what seemed like only a few minutes when I flush the toilet one more time to get rid of all the acid that my stomach managed to upchuck. I can't help but sit helplessly in this position, straddling the toilet. It's so quiet in the house that I am sure Justice has left. My heart sinks. I know I shouldn't expect anything more, but that doesn't stop me from wishing for it. Part of me hoped he would come to my rescue and that part of me may never go away.

I sigh and rustle my hand on the floor, looking for my phone. I am reminded and disgusted all at the same time of the cracked screen from last night. Somehow, it has magically started working. I have just opened the Panera Bread app icon to place an order for soup when I hear the front door open and close again. Did Justice just leave? I assumed he left earlier when he didn't say anything. Confused and concerned this time it might actually be a serial killer, I whisper-shout, "Hellllooo?..."

There is a knock on the bathroom door. To my surprise, I hear Justice call out, "Heyy... uhh, I ran out and got you some food. Even if you are not feeling good, you should probably eat something... I didn't really see anything in the refrigerator or pantry that's edible. I can leave it on the kitchen coun-".

I cut him off and call out, "Come in!" It may not be how the feminists out there would want me to feel, but my heart leaps for joy. Yes, please come in. He slowly opens the door, and I realize it is the first time I have truly seen him since we had our talk about our relationship. For over a month, we have been dodging each other, successfully if I might add. Now, as he opens the door and lets himself into our bathroom, I can see he has lost weight. His cheekbones are slightly hollow, his build is still muscular, but more athletic than usual. Regardless, he is the same Justice. Handsome as ever. And he is holding a Panera Bread to-go bag!

Justice lifts the bag up and says, "I figured you would only want soup, so I got you a soup and bread bowl from Panera."

I smile before I can even think to hide my excitement. "Thank you!"

Justice sets it on the bed and begins walking backwards. He is heading towards the door when he says, "Let me know if you need anything else."

And before he completely closes the door, I blurt out, "Justice!" he opens the door a little more and turns to face me. "What are you doing today?"

"Not much," Justice replies. I'm not sure if it is the time spent away from each other, but somehow, I could tell, even from that little response, that he was happy to stay with me.

"Would you mind staying?" I ask nervously.

"Of course," he replies with a smile. He makes his way around the bed to his side. We turn the television on and spend the rest of the day just like that.

JUSTICE

I have been sleeping at Revel's ever since the night of my corporate work event, which was over a week ago. I cannot sleep next to Carrie knowing that I kissed someone else. Although that was part of the agreement, I still cannot in good conscious lay next to her knowing my lips touched another's. She proposed this 'open' relationship agreement, and I am not sure whether she has made good on the deal, but, truthfully, it was never my intention to. The shame is eating at me. So, when I returned home from Miami, I grabbed a bag of my stuff and moved it to Revel's. This is the longest time I have ever physically spent away from Carrie. It irks me to be away from her. I know I can't sleep in the same bed or stay in the same house because of what I did. But it also reminded me that I don't want to be with anyone else. I regret it. I moved out because I respect Carrie too much to pretend like that didn't matter. But all I want now is to see her.

I head down the stairs of Revel's place and pass by him on my way out the door. "Hey, late night last night?" Revel went to a dinner party or something for work. He was a little vague and evasive when I asked where he was going in a fancy suit.

"Uhh, yah," he nods but avoids making eye contact, "But, you know, I managed to dodge out of there pretty quickly." A little twinge on the corner of his mouth lifts up, but his eyes are serious. He walks around me and up the stairs before stopping and asking. "Wait, where are you going?... And, are you... smiling?"

I scoff. "What? No... No, no, I am just heading over to our house to get something I left."

Revel turns his hips around to face me directly now. "You are going to see Carrie?"

"Well, I am not sure if she is there. I am just going to stop by and then I'm coming back," I hesitate. I am not sure if I should tell Revel what is really going on. "Ya, okay, I guess, I wish she will be there."

Revel turns around, immediately, and heads up the stairs before shouting, "Sounds good!"

Okay, that was strange. Not to be self-pitying, but I thought Revel might be a little happier since he kept pushing me to see her for so long. Is he upset with me that it took me this long? Whatever. I'll deal with that later.

--

When I enter the house, I can hear someone puking in the bedroom bathroom. Is that Carrie? I knock, "Carrie, are you okay?"

In between heaves and the sound of the toilet flushing, she replies, "Uhh, yah I'm fine."

She is hiding her pain from me. Before all of this, she would have made sure I was busy assisting her in her time of need. Maybe she doesn't need me... and, suddenly, I realize I don't like that feeling. Almost involuntarily, I decide to pick her up something at Panera Bread down the street.

I head out and make it back 15 minutes later. I walk towards the bedroom door and, rather than hearing puking again, I hear Carrie call out with trepidation, "Helllllooo?"

Hearing her questioning tone, I begin to second guess myself. Is it weird that I ran out suddenly? Am I overstepping? "Heyy... uhh, I ran out and got you some food. Even if you are not feeling good, you should probably eat something... I didn't really see anything in the refrigerator or pantry that's edible. I can leave it on the kitchen coun-".

Before I can finish my sentence, Carrie calls out, "Come in!" Tell me why I am nervous to walk in on her in our own room? I guess the truth is that our relationship isn't what it once was. I slowly open the door and make my way in. Carrie is still sitting on the bathroom floor with her back against the wall near the toilet. Her hair is in a bun on the top of her head and, although she is clearly sick, she looks beautiful nonetheless. Before I can overthink it all, I set the to-go bag down and reach out to help her up. She smiles and takes hold of it. Slowly, we make it to the bed, and she gets all tucked in. I want to be respectful of her space, so as much as I would like to stay and keep her company, I inch back towards the door.

I am closing the door slowly when she says, "Justice!" I open the door wide open again and turn my body to face her. "What are you doing today?"

"Not much," I reply with a nonchalant attitude, but my eyes tell a different story. I am not sure how to act around her nowadays, but she must know deep down that all I want to do in this moment is stay by her side to make sure she is okay. That is all I will ever want. In sickness and in health.

"Would you mind staying?" she asks.

"Of course," I reply with no hesitation. I head over to my side of the bed. This is where I am meant to be. Next to my girl. I turn on the television for us and willingly take up patrol duty to make sure Carrie is alright.

~ 33 ~

CARRIE

Sunday morning and my alarm clock blares. Ugh. I must've forgotten to turn it off. I fling my arm over to my bedside table, fishing for my phone whilst laying comfortably in the same position on my bed. Hmmm, my phone is not on my bedside table, and it is still going off obnoxiously. I bring my arm back to my side and open my eyes. My arm touches something on my hip and my eyes focus on it. Justice? Justice and I are spooning this morning, and I think my phone is on his side of the bed. After the 5th ring, Justice moves his arm and moves onto his back with an exasperated breath. He is awake. I turn around and notice he is still in his clothes from last night and so am I. We must have fallen asleep watching movies and moved into this position.

Justice looks at me, making the same realization as I just did, "Good morning."

"Morning," I say, and then turn back into the position I woke up in because I can't help but smile. Something in me tells me this is right. Why am I fighting him? Why am I fighting us?

I temporarily forget all the miscommunication and nights of endless crying, and Justice sits up, rubbing his eyes awake and looking so cute and charming. In this moment, I take in the changes from the month apart and wonder if beneath those eyes is a desperation for revival in us. Or is it just me?

Justice looks at me, breathes in and blows out a deep breath, "Want some coffee?"

"Ya, I would love some coffee."

"I have been trying new coffee shops lately. You know, to get out of the house. Want to try one?" he replies.

So, that is part of the reason he is gone so often and so early in the morning. The idea that he has been trying different coffee blends in the morning and not other women, while we have avoided each other, eases my mind. "Ya, let's go."

I hop off the bed and Justice starts heading out of the bedroom. "I will let you get ready first."

I nod in surprise. We haven't been in each other's company, so the challenge of having the same closet has not been an issue. Of course, changing in front of my husband, whom I have chosen to separate from, was not something that I thought about. But, I guess, I can be glad that Justice is a gentleman.

Justice closes the bedroom door and I throw something on quickly. I have found that when it comes to dressing and caring about what I look like lately, I have become more myself. Before, I was trying to catch Justice's eye or grab his attention. And, although I can't deny I feel butterflies as I get ready to grab coffee with my husband/ex, I am more confident in myself. Take it or leave it.

I walk out of the bedroom wearing a black tank and short workout set with a black purse over my shoulder and brown sandals. "Ready. I'll uh just wait out here." Why am I so awkward and giddy around him?

As I wait, I start questioning, 'What are we doing here? Is this smart?'

~ 34 ~

JUSTICE

I close the bedroom door behind me, and for the first time since Carrie and I started dating, I am questioning what to wear. She looked so effortlessly gorgeous when she walked out in her black outfit and natural curls. I don't know how she gets prettier without trying.

I am scanning my closet for any clues and decide to throw on a light blue Lululemon shirt and light grey shorts with my ON running sneakers. I might as well just embrace the runner side of me that has contributed to my weight loss over the past month. That and the loss of appetite. Yet, for once, this coffee date has me perked up and my stomach growling. Wait, coffee date? *Ya, what is this?* I wonder what Carrie thinks this is. *Ahhh whatever I can't over think it.* I look at myself in the mirror and brush through my hair with water. I grab my cologne from the bathroom counter next to Carrie's perfume and realize it has been a whole month since I used it. *Will it only be one torturous month without her? Can I finally come back and make her realize who we are? Will she stop having her doubts?*

I brush the questions away and can't wait to open the door and just to be close to her again. Two steps left and I see her sitting on the couch waiting patiently. She looks up from her phone and stands. "So, what coffee shop are we going to again?" she asks.

"I'll show you," I leave a little mystery to our coffee quest, knowing she has never been to this place before.

We head out awkwardly. This is the first time we have been alone together in the past month and it is undeniably weird. I am sure there are questions running through her mind just as much as mine. Like, are we rushing the ending of this separation? Should we be hanging out? I just hope she doesn't think on those questions for too long.

She gets in my truck, and I am so happy to see her sitting passenger again. I hand over the aux cord and suggest, "Would you like to play music?"

"What?" Carrie replies. "You never let me play music in your car. Why now?" Her eyebrow is raised, and her tone is quizzical.

Ok, she got me. I was territorial over my aux cable before, but I think both she and I know that she is all I am thinking of in this moment. I am a 'simp' to her. "Just take it," I tease her. She gladly keeps the cord and plugs in her phone. The first song she plays is by Ariana Grande. "Okay, I think I may be regretting this one," I joke.

"Shhh," she replies, laughing, "You can't take it back now."

We continue listening to Ariana Grande, Beyoncé, and Taylor Swift before we reach a hole-in-the-wall coffee shop. And thank God, because the urge to hold her hand like a giddy, goo-eyed teenage boy was overwhelming, just like back in college when I was pursuing her.

She is still singing to a new favorite Taylor Swift song when she spots the coffee shop. It is nothing special, but it is decorated with a succulent wall and wicker chairs that get her attention. "Oooo cute," she comments.

I park on the street, and we walk towards the coffee shop. I decide to be bold and grab her hand, leading her to the cashier. I can feel her hand squirm in consideration, but then grip my hand back. I look at her and see her relax into my assertiveness.

We are waiting in line behind a huge group of young adults, so it takes a lot longer than anticipated. The group ahead of us are handing out flyers for an event and asking the cashier if he minds placing them at the front of the shop.

"What would you like to drink?" I ask Carrie. "I'll order and you can grab a seat by the window over there."

"Yah, sure. I will have an iced vanilla latte." She heads towards the table for two as the group finishes placing their order.

I order our coffees and wait until the barista finishes making them. I sit across from Carrie and hand her coffee over. I am entranced by the sun shining through the windowsill, reflecting off Carrie's curls and freckled face. I am so distracted by the red and yellow tints reflecting off her hair from the sun rays that as I lean my head to take a sip, my mouth completely misses the straw. Embarrassingly enough, Carrie witnesses the whole thing and bursts out laughing so hard that a little coffee spurts out. She stops laughing once she realizes she just spit out coffee in public, and, in return, I laugh at her. The karma was instant, and as soon as we realized it, we started laughing again. Once we calm down, I cannot help but ask, "So, how have you been?"

She looks at me with serious tenderness and says, "I am not sure yet."

Confused by that response, I try not to overthink it. She probably feels the same way I do. We just needed some space. Involuntarily, I ask her, "I know we didn't communicate very well. But, overall, we were happy. Weren't we?"

Carrie grins, but then almost immediately shakes her head. "No, Justice. I wasn't." I am taken aback, and I think she notices my confusion because she adds, "I think there is supposed to be more to just being together. There needs to be more than just love. We need respect for each other and the hope of uplifting each other. And, I do not know how to do that, yet."

"Carrie, we have respect for each other, and I can uplift you," I assure her. I truly do not know how much more I can do, but I must convince her that we can work this out. I need her.

Carrie pulls away from my gaze and looks at the barista pouring espresso over ice behind the counter. She shakes her head and says, "No, I knew this was not a good idea."

"What is not a good idea?"

She looks back at me, sternly. "This," she points at the table with our coffees, "What are we doing right now? I need more time. I haven't been my best self for a long time."

"I think you are perfect," I reassure her.

"I'm not perfect. Believe me."

~ 35 ~

CARRIE

Justice drives us home, and I go straight to my room. I need time to decompress after that coffee date. I mean, how can he act like our relationship didn't implode just a month or so ago? Does he have amnesia? If there were no problems with us, then I wouldn't have declared this separation, and he would have spoken up and protested when I suggested it, and I would not have kissed his best friend!

Before I lose my mind, I call Sarai. She picks up after a couple of rings. "Hey, want to go shopping?" To my pleasure, she accepts. I grab my purse and notice the flyer I took from the coffee shop. I am not sure what came over me when I grabbed it, but I reason it must be desperation or curiosity, because why else would I pick up a flyer welcoming people to attend a church nearby? If I had known that is what it was, there is no way I would have reached for it. Now, I have a paper with bold, orange letters saying, "Come Visit Revival!" I shake the image out of my head and run out the door.

As always, Sarai greets me with a big smile and excitement bursting out of her pores. It significantly relieves the pressure I was feeling a moment ago.

"Hey boo thang!"

"Hey girl!" I respond.

She climbs into my car and asks, "So what's up? What are we shopping for?"

"My dignity." I laugh at my own joke.

Sarai looks at me with a smile and replies, "Does this have to do with the tall, handsome guy I saw you with the other night?"

"Oh no, did everyone see me with him?" The idea of everyone in the office spotting me with another man who is not my husband was a glimpse into my personal life that I did not want anyone to see.

Sarai can sense my anxiousness and replies, "No, calm down. I was just keeping a watchful eye on my girl after the third drink she ordered." She giggles and, again, reassures me, "No one noticed that either! He was quite the gentleman, getting you out of there before anyone did notice." She is smiling ear to ear as if it was about time that I let a guy come between Justice and me. Little does she know it is his best friend.

My stomach grumbles and, somehow, I am feeling a little nauseous again. "It's not as good as you think. Hold on let's get to the mall. I need food and I will tell you everything."

--

I am picking at the half-eaten croissant breakfast sandwich in front of me that is not settling in my stomach as I had expected it to, as I sum up everything that happened this weekend. "So, it is not good because I can tell Justice wants to get back together, but if he knew that I kissed Revel, then he would freak. Plus, I am not sure how I feel about Justice. Obviously, I still love him and want him, but has anything really changed? I don't know. It is all just a mess."

Shockingly, Sarai let me speak the whole time, but I had to keep my gaze on my croissant as I spoke. Every time I glanced at her, I saw a glimmer of pride in her. So, before she even responded, I knew her stance and I was not sure if I liked it.

"Oh my god, Carrie! I am impressed. This is what you needed. You needed an awakening, and, honestly, forget what Justice will think. It is no surprise that his best friend kissed you because I am sure he can see in you what we all can see and what Justice has been neglecting for so long."

Her words were meant to cheer me up, but they felt empty. I did not feel special, and to me, my actions were selfish. Justice may be as bad as she paints him, or he may not. But, even so, I do not want to stoop to this level. Like a lightbulb going off in my head, I realized I did this all wrong. I have been listening to everyone around me because I was riddled with doubt. My emotions were so up and down that I could no longer trust them. So, I put my trust in those around me. Thinking that it was my last choice, it led me to this point. In this moment, all I can do is nod my head at my friend with all her good intentions. She wouldn't understand, but I know I have to turn everything around somehow.

--

A week has gone by since Justice and I grabbed coffee, and since talking to Sarai about it. I spent the week buried in my work and resisting spending time with anyone. I needed to decompress, and something tells me I will not have the energy to be around my friends for a while. They have been so great during this time, but I can handle it from here.

I am sitting on the couch watching trash television when my phone dings. It's a text from Justice and my heart immediately starts racing.

'Hey, we need to talk.' Justice is still typing. The next message pops up, 'I miss you'.

My heart pounds when I read the second text, and the butterflies in my stomach whirl around ferociously. I do not want to give away too much of how I am feeling, 'when? where?'

The first bubble reads: 'I can come by the house tomorrow around 10 A.M.'

The second bubble reads: 'I would like to see you sooner than later.'

My heart leaps a second time before my stomach flips and lands into a pit of emotions. All of a sudden, I am fearful. I must tell him about my kiss with Revel and I do not know how he is going to take it. My heart is racing, and my fingers are shaking as I type, 'Ok, see you at 10."

~ 36 ~

JUSTICE

I longingly stare at Carrie. My hand is grasping the twinged hairs curled around her face. I can tell from her pursed lips and the way she can't look me straight in the eyes that she has been with another person, too. My heart is thumping faster and faster as I anticipate the words that are seconds from falling out of her mouth. At any moment, my heart will crack. Could it be a one-night stand?

By the way she is leaning into my hand and agreed to meet me here today, I can tell she wants to give us a try. I feel the magnetic pull between us that brought us together and is still present in this moment. There would not be this spark if there were someone else that she had fallen for. So, it is okay then. She can tell me anything and I would still love her.

Carrie lets out a deep sigh and steps away for a second. "It's okay, Carrie. You can tell me," I assure her. I can tell she is having a hard time telling me. I am having a hard time as well. The kiss I shared with someone else is eating me alive. Her lips were supposed to be the only ones I kissed for the rest of my life. "Carrie, you can tell me. I kissed someone else, too."

Her eyes flicker up at me and I see the pang of hurt that I was expecting to feel myself. "Who?" she replies.

"Megan... from work. They came to Florida for a corporate event," I explained. I see a tear escape, and just as I reach out to brush it away with my thumb, she pulls away. Carrie takes two steps back and is shaking her head from side to side. This is clearly affecting her a lot because she has barely gotten two words out since we met up. I have been waiting for her to respond, and all she is doing is shaking her head. "We only kissed, and it was brief, but it has not felt right ever since."

"What have we done, Justice?"

I try to move towards her, but she only backs away further. We are about three feet apart and the distance makes it even worse. I want this separation to be over. I want to close the gap between us and embrace her with every fiber of my being. Her face is the only thing stopping me. Her eyes are swollen and gleaming with tears. Those big, green eyes that I have missed, whether they are tear-soaked or not. But it is not the tears that stop me in my tracks. It is how wide her big, green eyes get the closer she gets to spilling whatever she is hiding. The right corner of her mouth is quivering with fear. Why is she so afraid of what she must tell me?

"I mean... what have I done? I can't believe what I have done, Justice," Carrie admits.

Whatever it is, I will always love her. She must have slept with someone else, and if that is the case, we will find our way back to each other. "Carrie, I will always love you no matter what."

She stares down at her feet, and I take the chance to close the gap a little, stepping forward so there are only two feet between us. I stare at her with pleading eyes because all I want is for her to clear the air. I want her to know that she can tell me anything and it will never change how I feel about her.

She turns around for a brief second and lifts her arms into her hair, scrunching the curls and pulling her hands over her face. Finally, she removes her hands from her face and looks me straight in the eyes.

"Revel and I kissed."

"What?" I don't even hear myself say it. My body is frozen in place, and I can feel a fire burning up in my stomach. Revel? My best friend, Revel? My best man, Revel? My friend, who should know my wife is off-limits, Revel?

"I don't know how it happened. I was drunk and was not thinking about how it would affect you," Carrie word vomits. Now that her secret is out, she has opened the floodgates and the whole story pours out. "I was really upset at the time, and I can see now that I was being selfish... Justice, it was nothing."

I am still frozen in place when she starts closing the gap between us. She reaches out to brush my arm, but I flinch and pull away. I can't process this. Never in a million years would I believe that my best friend and wife would betray me like this. I back away from Carrie and shift my eyesight. I can't look at her right now. It is sending images to my mind that I can't handle. We are now five feet away from each other, and the distance that was a discomfort at first has become my security blanket.

"Justice, please say something…" Carrie pleads. I lift my arms above my head and brush my hands through my hair. My chest is heaving. I need to get out of here.

"I need to go." It takes everything in me to remain calm and blurt out those four words. I turn around, shaking my head in disbelief. How could he do this to me? I speed up with every step as I make my way to my car in the driveway. I slam the car door loudly and white-knuckle the steering wheel as my eyes narrow at our house in front of me. I put the car in reverse and everything goes blurry.

~ 37 ~

CARRIE

I feel sick again. Sick because Justice clearly hates me, but also just *sick*! I am driving aimlessly, now. I left after Justice and I drove because I needed to do something. I wanted to clear my head, but as soon as I started driving, I realized I had nowhere to go. I don't want to confide in Sarai anymore. I have no one and nowhere to go.

I can feel my stomach unsettled as bile makes its way up. I pull over to the closest store in sight, a CVS. I run for the bathroom in my faint, weakened state. It's grungy and small, but that does not stop me from vomiting in it. My stomach quickly settles once I am done. Why have I been puking and feeling so sick lately? It is not like me to puke even after a night of drinking. However, I have puked more in the past couple of weeks than I have in years. Well, if I am not sick, what else could it be? ... Fuck. Am I pregnant?

I force myself to stand from the disgusting public bathroom floor and feel woozy all over again. I need to be sure before I get myself all worked up about it. Grabbing a test from the aisles, I return to the bathroom with a paid pregnancy test. Ok, ok, how do I even use this thing? Okay, you open this part... and pee here...

--

Twenty minutes later...

I am standing in front of an industrial building with a sign that reads 'Revival'.

When I picked up the flyer, I never thought that I would follow through on it. But here I am, standing at the address on the flyer that I somehow remembered.

As I stand beneath the bold entrance to a new-age church, I feel smaller than I ever have before and far from hopeful that it will change. I could have spent the entire day driving around aimlessly before finding out I am pregnant. Once, I saw those two pink lines, I fell to my knees.

The person who mattered most in my life turned away from me in disgust. And the tipping point is knowing we are having a child together amidst the mess. Suddenly, a 'Revival' sounded exactly like what I needed.

I find myself behind the big double doors listening to a church band singing in the background, "He is a good, gooood fatherrr..." I am not sure what has brought me here other than the fear that I have no other option. To do right by my child, I need to find my way and so far, everything I have tried has made it all so much worse.

I take one more look at the blazing sign above my head and open one side of the billowing door, the air conditioning hitting me in the face. At least, the cold air helps me feel less woozy than the effects of the humidity outside.

I must have arrived mid-mass because no one is bombarding me with pamphlets and a good morning welcome. And thank God for that. I remember attending church with one of my friends when I was in high school. We were friends for a brief time before I found out that she and her church friends were the most cliquey group I ever tried to be a part of. The day she brought me to church with her, we showed up 20 minutes early to find her friends and say 'hi' to everyone before listening to the pastor for an entire hour. I went one or two times after that, but was thankful not to spend any more Sunday mornings being aggressively greeted with a "Good Morning, blessed day!"

Here I am, more than ten years after my last experience at a church, only to expose myself to the hysterics once again.

I open the second set of doors, repressing the inner PTSD and allowing the small voice in my head to call out for help. Everyone is worshipping with their hands in the air and the lights are dim, so no one notices me sneak into the back pew. I am standing for another three minutes when the music comes to an end and the musicians lay their instruments on their stands and leave the stage. As glad as I am to take a seat, the singer and bandmates exceeded my expectations of a church band. Maybe it is because we are in the presence of the Lord, but her voice was like an angel's.

Once the band exits, volunteers assemble couch-like chairs on the stage in front of the instruments. I assume this is an intermission when the people begin chattering in their pews. I take this time to observe my surroundings. On the outside, the church was just a simple industrial building with a bold sign. Yet, inside the building is a traditional-looking church with modern changes. There are pews and pillars that give off the cathedral feel of older churches, but there is a modernized interior design that you can tell came from a recent renovation. The chairs on the stage are brown leather and emerald velvet with faux animal furs thrown across them. I am impressed by the design, and I cannot deny how cozy the room feels.

As I watch a volunteer adjust one of the throws, a tall man climbs the stairs to the stage and taps the microphone in his hand. "Test, test," the man mumbles into the microphone. The man smiles at the crowd and continues, "Good morning, everyone!" I knew that was coming. "I am Pastor Noah for any of you that do not know me or are firstcomers to the church. I speak at this church alongside other members, but today I am not here to provide a sermon. Rather, today, we have the special opportunity of providing you with a panel comprised of a few married members of our church for a Q&A."

Oh great. I drag myself to church and there is no sermon for me to listen to. Instead, there is a panel of married couples ready to mock me. Of course, staring me blindly in the face as soon as I enter a church is shame. Perfect couples sitting in chairs on a smaller-scale stage but, regardless, superior to the mess of a marriage I am in. A marriage that, no matter how you paint it, includes infidelity and is on the brink of a divorce. I hope I do not regret this.

"So, welcome the couples who have put themselves in a vulnerable position to provide advice and insight into their day-to-day married lives." The audience claps for a moment before the pastor carries on, "My plan is to ask some questions submitted by the audience after last Sunday's service. Then, any one of the couples that has something to say or would like to answer can chime in. Our first question is... What helps you communicate, especially when your husband is, by nature, a quiet man? Oh, I like that."

One of the wives in the panel looks around at the other couples, probably gauging whether anyone wants to speak up. After the other couples give her the nod to go ahead, she chimes in, "Yes, that is a good question and one I particularly resonate with. My husband, Levi, here does not tap into his emotions as well as I do." And, with that comment, she lets out a giggle, and the audience roars. "I think it is common for many women to struggle with communicating with their husbands because we are inherently more sensitive, aware, or empathetic. And I think the most important thing to remember is that it takes time. It took years for my husband and me to come to level ground and it was not for lack of trying. Unfortunately, I was asking him to tap into a side of him that he had never had to for the many years he lived on his own and expecting him to understand the depth of my emotions. So, number one, it takes time. Number two, there were many times that it would bring me to the brink of my emotions because communication affected all areas of our relationship. So, if you find that you are struggling intimacy-wise or quality time, whatever it may be, it is probably coming from a lack of communication. Now, number three, communication is not always what you may expect it to be. It could simply be the touch of the other's hand or the pursuit for the other's time. Levi and I communicated, over and over, until eventually, we understood each other. Now, Levi knows when I simply just need his presence or when I need him to listen rather than fix the situation. You have to get it out of your head that things come easy in this life. Marriage is not easy, and we are not always perfect, but God can mend anything. It is the work and holding on for dear life that makes it all worth it in the end. Only God can make sure change happens." She brings the microphone back to her lap and the audience roars with another round of applause.

My jaw drops. That's it? It takes time and only God can mend things. How can I leave my life in the hands of a non-tangible being? My mind is screaming, trying to convince myself that this is crazy. There is no way that a higher power could change my life for the better. I have screwed it up beyond repair. If anything, when I listen to these people, my mind rationalizes that everything that happens for the better is simply a coincidence. Yet, I can't help but notice my heart feels lighter. Truthfully, I am so exhausted by all my own efforts to control my life that, overall, I am relieved to think that my fate is not up to me. Could God help mend things for Justice, the baby, and me?

"Thank you for that, Emma. I appreciate all the points you mentioned and that you ended with God at the center of everything. How can a marriage last if we do not have

God at the center? Humans are by nature imperfect beings, and so without a perfect being, such as Christ, at the center of our relationship, it will continue to be flawed. So, thank you for that..." The pastor nods his head at the woman who spoke in appreciation. "The next question is a special one and an important one to answer... 'I am thinking about getting married, but am not sure it is what God has called for me? How do I know my partner is the one?' Any advice you would give this young lady or man?"

To my surprise, one of the husbands raises his microphone to his mouth and responds, "Ya, I think I may have an answer for that. My wife and I were very young when I got on one knee and proposed to her. I was twenty-one years old, and she was twenty. I had some doubts about whether I was making the right decision. Of course, I was in love, and that overpowered anything when I ultimately made my decision. However, at the time, I remember thinking, 'Is this the person God intended for me or am I too young to be proposing?' What I came to realize, shortly, at the beginning of our marriage, was that there is no such thing as 'The One'. God does not have one person in mind for us. Rather, choosing a partner is part of the free will that God gifts us. In that, it is God's hope that we bring him into the partnership to make it holy. As a couple, we found out quickly that as much as we loved each other, we would never be enough for each other. In the end, 'The One' is God." The man lowers the microphone and, again, the crowd claps at his answer.

I, on the other hand, am sitting still with the words 'We would never be enough for each other' ringing in my mind.

I was so sure that Justice and I would always have each other at the end of the day, but I was wrong. 'We would never be enough for each other.' The more people talk, the more I relate to them. It seems so obvious that every one of these couples has struggled and they humble themselves to their god.

I sit through the rest of the questions, with each panelist answering at least one. The hour flew by and each answer kept me a little more engaged than the last. Before today, I had never heard from other married couples. None of the people in my life are married and marriage is rarely talked about in the media. Therefore, I had always felt alone in my struggles–until today.

I walked into this church thinking that Justice and I were not meant to be together. That we had done all that we could, and it was not meant to be. I am leaving with the hope that Justice and I can be restored. If not for my own desire, then for our baby.

All of this is running through my head as the pastor closes out in prayer. It is hard to close your eyes and pay attention to prayer when you have not been trained to do so your entire life. So, when the prayer is over, I open my eyes and mimic the audience, "Amen."

The pastor finishes with, "Thank you for coming and please check out the guest booth if it is your first time here."

In an instant, everyone in the room vacates the pews and makes their way, single file, into the hall outside the doors. Just as I was the last to enter the room, I let everyone push ahead so I can stay in the back, invisible. I follow behind the herd of people with only an older couple behind me. The guest booth is right next to the exit and the volunteers at the booth are wide-eyed and ready to pounce on any new-comers. Or maybe I am just jaded. Of course, the herd of people I was following have dispersed between the coffee shop on one side or to mingle with others in the hall.

I accidentally make eye contact with one of the volunteers. Fight or flight? Flight! I break eye contact and immediately pivot to the left, where there is a crowd waiting in line for coffee. I could use a coffee!

I overhear a woman behind me asking her husband what he would like. The woman reiterates, "ok, so I will get you an iced caramel macchiato? Anything else?" The husband is clearly shy about ordering a sugary, typical Starbucks order because he only nods his head in affirmation and whispers 'no.'

His order makes me giggle a little to myself. I cannot imagine ordering such a thing for Justice. He probably would have taken one look at the iced latte, filled halfway with milk and drizzled with caramel, and scoffed at me. I can just picture what he would say, "Carrie, why is my coffee watered down with milk and topped off with sprinkles?"

I am glad I got in line, so now I can listen to those around me and people-watch without feeling like the spotlight is on me. You would think that Christian people aren't supposed to judge, but it is hard to come to church and not feel like that is exactly what's happening. I don't know if it is para-noia, but I can't help but feel like an outsider.

The coffee shop is connected to the auditorium where the service took place, but it opens into another room. To be honest, I am quite impressed by the setup. You can tell the room was mirrored after a Starbucks with dark wood features. There are multiple couches and coffee tables that people are comfortably sitting on. Fresh coffee cups are in one hand and children are held onto by the other. The children are hyper with excitement, looking like they just came out of a daycare or classroom nearby.

I spot one of the husbands from the panel trying to take a sip of his coffee while his kid yanks at his arm to show him the picture he drew in class. Unfortunately, the kid's attempt for attention results in the poor father's demise. Before his lips could contact the coffee cup, hot coffee swished out of the opening and onto his thin shirt, causing the father to yelp and stare at his son with astonishment. Yet, as fast as the commotion happened, his anger dissipated. The father kneels at the child's level. I cannot make out his words, but the son is nodding in agreement. I rest my hand on my stomach and wonder, will that be Justice one day?

The line is moving quickly so I am now second. I look at the menu above the cashier and decide I'll ask for a decaf lavender latte. Ugh, decaf. Looks like it will be a long nine months. At least they are offering lavender as a seasonal latte. I can't lie, I am a sucker for anything seasonal.

The guy ahead of me finishes putting in his order and walks away. I move closer to the cashier and, hesitantly, ask, "Can I have the 16 oz. decaf lavender latte?"

The cashier replies, "Of course. And, your name is…?"

"Carrie."

"Okay, that will be ready in just a second."

I take my credit card out, but the cashier looks like he is ready to move on to the next person. "Um, how much is it?" I ask hoping that he will notice me trying to pay.

"Oh, we do not charge on Sunday mornings," he replies with a smile. "We only have two services and offer certain drinks for free. The lavender latte is one of the lucky ones."

"Oh," I smile back and put my credit card away. "Thank you!"

I walk over to the back counter where they are setting the readied coffees. Free coffee? Regardless of how good the service was, I may be coming back here just for the free caffeine. The lady who was behind me in line is making her way over. Oh no, it looks like my attempt to blend in is blown. She is now making eye contact with me.

"Hi, my name is Sandy. Are you new here?" Her tone is calm and sweet, so I cannot help but find her introduction endearing.

"Yes, is it that obvious?" I reply.

"Oh no, honey. I am just an old timer," she assures me as she points at herself to point out the difference in age.

I laugh. For some reason, she does not portray the energy that she is here to poach me.

"The free coffee is one of the reasons I have attended this church for so long. Of course, my husband refuses to get the free options and asks for one of the specialty coffees," she grins. Her humility draws me in, and I love an old soul that uses deprecating humor. "I guess it is fine since he is the one paying for it." She winks at me.

I can feel my barriers coming down. "I did not expect anything to be free, but I guess it is a good way to get people like me with a caffeine addiction to keep coming back."

"Hooked me!" She replies. "So, where is your husband?" She points to the wedding ring on my finger.

I halt for a second. All the breath whooshes out of my lungs. How do you say, 'I no longer have one' or 'I am not sure whether he still wants to be my husband'?

"Um, he is at home. I kind of came on my own today."

"Oh, well, my husband and I run a mentorship and are always looking to grab coffee with newcomers or anyone looking to join the community. Here is my card. The two of you should give us a call if you are looking to get more coffee for free." Again, she flashes me a slight grin.

I accept the card. Do people still use business cards? I guess she is from the older generation. "Thank you." And, with the grace of God, my coffee is slid across the counter ahead of us. "Well, it was nice to meet you," I interject as I make my way over to my order. I grab my coffee, shoot her a grin back, and dart out of the room. Thankfully, the volunteers have left their posts at the guest booth and I sneak out.

~ 38 ~

REVEL

"Argghhhh," I let out a groan before turning over in my bed to face my side table, where my phone is persistently vibrating. Buzz, buzz, buzz! I pick up my phone and see 10 missed calls from Justice. The clock reads 11:45 a.m. Ugh, he is probably trying to wake me up so that we can watch the football games together this morning. I could care less about football, but somehow Justice always finds a way to rope me into watching every season. I fail to pick up the phone in time before the call ends. I consider calling Justice back, but figure there is no point since he will probably be home soon.

He is still staying here even after the day and night he spent with Carrie last week. The night after Carrie and I kissed. When he mentioned it, I was so caught off guard that I couldn't say much, except 'Sounds good!' I think he forgot about how weird I acted because he came back that Sunday and hasn't mentioned it. He seemed lost in thought, but also happier than I have seen him in a while. It made me anxious. I wanted to ask him about his time with Carrie, yet at the same time couldn't bring myself to find out if they reconciled after all. Whoa, the shitstorm I have put myself in this time is unbelievable.

I climb out of bed to put the game on and hear Justice's call pull up in the driveway just as I set two open beers on the coffee table. I head to the kitchen to grab chips when I hear the front door slam. I head back towards the living room with bags of opened chips, questioning the commotion when a force pounds me in the face, and the chips go flying.

"Ahhh, fuck," I yell. I think Justice just sucker punched me. "What the hell, Justice?"

"Thanks for letting me use your spare room, but I'm done coming over. I will be moving out and staying at Aaron's," Justice replies.

"Aaron? Does he even have an extra room?"

"No, but he has a couch and hasn't made out with my wife!" Justice seethes.

Fuck. Carrie told him. I thought we weren't going to tell him, and at the very least, I assumed she would tell me beforehand. Then, maybe, I could have talked him off the ledge he is teetering on at the moment. "It was a mistake, Justice. We both regret it and weren't thinking at the time."

"I am done talking to you." Justice takes off through the living room and back out the front door as quickly as he came in.

~ 39 ~

CARRIE

My drive home was not the easiest. Apparently, the mixture of decaf coffee on an empty stomach has upset the baby growing inside me. Except I didn't eat beforehand because that seemed to also make the baby queasy. Figuring out what the baby needs has turned out to be more difficult than I could have imagined. Not only am I overwhelmed by the change that this baby will make externally, but internally, the baby has already rearranged my insides. It takes everything inside me to drive through the nausea when all I want to do is lay in my bed with a box of saltine crackers and rest.

As I pull into my driveway, I am surprised to see Revel standing by the front door. I have not seen him since we kissed. He looks very serious. Serious? Or, angry? Oh no, did Justice tell him already? My curiosity is piqued and I forget how sick I feel.

I hear him as soon as I park and open the door, "You told him?! Why would you tell him?!" I'm in shock, climbing out of the car and staring at him as I make my way to my front door and let myself in.

"Did you want to ruin our friendship? I am the only person he had left. Do you get that?"

I turn my head to see him struggling immensely. Revel is not as angry as he just looks sad. His eyes have welled with tears from the intensity fuming inside. His face is scrunched and I can see as clear as day which eye Justice took his best shot at.

"I'm sorry, Revel. I had to." A wave of peace and relief comes over me. There was nothing *I could* do. I had to be truthful and ask for forgiveness. Only that way could I accept that it truly is out of my hands and up to a higher power. However, as soon as I felt peace from within, my stomach contents want out. My hand instinctively moves in front of my face just as the back of my throat spasms and I am forced to gag loudly.

Revel is still fuming, "What do you mean you had to? Please explain why..." before stopping mid-sentence to process what is happening before his eyes.

I open the door and run for the bathroom as fast as I can. And then the heaving begins again. I let the baby take over. In these moments, there is nothing that I can do but give up control. I heave one more time and look up after flushing the contents to see Revel standing in the doorway with a concerned look.

"Oh God, are you okay?" he asks.

"For now," I reply. Why is it always the last person you want it to be that sees you at your worst?

"Are you sick?"

I don't want to lie. I don't want to lie. Some part of me wants to change and be honest with myself and others. I want to do right by this baby and be better for it, but Revel cannot be the first person that I tell I am pregnant. *You're real, real funny, God.* Here it goes.

"No, I am pregnant."

Shock washes over Revel's face. Man, I really wish I had a camera in this moment. I can't believe how surprised he is for someone who doesn't have to take care of the little bundle. I stand up from the bathroom mat and snap my fingers in front of his face, waking him from his trance as he shuts his mouth. However, his gaze is still stuck staring at the wall behind me. I shake my head and move past him to make myself a PB&J sandwich. And, frankly, if Revel needs to spend more time processing, then so be it. God knows I have still not fully processed it myself yet.

I am assembling my sandwich when I hear Revel's back slowly slide to an upright position against the doorway he was frozen to. With hands in his pockets, he slowly makes his way over to the kitchen and looks at me with soft, pitiful eyes. I guess admitting that I am pregnant is enough to turn anyone from raging anger to quietly sympathetic. I continue focusing on spreading peanut butter to avoid his pitying gaze.

"Did you tell him?" The words escape his mouth ever so slightly alongside his next breath.

"No," I say matter-of-factly and take a bite out of the sandwich I have masterfully assembled.

"When are you going to tell him?" Revel steps forward, clearly trying to grab my attention.

"I don't want to tell him. I mean, look at you! He still hates me for kissing you," I reply with worry that I was trying to mask during the sandwich-making process.

Revel's brow twinges at that remark and I can tell he regrets the kiss even more now. "About that, I'm sorry for kissing you. There was something pulling me towards you. I know it's dumb, but it wasn't out of nowhere."

"It's okay, Revel. You liked a version of me that wasn't really me to begin with. And, I wasn't totally blameless either."

Revel lets out a sigh, "Well, maybe I can talk to him about it."

"No, Revel! You can't tell him yet," I exclaim. I know he is trying to help, but I don't think this news coming from him will make the situation better.

Revel looks at me with those pitying eyes again. Except this time, I can see that it is not just for me. The pity is for all of us. Justice. Revel. Me. The baby. What a mess we have made. I look at him with the same sorrowful expression and we share a moment of compassion for each other.

"Ok, I won't say anything. But, please, let me know if you need anything. Because even if the guy doesn't know and may hate my guts, I know he would want me to make sure you are okay."

I nod and hope that what he says is true. Revel nods back with assurance and leaves me alone with my thoughts. Instead of sitting with my fears and doubts, I bow my head and intertwine my fingers as I have seen others who have prayed do. I close my eyes and call out to Him:

"God, I am not sure what I am doing. I am lost when it comes to praying and, truthfully, I am lost in my life. Justice and I were not perfect, but we weren't wrong. I thought I was doing everything right. I thought I deserved better or that we wanted different things. Now, I think that I was listening to all the wrong voices. Please have him forgive me."

I keep my head bowed and whisper, "Amen". I open my eyes and raise my head, catching a glimpse of the business card from the woman at the church service sitting on the kitchen island. When I ran into the bathroom, I had thrown my purse onto the island counter and had not noticed that the purse had toppled over. The card must have fallen out, awaiting me to act. God, is this a sign? I mean, I call out to you, and this is what you present in front of me. As much as it may seem like a coincidence, my gut is telling me otherwise. I grab my phone from my bag and type the number from the card into my contacts. There is no way I am getting on the phone to call this random lady to ask her on a date. Instead, I type out a text message.

"Hi Sandy, this is Carrie, the church newcomer from today. It was nice to meet you. Would you like to meet for coffee sometime this week? I am interested in learning more about the church."

Oh no, she did ask that my husband and I reach out to her. For a second, I rethink the text, but something tears me from the insecurity that has riddled me for the past year. Somehow, I have hope and something is encouraging me to act. I send the text and think, 'Well, if she says no then I just won't go to that church anymore.' Just as quickly as that thought enters my brain, the ding on my phone goes off and a message appears. It is Sandy.

"Hi! I am so glad you reached out. Yes, does this Thursday work for you? I am out of town for a couple days, but then back to my regular, old boring routine by Thursday."

I think about it for a second, but not a second too long, before I can talk myself out of this. "Yes. 1pm?"

Another ding. "Perfect!"

Well, Thursday it is.

~ 40 ~

JUSTICE

I am out of a home, a wife, and a best friend. I moved all my stuff out of Revel's place and into Aaron's apartment. I hadn't talked to Aaron much since everything with Carrie happened. Aaron and Cruise had been hitting me up since, but I was not in the mood to be around anyone, so I would reply to their texts with, "Can't tonight. Next time!" When that was not enough of an excuse for them, I would lie and tell them Carrie and I had something planned. I was in complete denial.

So, when I heard the truth from Carrie, punched Revel in the face, and needed somewhere else to stay, I figured it was as good a time as any to call Aaron and tell him the truth.

Me: "Hey, can I stay at your place for a bit?"

Aaron: "Uhh, sure. I mean, I have a couch for you to crash on. Is it for the night?"

Me: "Umm, kind of longer than that. Things aren't going well at home."

Aaron: "Oh shit. Uhh well, yah stay as long as you want."

Short and simple. Not much to say. Aaron greeted me with a beer that I happily accepted. I didn't turn down any of the hard liquor he gave me later that night either.

It has been two weeks and the nightmare only gets worse. There is no space in Aaron's one-bedroom apartment, so I have been working at a coffee shop nearby. Having to work off my laptop in a nearby crowded coffee shop with the most uncomfortable chairs has been far from ideal. Plus, it has been a long week of putting up with Aaron and Cruise's antics. The two of them are stuck as representatives of frat boy century. Cruise being the Vice President and Aaron President of the club. Aaron is always trying to get a rise out of me and Cruise is there to hype him up. I have found that it is best to spend most of my time outside of his apartment, but after a long day of working at the coffee shop and going for a run, I finally came back to rest.

Aaron and Cruise were drinking beers when I arrived, with empty shot glasses next to each other. The two of them can drink, that is for sure. It is like they are caught in a never-ending cycle of drinking all night and waking up hungover the next day. So, the liquor only adds to the obnoxious questioning.

I sit on the couch when Aaron slurs, "So, what happened with you and Carrie, Jus?"

Cruise echoes, "Yah, you haven't told us anything."

The two of them have the side of their mouths twinging up in glee like my love life is a joke. Somehow, that doesn't make me want to be completely open to talking with them.

"Oh, you know, communication... and.. just not getting along."

"Fuck that!" Aaron shouts and Cruise laughs along. "I call bullshiiiitttt." His words are blending together.

Wanting to escape what feels like an incessant battle, I reply, "Yah, it is bullshit, and I am done with this conversation!"

It is quiet for a moment until Aaron breaks the silence, "Boohoo. Trouble in paradise for whittle Justy." Cruise bursts out in laughter, and I roll my eyes, falling asleep to their arguing about which players they think will perform better in the upcoming football season.

I don't blame them. I don't think they know how to read the room, plus I think they have their own issues that they are avoiding. It is easier to point and pick on me rather than focus on their own lives. I have always known it, I just never felt like I needed to acknowledge it. Now, I not only acknowledge it but am hit with the blaring truth of it. Carrie was right. They need to grow up and I need to stop getting dragged down by them. Then again, they weren't the friends that I designated to pull me out of my deepest depths. They were never the friend that Revel was to me. Revel. Every time I think about him, my whole body tightens.

The first week staying with Aaron was the worst, but since then, Aaron hasn't been around and neither has his sidekick, Cruise. I haven't even seen Aaron enough to even ask what he has been up to, but to be honest, I wouldn't jinx it by asking either. However, it is Friday night and the two of them have already texted me to let me know they are bringing over alcohol for another boy's night. The break from the two of them has put me in better spirits to handle them tonight so I replied, "Get me Spacedust!"

They make it back with a six-pack of IPA and a case of Michelob's. The boys are hassling me as usual, and I am swinging right back, Cruise and I even teaming up on Aaron about laying off the beers for a while.

"Yah, Aaron, might need to lay off the late-night drinking or you will never meet a respectable girl like that." I joke because a respectable girl was not something Aaron was on the lookout for.

Cruise gives Aaron a look and smiles widely, pointing at Aaron with his beer, he taunts, "Seems that he already did!"

My eyes widen at Aaron with curiosity. "You did?"

He looks away from both of us and, nonchalantly, replies, "Yah, I did." So, nonchalantly, it is as if this isn't the most bizarre, out-of-the-blue thing to happen. "Ya, that is where he has been all week. Sleeping at her place! The guy is whipped!" Aaron is not even putting up a fight as Cruise continues. "Oh, and she wants to meet us tomorrow night. Apparently, she wants to meet Aaron's friends." Cruise is laughing at how disarmed Aaron looks and I cannot help but smile along. "Justice, c'mon, we have to give her the run-around just like he would do!"

"No, dude. Come on, she is not like that," Aaron yelps.

I smile. "Well, okay then, I'll be there."

--

"Can I get you guys anything to drink?"

The hostess just sat Cruise and me at a table and the waitress wasted no time taking our order.

"Yah, I'll have the 'Husky'," I reply. I choose the double IPA at 8% IBV on the menu described as smooth, creamy, and rich.

Cruise responds with, "I'll take an 805, thanks."

We are seated at a brewery close to Aaron's place. I have been with the guys a couple of times in the past. It is a large warehouse space and is always crowded with all types of people. College kids, people here on a work event, family outings, and even birthday parties.

Tonight would be an addition to the types of people and outings found at this place. How about two guys meet their friends' new serious girlfriend? According to Cruise, Aaron has been seeing this girl for about a month, and she has really changed him. He used air quotes around the word change, rolled his eyes, and laughed at the comment.

"You mean, you don't think he really has?" I ask.

"I mean, occasionally, he has been acting differently. Like, he's been going to bed earlier on days that he promises he will drive her to work in the morning. I guess their schedules are sort of opposite, so that is his way of seeing her. And, before you moved in, she was staying almost every night. I hadn't even been over in weeks before you started crashing on the couch. You know how he was with other girls. Worse than me. He would invite me over to hang out and have them sit on the couch on nights they were sup-posed to hang out. He never changed his schedule or his routine for anyone. Now, he is not drinking as much, and he is being considerate!" Cruise lays back in the booth we are sitting at and lets out a tsk. "I mean, thank God you asked to stay at his place. I almost thought he was a goner until that first week you stayed over and he called me to hang out."

I laugh a little in disbelief. I mean, I always figured Cruise and Aaron would one day find the people they would commit to. Did I realize how bad they were before meeting the one and how much they would change when they found them? No, not at all. I guess I thought it was cool that they were completely themselves and that I could be myself in return. But if Aaron found someone who makes him better than I am more than happy for him.

"This is a good thing, though, isn't it?" I ask. Just then, the waitress places our beers in front of us. Cruise gives a nod and a wink as she walks away.

Cruise takes a sip. "Yah, sure, whatever! Doesn't mean I am not going to bust his balls when they get here." He laughs and uses the back of his hand to brush the beer off his top lip.

The two of us are close to finishing our first round when they arrive. Aaron walks towards us with his hand on the back of a woman's waist.

Cruise whispers, "Whipped." He winks and nods at me as if we are in agreement that the teasing will commence. Instead, as I watch her make her way over here, she looks at Aaron with excitement and shyness. Suddenly, I see Carrie in her. I am reminded of the times that being around Aaron and Cruise made her uncomfortable.

The day of the Superbowl when they called her out for wanting to go home when that should have been a conversation between the two of us. The annoyed look I read on her face was clearly the face of hurt. Pictures of her are flashing through my mind. My mind flickers to another point in time when we were going out for Aaron's birthday. We had planned to go bar hopping and hit up a few of our favorite dive bars. Carrie was getting ready and finishing her makeup in the bathroom when she asked me how late we were staying out.

"I'm not sure."

"Well, I don't think I can go out later than 12:30pm tonight," she said. "I just feel really tired from the week, and I know how you guys get." She was laughing at that last part, but I took it as an attack. I always felt like she was trying to ruin my fun. Trying to put restrictions on my life when I was old enough to make my own decisions. There was one person I was celebrating that night, and it was not her. I realize now that I took the time we spent together for granted. Waking up to her and going to bed with her started to become so normal. All things that I miss so much now. I should have appreciated that she wanted to come out with my friends and leave with me. I should have jumped at the idea of taking her home early to spend the night together. Instead, I pushed her away and resented her.

"You don't have to come," I countered.

She looked at me, hurt, and that face is flickering through my mind. "What do you mean?"

"Well, I can't really come home early just for you."

"That's why I thought 12:30 would be okay." Her brows furrow together and her nose crinkles in confusion. I shrug and she asks, "Well, do you not want me to go then?"

"It just sounds like I might be doing you a favor if you stay," I retort. I had so much anger towards her and I don't even know why anymore. At the time, I laughed with Aaron and Cruise about how I left my wife at home so the boys could have a night out. It seemed so harmless. I ridiculed her for being sensitive and gave her the cold shoulder when she cried about it. I left her in a flurry of anger and deep sadness and woke up to a small wall between us that only grew bigger the following year.

As I look at Aaron with his arm around his new girl, I cannot help but think 'I bet he is not taking her for granted.' Once my friends find that one, as I did, they had better not make the same mistake. They'd better appreciate it.

Cruise snorts out, "Sup, guys," and I get up and shake her hand. Aaron smiles at me, eyes Cruise, and introduces the two of us.

"Hey, Justice. This is Stephanie."

I smile and reply, "Nice to meet you."

They move into the booth next to us, and Aaron points to Cruise, "And that is Cruise."

Cruise lifts his beer in a silent cheers. I can feel the tension in the air and try to break through, "...so I guess we can order now? Any idea what you guys want?" I am looking over the menu as an indication that they can take their time.

The waitress takes our order, and we exchange a little small talk, going over our jobs and how we all met, along with a few jabs that Cruise threw in throughout the conversation. When Stephanie mentions she is a fitness trainer and works at the local gym, Cruise responds, "Ever try to get this guy to go? He could use it!"

"Uhh no," she huffs out in confusion. "I don't think he needs it."

Clearly, she doesn't make fun of his weight like the boys do. Cruise is laughing to himself and jokes, "I would think you would know out of everyone at the table what is underneath those clothes."

Full body cringe.

I guess they acted like this when Carrie met them, and their behavior never changed. But, at this age, it is getting a little old. Not only is my body shivering from the sheer awkwardness of this conversation, but I have empathy for Stephanie more than anything. Something I didn't recognize before.

I take a few gulps of beer and redirect the conversation again. I will drive this conversation for the sake of Stephanie and hope that Cruise will get on board.

"So, how did you and Aaron meet?" I am looking between Stephanie and Aaron. Aaron looks at her goofily and she perks up at the question.

"It is kind of a funny story, actually," Stephanie replies. "He was my Uber driver." She pauses to let out a giggle at just hearing that sentence out loud. "I was out with some friends and, normally, I am not the drinking and going out type of person, but that night we were celebrating a friend's birthday. Well, I had a few too many drinks and I snuck out of the group, which was on their way to another bar for more, and ordered an Uber. Aaron pulled up, and because I had drunk more than usual, I asked him 'If I enter this car, you aren't going to murder me right?'... I watch too many murder documentaries and that week I had just watched one about a girl who was murdered by her Uber driver, and it only occurred to me once I opened the door. So, I thought there was no harm in asking, right? Well, Aaron started laughing and said something about how he wouldn't imagine getting his new leather seats dirty. I probably should have run the other way, but his comment was disarming and, well, we got to talking on the drive back... and he asked for my number... and the rest is history!"

The two of them are looking at each other with smiles on their faces. The puppy love emanating from them would make anyone within a 10-foot radius sick with affection. "So, Aaron, was telling me you are married!" she says, "She should have come. I would have loved to have met her."

My mouth is dry, and my mind is blank. For a moment, I am completely caught off guard and then, as if on instinct, I reply, "Ya, maybe next time."

As time goes on, I can tell that Carrie would like Stephanie. Stephanie has mentioned how taxing her job can be, yet on her free time, she finds time to get a workout in, much like Carrie. The two of them are superhero women. The type of women who inspire you to be better. Something I forgot was so intoxicating about her. Not to mention,

Stephanie can hold her own in this conversation with three men. Every so often, Cruise interjects with a crude comment or an inappropriate anecdote, but she shrugs it off. Carrie was always good about shrugging those comments off as well. I never thought anything of it. I always thought it never really bugged her, but over time, she started getting more sensitive, and I felt like I couldn't keep up with the change. Yet, as I watch Aaron get more uncomfortable by the comments and the small, inappropriate anecdotes, I realize now that acting okay with it is a big difference from actually being okay with it. And, maybe, Carrie was at first. But I should have expected that would change. That eventually the comments would become sour and ganging up on her would be juvenile. And, by staying out of it, I was acting juvenile too.

We say our goodbyes before Aaron can have the chance to explode on Cruise. Cruise waves bye to Aaron and Stephanie and I go in for a side hug. I say goodbye to Stephanie first. Then, face Aaron for a bear hug. Aaron whispers in my ear, "Thanks, man". And I know what he means. 'Thanks for being a good friend and respecting my girl.'

Though he never gave Carrie the same respect, I can see his perspective change, much like mine has. Maybe I was kidding myself when I thought I was more mature than them. I can see now that I was far from it.

CARRIE

It's been a month since I last spoke to Justice and my belly has formed a small curve to it. I continued attending Revival church and Sandy and I have kept up our Thursday coffee dates each week. I have been asking her all the tough questions about religion and God and some of the time she has a good answer to them, but most of the time we open our Bibles and ask God to answer our questions for us. She says that the bible is our greatest guide to living our best life and I must admit it is the only thing that has brought peace to me this whole month.

Sandy gifted me a bible that she had sitting around at home and told me to read it on my own time. I guess I was in a desperate state because I have implemented it into my daily routine and read it before heading to the office. On our third date, I could not help but confess everything to Sandy. She kept asking about my husband and I couldn't lie to her anymore after the rapport we had developed. I confessed that my husband and I are separated, that I am pregnant with his baby that he does not know about, and that he will not speak to me because I kissed his long-time best friend.

She took it all in with no judgment. Instead, she reached across the table and put her hand on mine. It was the first time in a while I had not felt alone. It felt like she knew exactly how I felt. She did not pity me or reply with a list of things to do. Rather, she radiated with love.

"I think God brought you to me for a reason, Carrie," Sandy replied. "My husband and I have been through our ups and downs, and I recall a story much like yours that almost broke us apart for good. See, we both had kids at the time, but we were struggling immensely. I had not realized it until then, but we were living life on our own terms, without God. I felt like he wasn't putting in enough effort with the kids, and he felt like the whole weight of the world was on his shoulders trying to provide for the family. We went through our own drama, but in the end, it was God who saved us."

In that moment, I knew I was no longer alone and there was hope for everything to work out. My doubts and fears shrank two sizes and the surge of hope overpowered them. I wanted to embrace His plan for me, so I did something way out of character and asked Sandy to pray for Justice and I and our family to be. Somehow, I know it is not over for us. I just don't know how it will be repaired, but anything is possible if I give it all to God.

I am not waiting or hanging on to hope that Justice will magically appear and forgive me for everything. Instead, I am giving him his time as I adapt to becoming a mother.

Thankfully, I have been surrounded by support from friends. I came clean to Sarai since I was constantly throwing up in the bathroom at the office. I needed her to divert everyone's attention as I puked my brains out. Or have her change the subject if anyone was suspicious that I was moodier than usual. I could have managed on my own, but I needed to tell someone. Preferably, someone who was not Revel.

However, as much as I did not want to tell Revel, he has really stepped up to support me as well. He brings me groceries each week to alleviate my workload. I mean, I always imagined that my husband would bring me weird food cravings when I got pregnant, but I guess his estranged best friend will have to do for now. Also, he reminds me constantly to let him know if I ever need anything. I know he wants to be here for me since Justice still does not know and isn't here himself. I see now why Justice was friends with him. Revel knows how important I am to Justice; therefore, he treats me like family. Even if we bicker and fuck up, he shows up at the end of the day.

Today is Sunday, the day Revel normally shows up to drop off the goods. It has been a couple of hours since I got home from church, and I am starving! I have entered my second trimester, so I blame my constant eating habits on the little one. Apparently, the second and third trimesters are when pregnant women gain most of their 'calories,' as the books describe it, but let's just be real and call it what it is: weight. This is when I start gaining weight. I am becoming more and more aware that I need to begin telling people I am pregnant because of how tight my clothes are fitting around my waist. But it does not feel right to tell anyone else before I tell Justice. Until then, I am wearing my baggiest clothes, so people wonder whether I have a figure instead of thinking about how big it's gotten.

Ding Dong! "Oooooh food is here," I shriek, craving pickles and anything salty. I reach for one of the grocery bags as soon as I open the door. We shimmy inside with bags in hand. I am only allowed one bag because Revel is afraid that it will hurt the baby if I carry anything too heavy. Works for me!

"Hey, Revel! Thank you, thank you, thank you," I shriek again with excitement.

"Anytime," Revel replies with a friendly smile. Revel helps unpack the groceries. Honestly, I am glad for his help around the house because cleaning is the last thing I want to do these days. So, I take a seat on one of the barstools and allow him to assist me. As Revel puts away my favorite premade Sprouts foods in the refrigerator, he hesitates, "So I see you are starting to show a little."

I am caught off guard. "Revel, are you calling me fat?" I let out a laugh and look at him with a teasing, quizzical look.

Oblivious that his statement implied I had gained weight, Revel tries to backtrack, "No, I didn't mean that... I mean, you still look good... No, I just meant... have you thought about telling Justice?"

I knew what he meant, but the subject has not gotten any easier over the past month. I still feel like we need time or that Justice needs time. I am trying to practice patience and resist the urge to take control.

"It will happen when it happens. I am not sure, yet."

Revel looks at me quizzically. It looks like he is about to disagree, but then shuts his mouth and finishes putting away the groceries. He is about to stow the pickle jar when I stop him and gesture for him to place it in front of me. He smiles and slides it over. I open the jar and pull out a pickle spear.

I am biting into the pickle when Revel speaks again, "Okay, well, there are your groceries for the week. Now, if you need anything, and I mean anything, please just text me." Revel never fails to assure me he is here to help, and I am very appreciative. I smile and nod. He gives me another assuring smile and heads out the door.

~ 42 ~

JUSTICE

I went from being a husband and owning a quaint home to couch-hopping and working out of coffee shops with free Wi-Fi. It has been over a month since I have spoken to Carrie, Revel, or Megan. Aaron is spending most days with his beloved, and I avoid Cruises' advances to hang out after work. Frankly, I need the space.

The isolation has allowed me to grow as a person and figure out what is important to me. I guess it took hitting rock bottom to recognize how stagnant my life had become. Once it derailed, the noise drained, and I could concentrate on who I was before I got comfortable. I just hope it is not too late.

Since my lunch with Aaron, Stephanie, and Cruise, it all started to sink in. Like looking in a mirror, I was the one sitting across from my friend and his girlfriend. Aaron went from being the guy in the group unwilling to grow up to being the one to take strides and grow for the woman he is dating. I was dumbfounded.

Relationships require growth from both people, and I stopped holding up my end a long time ago. I got comfortable and stayed stagnant in my job and around my friends. For a while, it took me forever to understand why. Why did I take Carrie's encouragement and recognition as an offense? Truth is, I was afraid of taking responsibility. I took her attempts to motivate me as her personal vendetta to push responsibility onto me. I ran from the responsibility of being in a relationship into the arms of my circle of friends, who were refusing to grow up.

My fear caused me to run and look at what I am left with. Avoiding responsibility at work has left me stagnant working at a job day in a day out that I have no interest in, achieving no financial benefit or fulfilling aspirations. I avoided responsibility and confided in immature friends that I see I no longer need. Lastly, I avoided taking responsibility for my actions in my relationship, and because of that, I have lost the only person in this world I truly care about and do not want to live without. Now, I must take responsibility for losing her.

For once, I see a clear vision for me in this life. One that Carrie had seen in me all along. After work, I have been putting in extra hours at the coffee shop with crappy Wi-Fi, editing photos I captured on the weekends. Carrie was always right, and I wish I had realized it earlier. Photography has always been my passion, and it is time that I use my free time to pursue it. Over the past couple of weeks, I have put together a range of photos to create a portfolio. However, there is one person I want to show before distributing it to potential clients.

I am working up the courage to reunite with Carrie today. I miss her and I need her to know that. I want to show her the work that I have been putting in and I need her to know that we can make this work. We tried the separation, and for fuck's sake, she fooled around with my best friend, yet I still love her. At the end of the day, I choose her. If it seemed like it was hard work to please her before, it has proven to be a great deal harder to leave her. Truth is, she makes me a better person and that is all that she was trying to do. I know now that it was my own cowardice and selfishness that was resisting. All I can do is hope she forgives me.

I am minutes from my destination, the pile of photos that make up my portfolio is sitting on the passenger seat, and I am re-running what I am going to say to her in my head. My thoughts are racing and my excitement is growing as I approach our home. I spot another car in the driveway, and all my preparation goes out the window. Not just any car. Revel's car.

I look closely as I park across the street out of sight. Revel is at the front door with grocery bags. Carrie has just opened the door and picked up one of the bags before they head inside. Wait, why would Revel be over with grocery bags? Unless... are they together? My head is spinning. I am feeling lightheaded, and at the same time, fighting the anger erupting inside me. I don't understand. I know they kissed, but I never thought it would lead to this. I can't move. I need answers, but my limbs have gone numb. I wait.

A total of eight minutes go by, and I no longer feel anger, only sadness. I came here because I truly love Carrie and no matter the time that has passed, I continue to love her. Apparently, she does not feel the same. She has moved on.

I am hot and heavy with hopelessness. I can feel the remnants of a tear slide down my cheek. I brush it away. I can't quit now. I open the door and step out. Suddenly, the door to our house opens again and Revel steps out. He makes eye contact with me almost immediately. He is stunned.

He brings his hands up to his chest in a surrendering stance as one would before a squad of policemen with a firearm pointed at you. My clenched jaw and determined strut must be intimidating because he is cowering.

"Justice, this is not what it looks like. See… I have been wanting to tell you something. But, it is best it comes from Carrie," he exclaims as I make my way towards him. I am coming in hot and I can't resist throwing the first punch. As soon as I am close enough, I pull my arm back and swing big. Revel was anticipating it because he ducks just in time and my body jerks forward. I turn back around to face Revel, still in that surrender stance. "Justice, listen. This is not what it looks like."

I shake my head. "I know exactly what it looks like. You two are together now and you bring her groceries and all. But it doesn't matter! Because Carrie is my wife, and you'd better back off, Revel!" I lunge forward and take Revel down onto the lawn before he has time to say anything else. Grunting and panting, I hold him down with all my might before his adrenaline kicks in. Our strengths are well matched, and Revel resists, throwing a punch that allows him to break free. Now, Revel is seething at the mouth and lunges at me. I take the hit in the gut and fall to the ground, but I do not allow him the advantage. Instead, I pull myself up on top of him and straddle his body.

Revel aware of imminent defeat yells out, "She is pregnant!"

It is like the words are a loud gong to my brain. Pregnant? All the focus I had on kicking Revel's butt is now gone... pregnant?

My body falls to the ground next to Revel and it is just the two of us staring at the sky. "You mean you two aren't together?"

"No."

"And she is pregnant with... my kid?"

"Yes."

"She didn't tell me."

"No."

"But why not?"

Revel lets out a sigh, "She wanted to give you time. She thinks you still hate her."

"No, quite the opposite."

~ 43 ~

CARRIE

I am brushing my teeth after eating half the jar of pickles. As much as I am craving the taste of pickles, I am not fond of smelling like one all day. I am taking my time, contemplating my day. Today has been great and yet I feel irrevocably sad. I miss Justice, and I wish he was here to lay a hand on my stomach or tease me about my pickle craving. I feel like I should not be admitting how much I miss him because I should be finding solace in my solitude, but to deny it would be a lie.

Is it bad that I am feeling this way? I am supposed to be patiently waiting for God to work it all out. Yet here I am still wanting the same thing. All I want is Justice.

Ding Dong! Hmmm, who could that be? I spit, rinse the toothpaste out and run over to do the door. Maybe Revel forgot something? I do think he may have forgotten a bag of chips I requested. I mean, I was not going to say anything, but I didn't see him pack it away.

Justice is standing there with a big smile on his face. Revel is behind him, and it looks like the two of them have been rolling around in the grass. However, I couldn't care less about the state they are in, only the fact that Justice is standing before me. My heart is exuding joy and racing with anticipation!

"Aww, what the heck!" Justice blurts out before grabbing me by the waist and pulling me off the ground. He tucks his head between my neck and shoulder and squeezes me so tightly I can tell that he was missing me as much as I missed him. I lift my head for a second to read Revel's expression. He is standing there with anticipation.

Justice puts me down and meets my eyes, trying to read the situation. His eyes move down to my stomach. "I know."

Of course, he is happy because he knows I am pregnant. I look at Revel and he shrugs. Is he happy to find out I am pregnant, or does he feel like he needs to do this for me? And is he here for me or just the baby? I am still assessing the situation, "And...?"

"And, I love you, Carrie. And I will love this little guy." He puts his hand on my stomach and my wish comes true. I melt at his hand on my tummy. "Carrie, I came here to tell you I want to be with you and found Revel here. Umm, we had it out a little bit, but then he told me. I understand why you didn't tell me. But I know now, and it's the best news!"

I am reading his face as he pours out his feelings. I am examining every wrinkle around his eyes and his dimples as he talks. All the things that I miss seeing every day. Most importantly, I can tell he is genuine. He really was going to come here to tell me he wanted to be with me, and he still loves me. Not only that, but this child is the best news! All

my worries have subsided. Peace and solitude finally overcome me.

I smile, "I missed you."

Justice places his hand on my cheek. The moment I have
been waiting for so long is happening so fast. Justice leans
in and pulls me into a warm, loving kiss. This is not the way
I had expected the year to turn out or the reconciliation I
was expecting. Rather, I know now that it was God's plan to
stop me in my tracks and start again with a new foundation.

Our lips pull apart at last and Justice smiles with relief
as he repeats, "No, I missed you." His eyes are taking me in
and he looks at me like I am a glowing, fertile goddess. And
then, he snaps back to reality and announces, "Wait, I have
something to show you!" He turns away to head to his car
and points at Revel, "You, too!"

Stunned, I look at Revel. He points at himself and
mouths, "Me?" Apparently, he is surprised too.

Justice opens the passenger door, grabs something from
the car, and walks back over. It looks like a pile of papers.
Laminated papers? No, wait, photographs?

He makes his way to me first and shows me the stack of
photographs. "I put together a portfolio to start my photography business," he says.

I am speechless. "Wait, what?" I look through the photos
in disbelief. They are amazing.

He has captured different groups of people all over the
city. A photograph of a group of young girls out on the town.
But, in a different light than the attention they were expecting. Rather, Justice captured the smiles they had on their

face and the camaraderie they had with each other. The women looked like the best part of their night was spending time together in this moment. And he captured it perfectly. Another photo was of an older couple. They were sitting at a café together, sipping their morning coffee. The photo was cute, just the two of them, but what made it so special was that he zoomed in and emphasized the glass vase of flowers on the table. Behind the vase, the man's hand held the woman's. Justice captured the beauty that was almost invisible to the eye and so easily overlooked.

"That one is my favorite," Justice replies. "I sat across from that café watching them, thinking who is this couple? Are they married? For how long? Because they still seem smitten with each other. They were laughing behind their mugs of coffee, and I thought, 'how nice'. I would be lucky to spend every morning laughing with the woman I love. It was then that I got a closer look and saw the man reach for the woman's hand."

"These are really good, Jus."

Justice smiles and turns to face Revel, who is still standing awkwardly to the side. "I am going to need a tech guy to help with the website and digital stuff. I know it is way below your skill level, but I think it would be pretty cool to work with my best friend." Justice winks as he waits for Revel's response.

Revel blows out a breath and rubs his neck, perplexed, "Are you sure?"

"Yes, I don't blame you for what has happened this year. I take the blame for making a mess out of everything. You have been a good friend, Revel," Justice replies. It is like he can read Revel's mind because he goes on to say, "You made a mistake, but I have a feeling you won't make it again." Justice fake punches the air and we all laugh, knowing how that turned out the first time.

~ 44 ~

CARRIE

One year and six months later...

"Hi, Carrie. Honey latte today as usual?" Trevor, from behind the coffee cart register, asks me the way he does every Sunday. I am a regular attendee of the Revival church and a frequent customer.

"Yes, please, Trevor!" I step to the side to wait for my order. In the distance, I see small pigtails waddling their way towards me. She is hanging on to her dad's hands, swinging her with every step to help move her along. I am savoring this moment between father and daughter and hoping this picture lives on forever in my mind.

My daughter is more beautiful than I ever imagined, and her father is everything I could ask for in a partner. He radiates love and is gracious with his two girls. I used to worry that I would not be enough. There was no way I could be his only one. Now, I know that true love is a choice.

Graciousness, love, and patience are all virtues we need to be a better person and partner. Through Christ, Justice and I choose to better ourselves. And, when we fall short, we know that above all else, we choose to have love and respect for one another. Love is not easy. Love is not selfish. Love is not deserved. Love is a gift.

"Honey latte!" I peel my eyes from the beautiful image of Justice and our daughter to grab my coffee from the counter. I make sure to say thanks to Rita, our volunteer barista in the back, before heading over to Justice.

"Got your coffee? Are you happy, now?" Justice teases.

"Hush, you know I can't be my best self or mother without caffeine," I retort.

"Yes, I know that all too well," he chuckles and plants a quick kiss on my lips.

I smile at the gesture and take another sip. Breathing in the roasted coffee beans, a bubble of warmth fills me.

"Hi, honey!" Sandy comes up from behind and pulls me in for a hug.

"Hi, Sandy!" I gasp with pleasure.

"Hi, honey," She repeats herself, moving on to pull Justice in for a hug, "Hey, you!"

"Hey, Sandy!" Justice replies, releasing his grip on our daughter's hands to reciprocate the hug.

We have been attending church for over a year, so Sandy and her husband, Todd, are more like family. They have been a great example to look up to through the ups and downs in our marriage. Not to mention, they are always there to lend an ear. Something the church has taught me is to lean on others with more wisdom or experience. I am thankful to have Sandy for that.

"Hi, you two," Todd approaches, the shyer of the two.

"Hi, Todd," Justice and I say in unison.

"How's the business doing, Justice?" Todd asks. "I ask because we have a few friends who came across your photography page. I haven't seen it myself, but they were really interested in doing sessions with you and said they'd reach out."

Justice and I look at each other when Todd questions the Instagram page and try not to laugh at his lack of knowledge about social media.

"Yah, I always answer responses when they message me, even if it takes a few days. Surprisingly, I have gotten a lot more engagement than expected with the thanks of my business partner."

"Oh, right, Revel! Good guy!" Todd recollects. We have invited Revel to some dinners with Todd and Sandy since he is more a part of our family than ever, working with Justice and being the best uncle.

Justice looks down at his feet to check on our daughter, only to notice she is trying to crawl away. It is way too crowded this morning for her to crawl around, forcing people to stop to avoid stepping on little fingers. I am mortified as a new mother. I look at Justice, but he is already in stealth mode, ready to complete the mission of 'Tame Baby'.

"Faith!" Justice calls out as he rushes to pick her up amid the chaotic flow of people.

DEDICATION

This is dedicated to all those women out there that are struggling with their faith. To the women who fall prey to comparison. The women that know their worth yet forget the One and Only who can fulfill their desires. Women who are taken for granted and must be reminded of something or someone greater.

This world is broken. Unfairly and unjustly, we are called to walk amongst others who feel pain just as much as you do. There is a world of people who have fears and doubts that on any day can overwhelm them to a crisp. Crumpled, burnt, thin. Even with anxiety and mental health at the forefront of conversation today, we still struggle immensely. It is because we have the enemy working against us. The more we internalize the more the enemy uses our own words or our own thoughts against us. The enemy works overtime to create walls so that little by little we become more jaded and more isolated towards those around us. Of course, no one is aware of this until it eats at us in every aspect of our lives. At first, one compares their husband to a friend's boyfriend who gave them roses for no reason that day. This person cannot help in this moment but think why does my husband not make this effort? I know he loves me so, maybe, I am being sensitive. Then again, they think of all the times they have been disappointed in their husband's little effort to be romantic and their dwindling intimate life. This thought then snowballs into deeper issues... is he not fulfilling my needs? Am I not happy? Do I deserve better? It took two years of torturing myself until I was down on my knees begging the Lord to give me peace. I realized it took feeling secure in Christ and taking captive of your thoughts to prevent myself from spiraling again.

I used this book to paint a picture of what it can feel like when we self-destruct. Our lives can look so great on the outside, but the enemy can attack us or our partner or our family on the inside. The most perfect union will not survive without the help of God. So, those woman in marriage who are struggling with post-wedding blues or intimacy with their partner or commitment issues after saying 'I do', I remind you that marriage with your partner is not meant to make you feel secure. In fact, marriage can be more isolating. Therefore, it is important that you seek out Christ. That you look to Christ when you have tears falling down your face and your partner has just left the room. Seek Christ when your expectations for your partner are not met. I encourage you to go to the bible in these moments so you can uncover how to feel and what to do in these moments. God has all the answers. Let us not do a disservice to ourselves by beating ourselves up with questions on top of questions. Let us seek Christ first.

Of course, this book is for all believers and non-believers, married or single. We can all use the encouragement to seek Christ and the reminder of life with Him.

Lastly, I dedicate this to my husband, my best friend and companion. Life with me is not always easy. Life with you is not always easy. Yet, at the end of the day, we love each other enough to surrender everything to Christ with complete confidence that He will preserve our love. In Him, our love is eternal.